CHOCOLATE DIAMONDS

ALEC PECHE

GBSW PUBLISHING

ACKNOWLEDGEMENTS...

...

Thank you GMM for being my third cold eye. Many thanks to the blog site The Kill Zone for making me a better writer and helping me navigate this world of publishing.

CHAPTER 1

*D*r. Jill Quint was walking through the large terminal in Brussels, Belgium looking for her three friends, Jo, Angela, and Marie who had flown out from Wisconsin, while Jill departed California, for blissful days of eating, drinking, shopping, and sightseeing in Belgium and the Netherlands. It was early fall and the color of the trees was starting to change outside the airport. She couldn't wait to get outside and explore this part of the world.

Jill was a vintner growing the Muscat grape. Her first crop had hit the market a few weeks before and was doing well in sales. To supplement her income, she also maintained a forensic pathologist consulting business that provided second opinions for cause of death. She'd had her toughest case in the spring of this year.

It had been her first case in five years in which she had become a target after providing the San Francisco medical examiner with evidence that the case was a homicide rather than death by natural causes.

On occasion, her three friends assisted Jill with her investigations. They had full-time jobs, but she generally needed ten to twenty hours in research, which they could do at night or on the weekend. This last case was so complex it had required many hours from all of them, and now they could afford fancier hotels than they normally booked.

Jill had taken a break from consulting over the summer and concentrated on producing her first crop of Moscato wine. Once she returned from vacation, she planned to resume consulting.

She spied her three friends in the baggage area at the other end of the baggage carousel and headed their way. After hugs, stories, and each retrieving their own piece of luggage, they departed the arrivals hall looking for their transport to the hotel in Antwerp.

They spotted a driver holding a sign with Jo's last name and were soon settled in the van and heading toward Antwerp, which was an hour's drive in normal conditions. Ongoing construction made the trip a little longer, but nothing could spoil the sunshine and promise of a new city, and indeed, a new country to explore.

The women had a list of museums, churches, and libraries to visit. Of course, they also planned to eat chocolate, drink lots of beer, and celebrate having the time together to enjoy a country that none of them had explored before. They were also studying the facial features of passer-bys, looking for Jo's heritage in the people around them. Her ancestry was in this city.

It was midday when they settled into their hotel rooms. Although they were tired from the long flight to Brussels, they really wanted to stretch their legs, so headed out into the city. Using their travel guide, they followed a walking tour of the historical center of the city.

After gazing up at the beautiful Gothic Cathedral of Our Lady, they found their first Belgian beer pub. Belgians served beer in glasses specially designed for each beer brand. Spending the next hour comparing the size and the shape of the glasses, the alcohol content of the beer and the taste passed the afternoon in a most pleasurable way.

They strolled around the Grote Market, walking off the beer, window shopping, casually looking for a place to dine. In the end they decided to try a restaurant recommended by several Belgians.

They settled in at their table and were handed menus that were printed in Dutch but fortunately had English subtitles. The noise level was moderate as tables were fairly close together. It was fairly easy for Jill and her friends to listen in on the conversations around them. Jill was looking forward to trying Flemish stew. Angela had the vegetarian pasta, Marie also went with the Flemish stew, and Jo ordered a seafood stew. Another round of beer was a fine pairing with the dishes they'd chosen. Between the beer and the heavy meal, they knew they'd sleep well that night.

"Let's toast," said Jo

"Cheers, and here's to a great vacation," the other three said in unison with a laugh.

Just then there was a commotion at the next table. The four women looked over towards the sound. There was a lone diner at the next table looking panicked and clawing at her throat.

Jill stood up and quickly went to the diner's aid.

"I'm a doctor. What's wrong?"

Now was not the time to mention that she was a doctor to the dead – a pathologist.

"Nut allergy," said the woman in a very distressed manner.

"Do you have an EpiPen or some kind of injection in case of an emergency? What's your name?" asked Jill, with her eyes on the woman's purse.

"I'm Laura Peeters."

Jill was peripherally aware that Marie, Angela, Jo, and half of the diners and restaurant staff were gathered around her and the woman. There was near silence; everyone was concerned about Laura. Jill looked over her shoulder.

"Call for an ambulance. She needs to get to a hospital right away."

Jill looked back at the woman, whose condition was rapidly

deteriorating. She had reached for her purse, but seemed to have forgotten what she was looking for. Jill knew people with severe allergies could become confused quickly if their blood pressure dropped drastically due to the allergic reaction.

In most cases people with bad allergies puffed up in the lips and eyes. Laura seemed to be that rare five to ten percent who experience some difficulty breathing, but whose biggest problem was a large and possibly fatal blood pressure drop. If Laura hadn't said nut allergy, Jill would not have guessed that she was someone heading for anaphylactic shock.

"You seem to be having trouble finding your allergy medication in your purse. Let me help."

Jill quickly looked through the purse, but didn't see any medication to treat the allergic reaction. She did locate the woman's identification and saved that for the ambulance crew.

"How soon will the ambulance be here? She desperately needs medication!"

The woman was slumped over, with labored breathing. Jill didn't carry a medical bag with her in California, let alone in a foreign country. She could start CPR if the woman needed that, but that was about all she could do for her.

"The ambulance will arrive in five minutes," shouted a restaurant employee.

"Is there any medical help nearby? A doctor's office or anything?" asked Jill.

"No, madam, this is a tourist area. We have police but no doctors or emergency personnel. Five minutes is a good response time. It generally takes ten minutes."

Jill didn't think that Laura's condition could wait five minutes.

"Help me get her out of her chair and flat on the floor," Jill instructed to people that had gathered around the table.

She looked at Laura intently. "Laura, I know you're having trouble breathing, but I want to make sure your heart gets plenty of blood. I am going to get you flat on your back and put your feet up."

Jill knew this situation was heading in a bad direction. She looked over at Angela with the silent request for her to take control of the crowd while she tended to Laura.

"Let's give Jill and Laura some space," said Angela to the crowd that had gathered around the resuscitation effort. "Will someone go outside and wait for the ambulance so that they can be directed inside to help as soon as possible?"

A couple volunteered to go outside and wait for the ambulance. Two men stepped forward to assist Jill in getting the woman flat on the ground. Jill had been monitoring her pulse as it slowed. She asked for something to prop the woman's legs up on in hopes of keeping blood available to her heart and brain.

"Does anyone else know cardiopulmonary resuscitation?"

Jill made the gesture of what CPR looks like in case her English words were not understood.

Fortunately, Marie knelt down beside Jill, ready to assist when Jill determined it was time to start CPR. Three other restaurant patrons knew CPR and were also ready to assist. Jill could no longer feel Laura's pulse.

"One and two and three and four and five. . ." Jill started chest compressions.

Since Laura was suffering from an allergic reaction causing anaphylactic shock, Jill knew that performing CPR would be of little help. Laura needed a shot of epinephrine, quickly. Jill hoped that the ambulance carried medication for allergic reactions. She had no idea who staffed ambulances in Belgium, or what supplies they had.

CPR had been underway for three to four minutes when the ambulance arrived. The two responders carried a toolbox that thankfully had medication in it. One of the responders was a nurse. Marie took over for Jill doing chest compressions.

"I am Dr. Jill Quint, a physician licensed in the United States.

"Her heart rhythm is holding," said Jill to the nurse.

"We are pulling into the hospital now. Laura will be met by a team that is excellent," the nurse replied.

Jill could see the Emergency doors ahead and indeed, there was a team awaiting their arrival. The ambulance came to a stop and the doors were opened up.

The team looked upon Jill and Marie briefly with some curiosity. Laura's gurney slid out and she was taken inside. Jill glanced over at Marie.

"I'll just check to see if they need any information from you or me. Then I'll find out how to get a taxi back to our hotel. I don't know about you, but my adrenaline rush is over and I'm crashing. Not enough sleep, no food, and I'm carsick from the ambulance ride and the beer sloshing in my belly."

Marie looked at her and said, "It's been an astounding thirty minutes. I've had my CPR card for twenty years, but that's the first time I've done CPR on a real person. It was physically hard, and you did it for longer than I did. I'm not queasy, but otherwise I feel exactly like you do. When we get to our hotel, let's hope we can find some food. I was so happy when Laura's heart started beating on its own in the ambulance. I feel we need to toast her tonight."

"She's not out of the woods yet," Jill replied. "Let's go inside and leave our information there and maybe they will tell us how she's doing."

Jill and Marie walked inside the emergency unit and approached the central desk. The unit looked much the same as its American counterpart. There were multilingual signs in English, Dutch, German, and French.

They explained who they were to the attendant who seemed to be directing the flow of patients. After the explanation, the attendant took them into the employee break room and offered them cookies and coffee. He asked Jill and Marie to wait while he checked on Laura and her team to see if they needed any further information from them.

He returned in a few minutes with the request that they wait ten to fifteen minutes for a hospital staff member. The staff caring for Laura thought they would have her stabilized by then.

The two sat down in the lounge with a huge sigh. Jill was grateful for a can of ginger ale. The soda, combined with some saltine crackers, settled her stomach. Marie likewise had a drink and cookies.

"Wow, this is a wild start to our vacation. I feel exhilarated and exhausted and jet-lagged. Jill, what do you know about the Belgian health system?"

"I know it's good. Probably better than the U.S. in some regards. I worked with a pathologist educated in Brussels about ten years ago. He seemed to have an education equal to that provided in an American medical school. Other than the language barrier, since Dutch is the predominant language, I would feel pretty comfortable getting my care here."

Several minutes later, a man in surgical scrubs with the word 'dokter' in front of a name tag stepped into the lounge.

"Hello, I'm Dr. Janssens. I am the lead physician caring for Laura Peeters. I understand you cared for Laura until she arrived at our emergency room."

"Hello, I'm Dr. Jill Quint. I am an American physician on vacation. I happened to be seated next to Laura in the restaurant."

"Hi, I'm Marie Simon. I have no medical background but I know CPR so I shared the chest compression duty with Jill."

"Welcome to Belgium. Thank you for saving one of our citizens. Laura was fortunate to be seated next to you in the restaurant. Dr. Quint, what is your medical area of focus?"

"I am a forensic pathologist. I have examined a few bodies for anaphylactic shock. From an autopsy point of view, I'm very aware of the symptoms. If Laura had not told me before she lost consciousness that she had a nut allergy, I don't think I would've recognized her condition. Less than ten percent of patients display her symptoms while in anaphylactic shock."

"I am impressed with your knowledge, especially now that I know you don't routinely care for those of us among the living."

"I worked for the State of California crime lab for ten years. For the past five years, I have operated a vineyard, but I also provide consulting services that offer second opinions on the cause of death. A couple of months ago, I had a different opportunity to perform CPR on a FBI agent and she survived my treatment. I am getting really good at keeping people away from their local medical examiner!"

"Ah Dr. Quint, now I recognize your name. We actually discussed how you determined that a patient with necrotizing fasciitis was a homicide in our grand rounds a month ago. As I recall an article published by Dr. Meyer from the San Francisco Medical Examiner's office described the case. It was a very well-attended lecture. Will you be in our city for a few days? I would love to have you come and present at a medical staff meeting."

"I'll be in Antwerp for three nights with my friends before we move on to Amsterdam, and then finally to Brussels. If you like, I could arrange my sightseeing to give you an hour one day. If you have a business card, I'll leave you my contact information," Jill offered.

"Normally I would have slides to present a lecture, but I don't have time to put together a slide deck, and I don't have the data from my lab with me in Belgium. So if I could limit the lecture to say, ten minutes, and spend the rest of the time in questions and answers, that would be the best I could do. Would that style of lecture offend any of the physicians?"

"Dr. Quint, this was a fascinating case and I'm sure that you have other cases in your career that are just as captivating. Your lecture would be a welcome break to our routine. I'm going to reserve our largest lecture space as I am sure that even with just two or three days' advance notice, the lecture hall will be filled to capacity. I will also invite our own medical examiner. Thank you for agreeing to interrupt your vacation to provide a guest lecture."

"You're welcome, Dr. Janssens. We just arrived at noon today in Antwerp. Now that the adrenaline rush from saving Laura is gone, we both want nothing more than to return to our hotel, grab a quick dinner and fall asleep. Can you tell us on how to get a taxi to take us to our hotel?"

"Dr. Quint and Ms. Simon, after all the work you've done today, it would be rude to direct you to a taxi stand to get a ride back to your hotel. Give me a few minutes and I will find a ride for you."

Dr. Janssens left the room. Jill and Marie were left alone.

"Wow! I did not know I was traveling with a famous pathologist. I thought you were just an obscure winemaker!"

"I had no idea that Dr. Meyer's case synopsis of death by necrotizing fasciitis had reached international fame. I hate to interfere with our sightseeing, but I feel I have a duty to educate whenever possible."

"I'm just glad he's arranging for a ride since neither of us remembered our purses when we left in the ambulance. It would be embarrassing to pull up in front of our fancy hotel and then make the taxi driver wait while we ran in to get some cash. Angela and Jo might not be back from dinner, and then what would we do, without our purses?"

"Good point. I was so caught up in thinking about how to design a lecture, that I forgot we didn't have our purses."

Dr. Janssens returned.

"We have a medical transport car that will take you to your hotel. It is waiting now outside our entrance. Let me take you there."

They exited the employee lounge. A staff member hurriedly walked up to Dr. Janssens.

"Je bent meteen in de kamer met Laura Peeters nodig."

Jill and Marie did not speak Dutch, but with the mention of

Laura's name and the urgency in the staff person's voice, they suspected that there was a problem with Laura.

"We will find our way to the exit. You go take care of your patient."

Dr. Janssens uttered a "thank-you" as he hurried off to Laura's bedside.

CHAPTER 2

*J*ill and Marie left the emergency area and spotted a medical transportation car. They walked toward the vehicle and a driver got out.

"Hi. Were you asked to give two people a ride to their hotel?" Jill asked.

"Yes, Madame. Dr. Janssens made a special request for us to transport two people who saved a woman's life tonight. What hotel are you staying at and do you know the address?"

"We just arrived from the United States today. We are staying at the DeWitt Hotel. We don't have an address for the hotel. Have you heard of it? Do you know where it's located?"

"Ah yes. I am familiar with the DeWitt Hotel. Please, have a seat in the car and I will take you there. It is a short drive."

"Thank you. I'm Jill, and this is Marie. What's your name?"

"I am pleased to meet you. My name is Thomas."

They got in the back seat as the passenger front seat had a big box on it. The two women spent a very pleasant ten minutes chatting with Thomas about his country. After the car stopped in front of the hotel, they got out of the car and leaned into the driver's window.

"Thank you very much for the ride, Thomas, and the tips on what to see and where to eat in Antwerp. Have a pleasant night."

"Goodbye, ladies."

Jill and Marie entered the hotel and approached registration for a key. The hotel did not recognize them as guests and they had no identification on them. After explaining their unusual story to registration, a staff member checked the room that Angela and Jo were staying in to see if they were available to verify their identity. Fortunately, the women were in the room and volunteered to come down to the lobby and meet them. A minute later the foursome was re-united in the lobby.

"Did the woman make it to the hospital alive?" asked Angela.

"She did make it although there was some emergency with her as we were leaving the hospital," Jill responded. "So she's not out of the woods yet."

"I bet you guys are hungry," suggested Jo. "When we returned to the hotel we asked what the food options were in this neighborhood. If you want to grab a jacket and your purse from upstairs, we can head over to the pub next door."

The four friends headed upstairs to do just that. A few minutes later they were seated in a pub. Angela and Jo had finished their dinner at the restaurant, so they settled for beer.

Marie was adventurous with food so she tried the mussels. Jill's stomach was still fragile, so she wanted something salty. She convinced the waitress to melt some cheese on top of pommes frites. Cheesy french fries were just the sort of bland, salty food that she needed to settle her stomach. She ordered a ginger ale to quench her thirst.

"How was your meal? I was really looking forward to trying the Flemish stew. I'm grateful I only had a few bites before we got in the back of the ambulance. You know how easily I get carsick under the best of circumstances. By the time we arrived at the hospital, I had grabbed a plastic bag and was ready to puke."

"It took the restaurant a few minutes to settle down once you left in the ambulance," said Jo. "After everything returned to normal, the owner came over to our table for a quick chat. He had never had an emergency in his restaurant before and wanted to assure us there was nothing wrong with the food."

Angela added, "I overheard Laura say she had a nut allergy. So I explained to him from my layman's view what allergies were. Once I mention a nut allergy he understood and was reassured there was nothing wrong with his food, unless he had told her that there were no nuts in a dish but in fact the cook put nuts in. He said he had not brought her any food as she was waiting to meet someone for dinner, so I assured him he was in the clear."

"He was so pleased that we had handled the situation with Laura that he gave us our meal for free and invited you back on another night. He said he uses his grandmother's recipe for Flemish stew and you'll want to taste it at his restaurant. The food was good and I wouldn't mind going back if we have time."

"I was so glad you guys went back to the hotel. Marie and I are running around in a foreign country with no cash, no identification, and no room key. The hospital arranged a ride back to the hotel for us. Our options were really limited without our purses," Jill said.

Marie smiled. "So until tonight, I had no idea how famous Jill is in the world of academic medicine. When she introduced herself to the physician in the emergency room, he invited her to deliver a lecture on the Graeme St. Louis case before she leaves Antwerp. Apparently they'd discussed the case in Grand Rounds. Can you believe that? Over five-thousand miles away and they've heard of Jill!"

"Really," said Jo, "that's cool. I knew the case was dangerous and full of intrigue, but I'm surprised that they're discussing it in Belgium. Did you publish an article?"

"The San Francisco medical examiner published an article," Jill responded. "He devoted a paragraph to my work and the context of the case. I explained to Dr. Janssens that I didn't have my data or a slide deck with me on vacation, so I asked if I could do like a ten-minute lecture off the cuff and leave the remaining minutes for Q and A. He said that was fine."

"How about if all of us attend the lecture," suggested Jill. "I would like to introduce you and give you credit for helping me break the case and keep me alive. Some of the questions may be in your areas of expertise and it would be best to hear the answers from you. It will mean giving up about two to three hours of our vacation, but it might be fun and we might meet new friends or someone to hang out with in the pubs."

"I'm in!" said Angela.

"I can't imagine they would have any questions on the financial trail of evidence, but it will be a unique vacation experience so count me in," said Jo.

"Well, I guess if everyone else is attending, I'll go too," said Marie.

Lifting their drinks, they toasted.

"All for one and one for all!"

They finished their meal and returned to the hotel. Jill could barely keep her eyes open. As they passed through the lobby, one of the hotel staff approached them with a note in her hand.

"Dr. Jill Quint?"

"Yes, that is me."

"I have a note for you from Dr. Janssens."

She handed the note to Jill, who proceeded to open and read it.

"Wow, he works fast. The lecture has been scheduled at noon two days from now. He will send a taxi to fetch us to the lecture hall," said Jill.

"I'm going to send a message to him letting him know that he's getting the whole team for free and to warn the audience that we will be casually dressed tourists."

They headed up to their rooms and quickly dropped off into sleep.

CHAPTER 3

*T*he friends met at breakfast to plan their stay in Antwerp. Each of them took a turn picking a favorite must-see site.

"I think we should visit the Royal Art Museum and the Rubens House."

"We also want to take a day trip on the train to Bruges."

"I want to see the diamond district."

"I want to visit lots of chocolate shops."

"Okay how about if we take the train to Bruges today, do the diamond district tomorrow morning, do the lecture thing in the middle of the day, then visit Rubens House and St. Bartholomew's Church. The following day we can do more museums and churches. Shop and eat chocolate wherever we go."

Marie was the organizer. She was always quick to come up with a great itinerary.

They finished breakfast and returned to their rooms. Jill used the hotel business center to get a note to Dr. Janssens confirming the team's appearance for the lecture the next day. They collected their coats, purses, cameras, and umbrellas and set off for the train station.

The ninety-minute train ride was beautiful. The fall colors were out in full force. It was interesting to observe the architecture of homes as they whizzed by. Bicyclists were everywhere, dressed in clothes signifying that they were riding to work. Very few were decked out as though they were racing in the Tour de France.

The gentle rocking of the train lulled Jill and Jo to sleep. Angela was keeping an eye open to make sure they didn't miss their stop.

"Hey, ladies, wake up, our stop is coming up."

They gathered up their belongings and exited the train, then took a taxi to the clock tower. They spent the day touring the canals, two churches, a brewery, and some amazing chocolate stores.

The group caught the late train back to Antwerp. Tired from the time difference and a very busy day, again they all fell asleep on the train, depending on Angela to wake them for the Antwerp station.

"Taxi or walk back to the hotel?" asked Marie.

"Let's walk," replied Angela. "Nighttime always gives you a different perspective on the city. It certainly gives me different pictures to take of our travels."

They walked back toward their hotel, pausing for Angela to take pictures. Photography was her profession and she did a fabulous job on their vacations documenting their travels.

When they arrived back at the hotel again, it was nearly ten at night Belgian time, which meant it was much earlier in the United States. They were exhausted from their day, but not ready to go to bed because their bodies had not yet adjusted to European time. A staff member approached them.

"Dr. Quint I have a message for you."

It was the same staff member from the previous night. Jill opened the message and read it.

"This is strange. A Dr. DeGroot would like to speak with me.

He was referred to me by Dr. Janssens, the note states. It is signed 'Chief medical examiner, St. Elizabeth's Hospital'. Hmmm, I wonder why he wants to talk to me? It's kind of late, so I'll call him in the morning."

""You're becoming famous and in demand," said Jo with a smile. "Are you still going to take vacations with your friends? Maybe the paparazzi will keep us separated in the future."

"I didn't know that I was famous in Belgium," said Jill with a smirk. "Certainly the paparazzi don't trail me around in the United States."

They all headed for the suite. No one was quite ready to go to sleep yet, so they had a bottle of wine and chitchatted for another hour before Jill started nodding off. One by one they left the living room of the suite to retire to their bedroom.

Shortly after breakfast, Jill took a moment and dialed the number for Dr. DeGroot.

"This is Dr. Quint. I am looking for a Dr. DeGroot."

"This is Dr. DeGroot. Thank you for calling me back. Dr. Janssens told me you were on vacation in Antwerp. I am aware of your work in the United States. Unfortunately, Laura Peeters expired the day before yesterday in the hospital after you left. I am responsible for her autopsy and I have some questions."

"She died the day before yesterday? She was alive when we left. That's unfortunate. Allergic reactions rarely cause death when the person gets to the hospital in time. Her allergy had unusual symptoms. If she hadn't told me she had a nut allergy, I'm not sure I would've recognized anaphylactic shock. As you know, she really had no rash, no swollen lips, no swollen eyes, but instead had low blood pressure. Less than ten percent of allergic reactions exhibit Laura's symptoms. What have you determined to be her cause of death?"

"Officially, Laura Peeters expired from empty vena cava/empty ventricle syndrome. She assumed an upright position, and all of the blood left her heart."

"I'm surprised the staff sat her up. It's well known that victims of anaphylactic shock should be kept flat on their back with their feet raised. What happened?"

"Someone had her sit up. None of the staff admits to it and she was doing well and even had a second injection of epinephrine about five minutes before she flat lined. No one was in the room to see her sit up and the staff was notified when the alarms went off on her heart monitor. She was found slumped sideways on the gurney, feet hanging over the edge."

"Did anyone instruct her to stay flat on her back?"

"Yes it is written in the chart that she was instructed to stay flat on her back, and Laura acknowledged that she understood the reason for the requirement."

"As I recall from my brief exposure to the staff at St. Elizabeth's, they carried a communication device that might have GPS. Was that looked at? Who was at her bedside according to the GPS system when she flat lined?"

"Dr. Quint, let me explain how deaths are investigated in Belgium. There are no private autopsies. Less than two percent of deaths undergo an autopsy and we're wrong about the cause of death on ten percent of cases. The perfect murder really does exist here.

"We don't have coroners or medical examiners that routinely look at "killing cases" as we call them in Belgium. The vast majority of my time is spent looking at expected deaths in our hospitals. I don't look at deaths that occur outside the hospital walls. If it weren't for criminals injured while committing a crime, brought here by police and dying, I would never have the opportunity to look at a death and debate if it is a killing. It either is or it isn't, and I know that at the start of my examination.

"This is around-about way of saying I would appreciate if you would consult on this case, as it would be an exceptional learning opportunity for the police and I."

Jill was very conflicted. This was supposed to be a best-friends-forever vacation. If she took herself out of the tourist activities, it would weigh on the other three. If she involved them in the case, then it wouldn't be a vacation.

She also had a passion for helping her fellow pathologists. Getting the cause of death correct was important to the deceased, their family, the police, and the justice system. Naïvely she wondered if her involvement in a case in Antwerp might start a revolution to improve forensic pathology in Belgium.

Maybe she could do a little of both – be a tourist and be a forensic pathologist.

"Dr. DeGroot as you know, I'm here on vacation. With me is the team that helped crack the Graeme St. Louis case of necrotizing fasciitis. They're not medical people. Their area of expertise is interrogation, background investigation, and financial sleuthing. Let me talk with them to see if we can both tour Belgium and assist you with this case. At the very least, I'll give you some suggestions of things to look for during the autopsy and tests to perform on Laura's body.

"I'll prepare a list of those suggestions and deliver it while at my lecture at the university. Dr. Janssens graciously and quickly set up a teaching opportunity today at noon on your campus. If you're not planning to attend that lecture, I'll find some way to get my notes to you."

"Dr. Quint, that is very gracious of you. I appreciate any assistance you and your team can deliver. I did hear of your lecture and was planning to attend, so we will meet face-to-face and I'll get your suggestions at that time. Thank you for taking the time, Dr. Quint, to speak with me this morning."

Jill's friends were waiting for her after she completed the call. On the way to the diamond district, she told them about Dr. DeGroot's request.

They all felt bad about Laura's death. One moment she was a random stranger sitting next to them in a restaurant, and in the next moment, they'd tried to save her life. She'd looked to be younger than the four of them.

They agreed that they did not want to change their vacation plans or itinerary. They could, however, help Dr. DeGroot with his investigation. Marie had her iPad with her and if they could find pubs with Wi-Fi, she would be very happy to drink beer and work on the case.

Angela, Jo, and Marie had never before met the victim of one of their investigations. They thought that Jill's job in the state crime lab had been a fairly disturbing occupation. They'ld stay out of Dr. DeGroot's autopsy room, but gladly supply him with the threads of an investigation from a distance.

They stopped in at a little café for coffee and pastries for breakfast. While they dined, they developed a list of questions to give to Dr. DeGroot.

"We can either start with the beginning or the end of Laura Peeters' life," said Jill.

"Let's start with the end and work backwards," suggested Angela. "I know where the end was, I just don't know where the start is. So better to keep working backwards until we feel like we've reached the start."

"It's much easier to think this through when you know your country's resources," commented Jo, who was concerned about how she would find financial information in Europe. "I assume they have an IRS-like agency that provides law enforcement with financial data on people. You know me - I'm the queen of financial information."

"Since I already do candidate background checks internationally, I can do an easy checklist of sources for Dr. DeGroot to investigate. In fact, I think I might have a checklist on my iPad that I could just mail him," remarked Marie.

"Okay, we should create that list for him," said Jill, pulling out pen and paper. "We need to have him check with the hospital to see what locator badges served Laura."

Marie added, "He should check for cameras around the hospital and in the emergency room."

"I'll ask him to let me view the medical record so I can comment on any care that was different than the standard for anaphylactic shock," said Jill.

Angela put aside her tea and added, "He should interview the staff that cared for her in the emergency room to get a full vision of what she said. Likely not everything she said was written down in the medical record."

Jill was tapping away at her phone "I have a list of routine autopsy tests on my iPhone. I'll mail those to him and attach the WHO guidelines on testing for anaphylactic shock."

Marie got up to fetch another cup of coffee and said, "If he'll give me her name, a picture, and the DOB, I can probably research her while we're in the lecture hall today."

"I'll develop a list of things to look for financially. Since I'm completely unfamiliar with the European regulatory bodies and reporting requirements, I'll leave you guys to do the sleuthing for now," Jo said with a smile.

She was amused at how engaged her friends were trying to solve the mystery, if there was one, of Laura Peeters.

They paid their bill and had an enjoyable walk to the diamond district. Once there, they admired many beautiful pieces of expensive jewelry. None of them had a collection of real jewels, preferring cheaper imitations. Angela had fun photographing her friends wearing different baubles and the amazing store display windows.

Jill called the number that Dr. Janssens had given her about thirty minutes before they were due at the lecture hall. A car arrived at their location and they piled in and headed for Saint Elizabeth's hospital. They were to be met at the emergency room entrance and guided to the lecture hall.

With a full ten minutes to spare, they arrived in a large and noisy conference hall. The four of them were amazed at the crowd given the short notification of the lecture topic. The room consisted of long narrow tables with chairs behind each table. Apparently, unlike American lecture halls, Belgians were not afraid to sit in the front rows and the room was rapidly filling in. There was a podium for Jill to speak from and behind her on a large screen was her name in print along with some other words in Dutch. Jill liked the fact she could get cozy with the audience if she left the podium and walked the aisles. Between school, training, and later, work; she had pretty much been in every possible lecture set-up.

CHAPTER 4

*J*ill introduced Angela and Jo to Dr. Janssens. The room continued to fill and in the end there were two to three hundred people in attendance by Jill's estimate. Dr. Janssens opened the meeting.

"For those of you who don't know me, I'm Dr. Janssens, Chief of Emergency Medicine. Some of you in the room may remember that we had a Grand Rounds discussion about two months ago about a case of necrotizing fasciitis that resulted from a killing in the United States.

"Two days ago a woman needed emergency medical care in an Antwerp restaurant for a nut allergy. She was fortunate that seated at the next table were a group of tourists newly arrived from the United States - Dr. Jill Quint and her team. As you may recall, she is the pathologist who made the discovery of a killing by bacterial infection that we discussed at Grand Rounds.

"Dr. Quint started CPR at the restaurant alternating chest compressions with Marie Simon," said Dr. Janssens introducing the two of them with Jill off to his side and Marie at the back of the room. "I had the great pleasure of meeting them in our emergency room as they continued CPR in the ambulance on the way to St. Elizabeth's. Dr. Quint has graciously agreed to give a short lecture to this group. She also has her team with her in case any of the audience has questions relevant to their areas."

Dr. Janssens continued with the introductions, "As she had not planned to lecture while on vacation in Belgium, Dr. Quint does not have a business suit, scientific data, or a PowerPoint deck, to present her findings. Instead, she will provide us a ten to fifteen minute outline of the case and leave the rest of this lecture open to questions and answers."

The hall erupted in appreciative applause of her team's sacrifice of their vacation time. Jill approached the microphone.

"Hello, and thank you for the warm welcome. I had no idea that the case of necrotizing fasciitis reached much outside of San Francisco, let alone to Belgium. I'll have to congratulate Dr. Meyer on his excellent presentation of the case.

"Let me give you a brief biography of my team and me. I was trained as a forensic pathologist in California, and I spent more than fifteen years in their Bureau of Forensic Services assisting law enforcement throughout the state with investigations and evidence.

"Unfortunately, the more I had to testify in court, the less I enjoyed my job. After a lot of soul-searching, I decided to buy land to run a vineyard. I operate Quixotic Winery in the Palisades Valley of California. A month ago, I began selling my first vintage of Moscato wine. Several years ago, as I began creating the winery, I converted one of the barns to contain a variety of laboratory analyzers. I used some of the analyzers to perfect my organic nutrients and pest-control substances for the grape-vines.

"I had been away from the forensic bureau for about three months when I got a call from a law enforcement friend in Southern California. He was unhappy with the quality of the autopsy performed. My friend was convinced that the case was a homicide, but the medical examiner had ruled death by natural causes. He was able to convince the family to request that I perform a private autopsy, and I did. It was a homicide, and my findings allowed law enforcement to proceed with solving the case. Now I do a cause-of-death consult on eight to twelve cases a year.

"My teammates," said Jill while pointing out each of her friends. "Jo Pringle, Marie Simon, and Angela Weber joined me in my investigations by the time I was engaged with my third client. Jo is an expert at examining the financial records of the victim and any suspects. Marie finds and compiles a background check on anyone. The digital foot-print we all leave on the Internet and elsewhere in the world is very informative. And Angela has this special force about her that makes anyone spill their guts during an interview."

This last comment drew a laugh from the conference hall audience.

"So let me move on to the case in San Francisco. Usually a loved one of the deceased contacts me within twenty-four hours of a death. It is best if I can begin before a mortician embalms the deceased. In this case, I fortunately was able to examine the victim before the mortician began his work to prepare the body for the funeral.

"The victim was a thirty-something otherwise healthy male who died from necrotizing fasciitis after being cut by coral underwater while scuba diving. At the time I took the case, I thought it was highly likely that the victim had died due to septic shock, and he did, but it was from unnatural causes.

"Given that the known cause of death in this case was an over-whelming infection, I took care to look at the infection from as many angles as I could. I swabbed and cultured the bacteria around his leg wound and an IV site in his upper arm, and ran several DNA studies on the bacteria."

As Jill continued to provide an overview of the case to those attending, Marie entered the notes that Jill had created earlier for Dr. DeGroot into her iPad. Once she completed typing the list, she began her Internet search on Laura Peeters.

"As Dr. Janssen mentioned, we are on vacation in Belgium, so I lack my slides to show you a DNA match in bacterial growth. What other questions can I answer for you related to the case of necrotizing fasciitis, other unusual causes of death, or questions you may have related to the field of forensic pathology?"

Jill paused and took a swig of water. She wasn't sure what would come next as far as questions. She thought that the attendance at the event was an indication of the interest in her work. But she was in a different culture and she couldn't begin to guess the behavior of physicians, residents, and medical students.

What followed proved to be one of the most engaging conversations she'd had within her profession. Like the United States, the European Union television networks carried their fair share of cops and robbers dramas. It was evident that those dramas had colored the audience's view of forensic pathology. They probably had another two hours of questions for Jill, but she ended the lecture on time. Her friends had been very supportive in coming with her to the lecture Hall, but they were all eager to get on with the search for the best chocolate.

At the end of the lecture, several people approached Jill wanting her contact information. She provided it to Dr. Janssens and the room quickly emptied. Finally, Dr. DeGroot approached the group as they were packing up to leave.

"Hello, Dr. Quint. It is nice to meet you in person. I'm Dr. DeGroot and we spoke this morning."

"Nice to meet you, Dr. DeGroot. We put together some checklists of what we usually look at for any case. If you give me your e-mail address, Marie will send those to you right now."

Marie had the iPad ready to send him the attachments, and she handed it over to him to enter his e-mail address. Pretty soon they heard the swish sound of a sent e-mail.

"Marie, what were you able to find on the victim Laura Peeters?"

Jill looked over at Dr. DeGroot and said "She was using your Wi-Fi to do a standard background check on your victim."

"Dr. DeGroot, I sent you a Word document that included my research on Laura. She has an unusual background. Based on my five years of working with Jill, her background is suspicious enough that it mirrors what we would find in working on a case of Jill's that was determined to be a homicide."

The women were all getting restless to return to their vacation state of mind, bored with talking about forensic pathology and homicide. They gave their contact information to Dr. DeGroot and exited the lecture hall.

They headed over to Ruben's House, one of the top attractions in Antwerp. Their new favorite chocolate shop was close by and they stopped in for a few pieces. Next, using a guidebook, they found a bar off the beaten path where the servers were extremely knowledgeable about beer. The four hundred page tome on beer gave them great conversation while they each drank two of their favorites from the book.

"Cheers! To a great vacation with fabulous friends!" toasted Angela.

"Cheers!" they all said in unison, with laughter and smiles, glasses raised.

"So Jill, have you been thinking about the mystery of Laura Peeters all afternoon?" asked Marie with a smirk. "I'm amazed that you had the willpower not to ask me what I found on that search while we were in the lecture hall."

"Since you asked, I've been dying to know what you found. It's only my respect for your vacation time that has kept me quiet."

"The three of us actually had a bet on you," said Marie. "While you were enjoying yourself in the lecture hall, Angela thought you would only last until we got out of that building. I thought you would hold back until sometime on our walk to Ruben's House. It appears that Jo knows you best she thought you'd hold out to the first beer."

"Really, you were all wrong. I made it through the first beer, and was working on my second. I still hadn't asked a question about Laura until you brought it up. I think that shows willpower!"

They all laughed at Jill's comment, as they were served their second choice of beer.

"Okay, I've been patient enough. Tell me your findings!"

"Laura Peeters, would have been age thirty-seven except she died, according to Belgian records, at age twenty-three. Native to Antwerp. Single, no children, no known partner. Family – adopted at age three by Marie and Josef Peeters, now deceased. No siblings, aunts, uncles, really no family. I have never, in over two-hundred searches, had a candidate with no family. Occupation – wanted by both the Belgian police and Interpol for over ten years for questioning in numerous diamond thefts and smuggling. Education – attended the International Gemological Institute in Antwerp. She was a certified gemstone scientist."

"I guess that background helps if you're going to steal diamonds," agreed Jo. "So, according to Belgian tax authorities, she's dead, but Interpol believed her to be alive and stealing. Maybe Dr. DeGroot can get her fingerprints and see if it's a match. I believe he mentioned that the ID that was with her at the hospital said her name was Julie DuPont. I remember that you located her wallet in her purse at the restaurant, but none of us looked at the identification. We may find more aliases as we dig deeper into this case. Just to reduce confusion, no matter the alias she is operating under, let's always call her Laura," Marie said.

After a moment, she added. "I suppose as a diamond thief you should try to steal the best stones, and it would be helpful to have the education to evaluate the stones. Laura left a calling card at some of the sites of her diamond heists, but they couldn't catch her."

"What kind of calling card?" asked Angela.

"She left a small piece of wrapped chocolate in lieu of the diamonds."

"Was it the same type of chocolate at each heist?" queried Jill.

"Funny you should ask I wondered the same myself. In my quick search, I couldn't find the answer to that question."

"How long had she been stealing diamonds, and exactly how many heists are attributable to Laura?" asked Jo.

"It looks like she was suspected to be involved in two major heists per year for nearly fifteen years. Is it any wonder that Interpol wanted her captured?"

"Were all of the heists in Antwerp?" asked Jill. "Were they all retail jewelry stores?"

"She stole diamonds from retail stores, manufacturers, and private homes throughout Europe, the UK, and South America."

"I think Laura should be our beer mystery while we are in Belgium and the Netherlands," stated Angela in all seriousness. "We can each do a little research on her every day, and discuss our findings each time we sit down for beer."

"Beer mystery?" questioned a laughing Jo.

"I agree. My gut is telling me that even though she died from anaphylactic shock, I think underneath it all, she's really a homicide case. I would love to help the Belgian authorities solve this case. I don't like to see anybody killed, even if Laura was a master diamond thief. Maybe if we solve the case, the police might find the diamonds or learn what she did with them. I assume the location of her diamond cache remains a mystery?" said Jill.

"You're correct. Most diamonds were traceable because of the setting, but none of Laura's stolen jewelry has ever been found," noted Marie, continuing with the story. "Loose diamonds could easily be sold anywhere in the world. Several of the private collections she raided, have substantial rewards posted for the return of the pieces. Maybe we can collect some of that reward money by finding Laura's stash!"

"Dream on," said Jo. "As if we could solve the case of the diamonds heists quicker than Interpol and the Belgian police! We're good, but we don't have half the resources they do."

"Yeah, but if we did, you could all quit your day jobs and do detective work when you wanted to work," reasoned Jill.

"But we like our day jobs most of the time," observed a smiling Angela.

"I can't argue with that sentiment. I love growing the Muscat grape. So we'll make Laura Peeters our beer mystery, and we'll attempt to solve her suspected homicide whenever we break for beer. Let's put together a game plan for our research," Jill directed. "We have four detectives and only two iPads."

She thought for a moment. "I bet that Dr. DeGroot will share the autopsy report with me. I want to find out more about her nut allergy and her circle of acquaintances. What did she eat unsuspectingly that had nuts in it? Who was close by to observe us doing CPR on her and then follow her to the hospital?" asked Jill starting the conversation.

"I took pictures inside the restaurant, so I'll take a look at those pictures and see if anyone looks suspicious," added Angela. "We could return to the same restaurant since you never got your Flemish stew, and while we dine, I'll question the restaurant staff."

"I'll follow the money," Jo declared. "I'll look into her bank accounts and tax statements if I can find them on the Internet. I'll also do some research on diamond sales and look into the value of the private collections she stole."

"I'm going to do more research into friends and family. I still can't believe she has no family. I'm also going to see if I can find any medical records of prior allergic reaction episodes. I want to figure out what the police know about how she carried out these heists. Most of all, you know how I love chocolate," Marie remarked with great enthusiasm. "I'm going to follow the chocolate route."

With their assignments laid out, they toasted to a successful resolution of the mystery of Laura Peeters, aka Julie DuPont.

CHAPTER 5

They left the pub and headed toward Saint Jacob's Church. Besides being the burial place of Rubens, it was over six hundred years old and full of side chapels and beautiful stained glass. From there they headed to the port, catching the Slaughterhouse Museum on the way.

They ended up at the restaurant from their first night. The manager remembered them and wanted to know what had happened to Laura. Angela took over the conversation gaining the manager's approval for her to talk to the staff. She'd had the opportunity while at the port, to view the pictures from the previous night at the restaurant. She thought two of the people captured in her pictures looked suspicious. She started with the manager.

"Did Ms. Peeters make a reservation or walk in from the street?"

"She arrived without a reservation. She'd eaten here before and I recognized her."

"Was she expecting someone to join her?"

"Yes, she said she was meeting a friend."

"Male or female?"

"She did not say. She just used the word 'friend'".

"Did you know she was allergic to nuts?"

"Yes. She questioned me about our food, making sure that what she ordered excluded nuts and it was prepared not in contact with nuts, but I didn't realized she was having an allergic reaction yesterday"

"Did she usually dine alone or with someone?"

"A little of each. Sometimes she dined alone, sometimes with friends."

"Friends as in more than one?"

He paused and considered the question.

"Mostly she dined with just a one friend – a male."

"Did they seem like friends, or more like boyfriend and girlfriend?"

"Hmm. More like a friend. They were very close, but nothing romantic."

"When she was here yesterday, had she been served any food?"

He paused and looked very uncomfortable.

"She had the bread we normally serve all customers. There was butter, water, and wine on the table. I did not notice what she ate or drank while she was waiting for her friend to arrive."

"Did anyone arrive to the restaurant looking for her?"

"I don't believe so, but let me check with my staff. As you can imagine, that night was full of confusion, yet I have vivid memories of what occurred."

"One final question – do you recognize this person in the picture?" asked Angela, showing the manager the images saved on her camera.

"No, madam, I don't recall seating that person that night. In fact, he doesn't look familiar at all."

"Thank you for your time. You've been very helpful. How would you like me to question the other staff? I don't want to interfere with the restaurant operation. I could wait until I finish my dinner and then question the staff back in your kitchen. It shouldn't take me more than two to three minutes with each staff person. Does that work for you?"

He looked around the restaurant, studying how the staff was moving and how the food was flowing from the kitchen. After doing some mental calculations, he nodded in agreement with Angela's plan. She joined the rest of her girlfriends to dine. She wrote some notes down, and told them what she found. They discussed any additional questions for the rest of the staff.

"When you go into the kitchen, ask them what dishes have nuts in them and have them show you where the nuts are stored," suggested Jill. "See if there is a back door and judge if someone could sneak in and add nuts to a dish."

"Ask if any of the wait staff noticed her relationship with the man she dined frequently with – if they'd overheard any conversations," suggested Marie.

"See if you can find out if she paid with cash or credit card and if they have any receipts from her prior meals," added Jo.

"I feel like we're having an adventure on the Orient Express with all of us trying to solve this case," said Angela with a smile while she took notes on their suggested questions. "It's a new aspect to a vacation!"

A waiter came over to take their orders. For Jill and Marie it was easy; they just ordered what they'd chosen on their previous visit to the restaurant. Angela and Jo were looking for something new. Angela tried chicken braised in beer, and Jo settled on soup that sounded delicious. Angela feared ordering seafood in Europe as she had once been unpleasantly surprised by getting the whole fish head, eyes included.

Marie and Jo settled on wine while Angela and Jill stayed with beer. It never worked for Jill's head if she mixed beer and wine within a few hours of each other. With drinks in hand, they talked about the day.

"I think it's safe to say, that this has been our most unusual day on vacation ever," mused Jo.

"It's not spoiling your vacation?" asked Jill.

"No, it's just unusual. Besides, how could I complain when we hit three museums, two major churches, and a few chocolate shops? The stop at the lecture hall was an interesting break. We got to watch every day citizens at work. I'm having a good time; you don't need to worry."

"Whew! You know me -I like to multitask," Jill said. "So solving the mystery of Laura Peeters while touring famous museums and churches is my idea of a great vacation. Of course, being with you guys is a minimum requirement."

"It's a shame we can't give them more research time," noted Marie. "We are limited both by our vacation and our access to the Internet. Maybe if we do happen to solve this case while we're here, we'll establish a reputation in Europe. Then we could get more cases here and travel often to Europe!"

"Huh! And you guys complain about me multitasking."

"So what was your favorite thing you viewed today?" queried Angela.

"Good question," exclaimed Jo. "I just enjoyed looking around the street thinking that I might be related to half of the people that we passed. I was soaking up my heritage."

"I liked the flash of the diamond district. There was a lot of ugly stuff in the windows, but at the same time, someone must buy it. I've never been around so many expensive diamonds in my life. I also liked the little pub we stopped at for beer," observed Jill.

"Personally, I could stop in a chocolate shop about every forty-five minutes on this vacation," Marie responded with a laugh. "The chocolate shop near Ruben's House was my favorite."

"I'ld have to say, I liked the cathedral and the square around it. I got some really great pictures of people in the square and the angles of the church," said Angela.

Just then, their waiter brought the entrees to the table. The conversation for the next several minutes was about the food. Jill and Marie loved their Flemish stew. Both Jo and Angela were happy with their choices as well. It really was a great restaurant.

They had an uneventful dinner with no one collapsing in the restaurant. After they finished eating, Jill, Jo, and Marie savored their beverages while Angela went to work on the restaurant staff. The manager had filled her in on all of their various roles in the restaurant. She opened the conversation with each staff member by confirming what he or she did for the restaurant; it was a way to put them at their ease.

"Were you the waiter of the woman that collapsed here two days ago?"

"Yes I was."

"Did you know her, had you served her before?"

"I might have, but I don't think so as I don't remember a conversation about nuts in the food and I think I would've remembered that."

"I'm surprised she asked you about nuts in the food as she'd dined here before, so I would've thought she knew your menu well."

"We change our menu seasonally to account for the availability of game on the menu. While we serve Flemish stew year-round, we only serve pheasant seasonally. She was considering ordering something from our fall menu, so the questions made sense."

"Okay. It looked to me like she had not eaten a main course. Had she ordered? Or was she waiting for someone to arrive?"

"I was told when she was seated that she was waiting on someone. I think she might've gotten an email or a text to say the person was running very late, because about five minutes later she said her friend was going to be late and to eat dinner without her. So she ordered and then, as usual, I brought bread and butter over to the table. Her order of food had not been delivered to the table."

"What kind of bread and butter? Did you notice if she ate any of it?"

"Yes, she did eat some of it as there were crumbs on her plate. It's just our house bread-and-butter that we make in the kitchen."

"Did you notice if she put butter on the bread?"

"She did."

"What would you guess was the time between when she ate the bread and when she looked ill?"

The waiter looked very uneasy about that question as Angela was trying to establish a link between the food and the onset of Laura's allergic reaction.

"Ten minutes."

"That's all the questions I have. Thank you so much for giving me a few minutes of your time," said Angela with a warm smile.

Angela spent another fifteen minutes questioning other staff in the restaurant. None of the waiters remembered her as a repeat customer. For the most part, they were college students working part-time so no surprise there. Her last interview was with the chef.

"I loved my chicken braised in beer tonight; thank you for creating such a delightful dish. As you know, there was a woman in the restaurant two days ago with a nut allergy. She had safely eaten here before, so clearly you're able to provide entrees without nuts. We don't know if she was exposed to nuts in the bread and butter at this restaurant, or if she had eaten something before she walked in. Can you show me where your nuts are stored in the kitchen?"

"We are conscious of nut allergies. She was not the only customer who was worried about nuts. We store almonds, pine nuts, peanuts, walnuts, and macadamia nuts for use in our recipes in airtight canisters on a separate shelf in our food storage area."

"If you have to grind or chop the nuts, where you do that?"

"We generally use small quantities of nuts. We keep a small food processor that changes the whole nuts to shaved, chopped, or nearly powdered nuts. The food processor is stored next to the canisters. Food moves from the canister to the processor to the mixing bowl or cooking pan. It does not touch any surface in the kitchen, nor do we use any knives to cut nuts."

Angela's mom, who was a renowned chef in her own right, would have loved to chat with this chef about food. She could see their conversation in her head, before she re-focused on the chef. "You seem to take a lot of nut allergy precautions."

"Several years ago someone worked at this restaurant that had a child with nut allergies. It permanently changed how we stored and prepared nuts at this restaurant. The child nearly died from eating in a restaurant that didn't pay attention to the separation of nuts from all other foods. It was a lifelong lesson for me, so we take precautions. I don't think it was something from this kitchen."

"Yes it seems very unlikely that the woman would have been exposed to nuts here."

"As I recall from conversations with the father of the child with nut allergies, he said that the allergy took one to two hours to show up after the child ate the wrong thing. She wasn't here that long."

"You've been very helpful; let me get out of your way so you can return to cooking."

Angela had one final question for the manager. She wanted to know if he remembered how Laura usually paid for her meals. She obviously had not had time to pay the other evening.

"Would you remember if Laura paid her bill with cash or a credit card on her previous visits to your restaurant?"

"I would not remember. After the restaurant closes, I can easily look at our credit receipts for say, the past two years, to see if her name comes up."

"That would be great. She also goes by the name Julie DuPont, so if you could look up that name as well. We're not looking for her credit card number, but if you could tell us if she used a MasterCard, Visa, or some other card. Here is my email address, if you wouldn't mind dropping a note to me," said Angela handing him a piece of paper with her information on it.

"I hope you find where she ate nuts unknowingly. I believe that it did not occur inside this restaurant. Have a nice evening, madam."

They left the restaurant, weaving their way through the streets of Antwerp. Once they were a few blocks away, Angela relayed her conversations with the restaurant staff. It was very unlikely that nuts could be in the bread as it had been baked that morning. She had looked at the doors in the kitchen, and perhaps someone could have entered and added nut powder to the butter, but it didn't feel right. A perpetrator would have to add nuts to all the bread and butter as he or she wouldn't know which slices and butter dishes would be delivered to Laura's table.

"Jill, the chef sounded well informed about nut allergies because a former employee had a child with a severe allergy. He made the comment that food allergies take one to two hours to impact someone. Is that true?"

"Yes, that's generally true and it would point to her consumption of nuts having occurred before she reached the restaurant."

"Jo, the manager couldn't remember if she paid by cash or credit. He will, however, access his credit card charges database to see if her name has appeared over the last two years. The big question is what name – Laura Peeters, Julie DuPont, or another name we haven't discovered yet. In theory, Laura is dead, so the credit card isn't likely in her name unless it is a popular name and she felt safe reverting to it in time. I gave him both names to look for in his database."

"I don't know if this tells us anything given that we don't think she ate nuts at the restaurant. We'll see what this investigation turns up over the next few days," Jo replied.

They headed over to a bar that had nice music and friendly conversation coming from it. Finding a table, they sat down and a waitress came over to take their order. People were enjoying the music and dancing to the beat. It was the perfect atmosphere to relax in.

Marie pulled her iPad out of her purse and checked to see if the bar had Wi-Fi so she could begin their beer mystery search in a very pleasant setting. Luckily, free Wi-Fi was available. She had organized the information she had learned in her earlier search. Marie hadn't had the time to finish that search and she needed to add the new information that Angela obtained earlier at the restaurant. She had a few things she wanted to explore, and then she would hand it over to Jo.

Marie was tapping her foot to the music and looking through her usual sources for mention of Laura's nut allergy. Jo was on the dance floor with Angela and a small group of dancing people. Jill was sitting next to Marie, looking at what she was finding on the Internet.

There were a few mentions of the allergy in such places as Facebook and Pinterest, but nothing significant. A few more minutes of exploration and they called it quits on the research for the night. All of the women spent a little more time on the dance floor before heading back to their hotel suite.

It was dark when they left the bar. The streets became darker and quieter as they left the main thoroughfare. Cars were parked bumper-to-bumper in this residential area. Jill felt uneasy even though the neighborhood looked deserted. There was an apartment with flowers up ahead. She nonchalantly drew her friends in to admire the flowers.

"Hey guys come over here and look at these beautiful flowers," said Jill. Then she lowered her voice and added, "I think someone is following us."

The other three looked down the street, but all they saw was a quiet residential section.

"Call me paranoid, but let's test if someone is out there. Let's slow our pace down as we approach the end of this street and the moment we get around the corner, let's sprint and hide in one of these front entrance alcoves. They look dark enough for us to hide in the shadows. If we see someone looking for us, then my feelings were spot-on. If we don't, my paranoia will get you all a drink at the bar when we return to the hotel. Deal?" asked Jill.

"I don't see anyone on the street, but you haven't been wrong up to this point about sensing strangers' intent on doing us harm. So I'm in agreement with your plan," replied Marie.

The others nodded in agreement and they set off at a slower pace to the end of the street. When they reached the corner, they sprinted to the first alcove and heaved a sigh of relief to see the gate was open. They ducked into the shadows, while Angela quickly closed the gate. Jill looked at her watch and decided to give it five minutes to see if anyone sinister-looking walked by. She wasn't sure what a sinister look was, but, she thought she would know when she saw it.

The seconds ticked by and Jill began to feel like an idiot. Her watch dial indicated that a minute had passed. Her knees were starting to feel uncomfortable against the cold concrete surface. Then she heard a sound. She looked at her three friends - they'd heard it too.

From their place in the shadows, they watched a figure jog by in a dark coat. It appeared to be a man. The figure was carrying something metallic in his hand. It wasn't clear whether it was a gun or knife.

"What should we do now?" whispered Jo.

Jill shrugged "I don't know, I hadn't thought that far ahead."

They listened a while longer and heard no other sounds.

"I think we should stay hidden in the shadows for another ten minutes. I would think our stranger would move beyond this street by then. What if we call for a taxi for pick-up here at the end of those ten minutes? I have no idea how fast service will be, but we can stay hidden until then," suggested Marie.

"Sounds like a plan," said Angela.

"What do we do when we reach the hotel? Does this person know where we are staying?" asked Jo.

They'd been whispering to each other, pausing at times to listen for footsteps. As they thought about Jo's question, they heard footsteps approaching. They hunched down and stayed quiet, watching the street through the wrought-iron fence.

The same stranger slowly passed by their gate, talking on a cell phone in a language they couldn't understand. They knew it wasn't German, Spanish or French. Beyond that, they couldn't tell if it was Dutch or a different language.

The four of them sat crouched in the shadows. They waited another five minutes but the stranger did not return. They returned to their plan, waited another five minutes, and then called a taxi.

While waiting for the taxi, they discussed what they should do to return to their hotel safely. They agreed that they would have the taxi drop them off two blocks from their hotel and they would look for a back entrance – perhaps through the kitchen or laundry area. If they didn't find a back entrance, they would split up and enter the hotel one at a time.

The taxi arrived soon and dropped them off close to their hotel. The women took a moment to evaluate the situation. They didn't see anyone lurking around the entrance to the hotel, and the road was too dark and they were too far away to really see into the parked cars. They took the long way around, looking for a back entrance to the hotel. Luck was with them - they found an employee taking a smoking break outside a back door. They showed him their room keys and proceeded in and up the stairs to their rooms. Despite the excitement of the past hour, jetlag was still washing over them, and they soon dropped off into sleep.

CHAPTER 6

*T*he next morning was to be their last in Antwerp before heading to Amsterdam on the train. A couple of hours on the train would give Jill and Jo time to do a little more research on Laura. After checking out of their hotel, they headed for the train station. It was an amazingly beautiful station with twin towers and large dome.

After locating the platform where their train was, they climbed aboard and stored their luggage overhead before settling in their seats. The countryside was beautiful as the train glided by. The bike paths were numerous and well used. Jill had always found it interesting to look at the architecture of homes in the country-side, and this was as fascinating as ever. In Europe, she was constantly amazed at how frequently nice homes were adjacent to the train tracks. As a light sleeper, she'd had a lifelong aversion to hotels and homes close to train tracks.

Eventually she settled in to her Internet search. She wanted to get a sense of how Europeans viewed nut allergies. Were these allergies as prevalent as in the United States? Was it routine that people with nut allergies carried EpiPens in Europe? Were nuts a basic ingredient in Flemish cooking? Certainly they were a staple in chocolate recipes. How many nuts did it take to generate an allergic reaction in someone with this allergy? Would one nut do it, or was it a minimum quantity, like a quarter of a cup? She enjoyed the intellectual exercise of refreshing her knowledge on nut allergies.

Jo knew everything about how to find financial information in the United States, but she knew nothing about it in Belgium. She started looking for tax returns and corporate tax filings, and she acquired a sense of the availability of financial information in Belgium.

She couldn't imagine that Laura Peeters had filed any tax information under her real name considering she was officially dead, but some of her aliases might have. She would start with the name of Julie DuPont. Somehow, it just seemed that someone whose occupation was "diamond thief" would not be likely to file tax returns.

Jo looked a little into the diamond market. If one stole loose diamonds, what was your potential market to sell them to? Had Laura set up a company that sold loose diamonds to retail jewelry stores in Antwerp, Europe, or the world? If she had set up a company, would there be corporate information about that company? It was a good place to start.

About thirty minutes into their search activities, Jill received an email from Dr. DeGroot. He was appreciative of the work the women were doing in trying to help him solve the mystery of Laura Peeters. He had reviewed the information that Marie was able to compile. Using Jill's checklist, he had performed a lot more analysis than his usual autopsy.

The four friends were facing each other, thanks to the seating arrangement on the train. When Jill had finished reading Dr. DeGroot's email, she lowered her voice and leaned in.

"Dr. DeGroot just sent me an email regarding Laura. He had some interesting findings. He found chocolate with nuts in her stomach contents, which had been ingested about an hour to an hour and a half prior to her arrival at the hospital. As we suspected, it was not in the bread or butter of the restaurant. Whoever sold her the chocolate had to have indicated to her that there were no nuts in the chocolate."

"Did she die from the empty heart condition you described?" asked Angela.

"Yes she did. The autopsy showed a minimal amount of blood in her heart chambers. That will kill you every time. They aren't sure, if she sat up herself or if someone sat her up. She was dusted for fingerprints and they are running the results through Interpol. I don't know if they'll get anywhere with fingerprints, because a lot of people cared for her in the emergency room, and even our fingerprints should have been on her. Hospital staff members are not routinely fingerprinted so they don't even have enough prints on file to eliminate legitimate staff."

"She must have been a chocolate fanatic," said Marie instantly sharing an affinity for Laura's preference. "Chocolate is one of the few foods in which you can consistently have traces of nuts. You would think for her own health, she would've just stayed away from chocolate. I love chocolate, but I would go cold turkey tomorrow if it was determined I had a nut allergy."

"What else did he say in the autopsy report?" said Angela.

"She had a little facial reconstruction done about ten years ago. I would guess that was to help her stay hidden from Interpol. There are a few comments about different organs and various skin marks. She had a tattoo on her right hip that is the logo of the International Gemological Institute. Interesting how important her profession was to her. His final comment, and this is certainly unusual: her stomach contents contained several carats' worth of diamonds. When he pulled her stomach out to weigh it, it was unusually heavy. He had to slice her stomach open as he was looking for nuts. Imagine his surprise on seeing diamonds."

"Was that her method of transporting diamonds, or did she

swallow them during the burglar process?" Angela probed. "Can I just say yuck to the retrieval process that would follow?"

"You would be amazed at what I have found in stomachs at the time of autopsy. Usually it's drugs. Diamonds would have been a pleasant surprise."

"Let me see if I can find anything on Interpol about her alleged style of burglary," offered Marie.

Jill passed the iPad over to Marie. They had another thirty minutes on the train before they would reach Amsterdam. As Marie began her search on diamond thieves, Jill and Angela enjoyed the scenery. The fall colors were amazing – vivid reds and yellows. Some trees looked like they were on fire, their leaves were so alive. The train stopped in Rotterdam, but there wasn't much to see of the city from the train station. Pretty soon they were packing up their belongings to get ready to disembark from the train at Amsterdam's Central Station. Jill gave the other passengers a glance as they exited the train. She thought she'd seen the man in the seat behind her previously, but that thought passed out of her head as she began to lug her heavy luggage off the train.

The gentleman in question had been seated behind the foursome and had been listening intently to their conversation. He was a computer hacker, among his many skills, and thanks to the unsecured Wi-Fi, was soon looking at Dr. DeGroot's email, as well as the sites they visited. He sent an email off to Antwerp with a summary of their activities. He hoped he wouldn't be ordered to kill them; he rather liked their looks and conversation. They had guts, a trait he always respected. He would continue to follow them and figure out what they were up to.

It took a lot of energy to heave their suitcases up and down the stairs at the train station. Their hotel was within half a mile of the train station, so they planned to walk loaded down with their luggage. They were all grateful that the suitcases had wheels on them. Carrying forty pounds any distance was beyond them.

Upon reaching the station exit, they came to a halt to look at the bicycles parked at the station. There were thousands of them. Everywhere you looked, there was a bicycle. Angela wondered aloud, "How do you find your bicycle?" From their vantage point, they all looked alike. They looked out onto the street where they were headed to see a hundred more bicyclists riding along the bike lanes. A tourist had to quickly get used to looking for bicyclists before crossing the street.

Soon they reached their hotel and checked in. Sitting down on the chairs in their suite, they planned their stay in Amsterdam. First, they decided to walk toward Anne Frank's house. Jill received another message from Dr. DeGroot asking her to give them a call. She planned to chat with him as they walked toward the house.

"Dr. DeGroot, this is Jill Quint. How may I help you?"

"Thank you, Dr. Quint, for returning my call. I am sorry to keep bothering you on your holiday, but I've never performed an autopsy like the one I did for Laura Peeters, and I feel so fortunate that I have a forensic expert to guide me in this investigation."

"I'm glad to help, Dr. DeGroot. My team and I are walking toward Anne Frank's house, so you're not interfering with my holiday. How can I help you with the investigation?"

"Did you see my earlier email with the results of the autopsy?"

"Yes, I did. You found diamonds in her stomach. You also found nuts in the chocolate in her stomach."

"I'm going to declare her death a killing. We don't use the word 'homicide' in Belgium. The police did extensive questioning of the staff in the emergency room that cared for her. That questioning suggests that a stranger was in the area near Laura. No one saw that stranger move her to an upright position. They were busy that night with a major auto accident and had thought that she was stabilized. So at the time, no one thought to follow up on the rumor of a stranger."

"Is the stranger in the area the only reason you have for calling it a killing?"

Jill would never label a death as a homicide based on the single piece of information about a stranger alone.

"I'm declaring it a killing because of the nut allergy. She told hospital staff that she always carried an emergency epinephrine pen in her purse. However, a man had taken the pen out of her purse and crushed it earlier that day and she had not had the opportunity to get her back-up pen. She told the staff that in thirty years she had never been without the pen, as she knew she had a severe allergy. The second thing she told hospital staff was that she purchased chocolate from a limited number of stores worldwide that she trusted not to put nuts in their chocolate. She had gone so far as to inspect their kitchens and have their chocolate tested for nuts before she consumed it. She'd been eating chocolate safely for ten years."

"Wow, that was wise of her. I had wondered why she would ever touch chocolate given her severe allergy and the propensity to manufacture chocolate close to nuts."

"Dr. Quint, based on what I have told you, would you agree that I have the basis to label this case a killing?"

"In the United States, we have a category called 'suspicious death.' It's a term used to say obviously that the death is suspicious, but the coroner needs further information from law enforcement's investigation to make a final determination. From what you have told me about Laura Peeters, she would fit the category of suspicious death in the United States."

"Let me contact the Belgian police to see if I can use that label for her death."

"Do you know if swallowing diamonds was her usual method of diamond theft?"

"From what law enforcement said to me, I would think that her swallowing the diamonds was unusual."

"Why?"

"She was caught on camera during a few thefts early in her career. That was how her calling card of chocolate was connected to her. She always carried her loot in a bag. The police believe she used her gemologist credentials to establish paperwork for the stolen diamonds. At one time she even had connections to the DeBeers mines in South Africa."

"Why there?"

"Dr. Quint, how much do you know about the diamond trade?"

"Not much. I likely own a diamond in a piece of jewelry, but I have never paid attention to carats or quality. I get bored with jewelry and stop wearing it, so it's best for me to own fake stuff. Tell me about South Africa."

"Most diamonds are mined in South Africa, and the largest theft of diamonds actually occurs in the mines. Miners often swallow raw diamonds as a means of stealing them. Mines have x-rays to randomly scan workers for swallowed diamonds, but they can't do it every day as the radiation exposure is too great. Some experts estimate that twenty-five percent of diamonds are stolen in the mines.

"Before diamonds are sold, they have to be certified by a gemologist for their cut and clarity. It's extremely hard to sell them without this documentation. Also for this reason, it is hard to resell stolen diamonds-especially famous diamonds or settings."

"So why would you think that Laura went out of character and swallowed diamonds to carry out a theft?"

"I don't know. The police and Interpol are looking into that angle. Dr. Quint, can you think of any other tests I should run on Laura Peeters that would give us more information?"

"Did you analyze the chocolate?"

"The chocolate?"

"You might be able to identify where she purchased the chocolate she consumed by analyzing its DNA. I would get a sample from, say, ten to fifteen prominent chocolate shops in Antwerp. I would compare the chocolate in her stomach contents to the samples from the stores to see if there is a match. I understand that chocolate in Belgium is a craft, so I would think that each brand of chocolate would be unique in an analysis. Knowing where she purchased the chocolate containing nuts would help the police with the investigation."

"An excellent suggestion, Dr. Quint. I remember a few years ago an announcement from someone in the chocolate industry about the genome sequence of chocolate. If I recall, they did the sequencing to improve the health of the cocoa tree. At the time, I thought it was superfluous research. Later, when I understood the agricultural benefit, I thought it was a good idea. Now, maybe it will help us solve this mystery.

"I'm going to send a student out to purchase chocolate as you suggested, and get to work on this DNA analysis. Thank you for your help and for taking my call today."

Jill closed out the call with Dr. DeGroot and switched back to vacation mode. Her friends had heard her comment about the chocolate.

"Did I hear you say that you recommend he run DNA tests on the chocolate in Laura's stomach?" asked Marie.

"About three years ago, some scientist mapped out the DNA of chocolate," replied Jill. "Being a chocolate lover, do you know much about the industry?"

"Not really," answered Marie with a grin. "I just enjoy eating it."

"Nearly all of the world's chocolate comes from small farmers in Africa. Ghana and the Ivory Coast produce something like 70 percent of the world's cocoa beans. The tree is relatively fragile and certain pests can do great damage to the crop and the industry. Scientists hypothesize that knowing the DNA of the different cocoa trees could help them design a tree more resilient to pests. It's very possible that each Belgian chocolatier purchases their chocolate from a different farmer and therefore it would have different DNA. Knowing the DNA will assist the police in identifying where Laura purchased the chocolate that caused her reaction."

"You know, Jill, your brain contains some of the most obscure facts of anyone I know," said Marie admiringly. "It's lucky for Laura that you know this stuff."

"Thanks! I think," said Jill with a laugh.

She caught a reflection in a storefront glass window. She slowed her pace and looked out of the corner of her eye. She rarely believed in coincidence, and this situation was too coincidental. She turned and hurried back a few steps.

"Excuse me, why are you following us?"

"I am not following you madam." said the man that Jill had noticed as they were getting off the train.

Jo, Marie, and Angela followed her and caught up.

"You were on the train about an hour ago that arrived from Antwerp. Now you are on the same street as us. Are you following us?" she asked again.

"You are mistaken. I did not take the train from Antwerp. You must be thinking of someone who looks like me. Excuse me, I must be on my way."

While Jill was confronting the man, Angela had gotten a nice shot of his face with her camera. Jill had always been really good at sensing people around her and if she thought she'd seen the man on the train, the other three knew it to be true.

"Jill, are you sure he was on the train? If he was, then he had to be following us since we detoured to the hotel first," reasoned Jo.

"Yes I am sure he was on the train," responded Jill. "You know how vigilant I am about keeping an eye open at all times looking for pickpockets. He was dumb to follow us so closely. He must have been trying to hear our conversation."

"Why is anyone following us?" asked Angela. "We're just a bunch of American tourists."

"It must have something to do with the Laura Peeters case. I can't think of a reason to observe us on our vacation. I'll have to pass this information on to Dr. DeGroot. There's nothing like having us followed that solidifies his impression that Laura was a victim of a homicide."

"After your last experience, Jill, I no longer think that forensic pathology is a safe occupation. Should we call the police here? Should we go shopping for some kind of self-defense item like pepper spray, or should we just all be on alert?" asked Marie.

"Good question. I don't think we have enough information to go to the police and pepper spray is illegal in Europe. How about the three of us stay on alert for people that are following us. Pay attention to clothing and faces. Jo, I know you're hopeless at paying attention to your surroundings. We will watch out for you," advised a smiling Jill.

"Hey, don't make disparaging remarks about me," Jo asserted. "I can pay attention when I need to. Angela, show me his picture and I'll start looking for him everywhere we go. At least, we can hope to bankrupt him with museum admission fees and bus tickets."

They all stared at the picture on Angela's camera memorizing it. They continued down the street, crossed a bridge over a canal and made a right turn to see Anne Frank's house. They spent a solemn two hours reading about and imagining the life of Anne Frank. It was a very sad time in world history.

After exiting the museum, they walked around the immediate neighborhood looking for a place to eat. They settled on an Indian restaurant. On one hand they felt a duty to eat Dutch food, but the Indian restaurant was packed, and the smells were enticing. The restaurant host approached them.

"Table for four?"

"Yes"

"Please have a seat in our waiting area. It will be about a fifteen minute wait."

"What do you think we should do next in regards to Laura Peeters?" asked Marie.

"This is our vacation. We should probably do nothing related to her suspected homicide" said Jill.

Her three friends looked at her with eyebrows raised in doubt. She gazed back at them in silence.

"This is Europe and I don't think rocket launching helicopters are going to be attacking us here, but I feel uneasy with doing nothing, especially since that man followed us on the train and then through the town. You know that I am the last person to ever work on a vacation," said Jo. "However, if we don't, we could unknowingly put our lives at risk. Let's continue sightseeing, watch out for bad people, and spend every spare moment researching this case."

Jo was right. When she went on a vacation, she never checked in with work. She did not check her e-mail, and made no calls to the office. Vacationing was about fun, friends, relaxation, and sightseeing. If she felt an urgent need to handle the Laura Peeters case in their spare time, then it meant she was really bothered.

Secretly Jill was itching to dive into the case, but respect for her friends and their vacation time had caused her to deeply bury that desire. She was glad that they'd arrived at the conclusion that continuing to research the case would be in all their best interests. So she would lay her cards on the table.

"Thanks, Jo. I think trying to solve this case is the right thing to do," agreed Jill. "I've been dying to help, but I also have great respect for your holiday time and I would never put the job before us enjoying our vacation."

"Ladies, your table is ready. Please come with me," said the host as he led them to a table.

The group of friends settled in to study the menu. The server came back with water, and took their drink and food orders. After a fabulous dinner of butter chicken, chicken marsala, daal, chole, and malai kofta, they began walking the streets back to their hotel. They wanted a peek at the notorious red-light district, and they thought it would be crowded enough that they would be safe. The district was just a little out of their way on the walk back to their hotel. While enjoying Amsterdam at night, they still were on guard, watching out for any suspicious strangers.

It was difficult evaluating the people they passed on the street. Added to that were the bicyclists and cars that gave them too many people to watch under the street-lights. In the end, Jill watched the pedestrians, Angela and Jo studied the bicyclists and Marie monitored the cars.

They walked around the area where they thought the district was located, but failed to find it. Finally, they stopped in an ice-cream shop and asked for directions. The young salesperson frowned at them and said there was really nothing to see in the district.

"Yes, I know you're right, but we have never seen such a thing, so our curiosity is driving us to find the red-light district," said Marie.

The salesperson provided directions and the women quickly found the area. They didn't know what to expect. They found women, usually wearing white lingerie, standing under black lighting, inside rooms with a red light on the exterior. They appeared to be in a room with a sliding glass door in the front, a door leading to an exit in the back, and there was a bed to one side of the room. The room was also outfitted with a shower, according to the tour book. The women were generally smoking a cigarette or reading and texting on a mobile phone. Some of the rooms were dark, so presumably either its tenant was occupied or it wasn't staffed that night.

They decided they wanted to watch the street to observe the transactions, and in particular who was buying that evening. They picked a spot where they could observe about eight different prostitutes available to conduct business. While the women were in a cluster talking about this unique Amsterdam industry, Jill noticed that they were being watched by two men. Given that they were in a red-light district, at first she thought perhaps they were being sized up for companionship, but something didn't seem right.

"Hey, there are two men watching us and I don't think it's for the same reason they're watching the other girls," Jill murmured. "They seem too alert and they are paying zero attention to the women in the window. Besides we are probably fifteen to twenty years older than those women, and we're wearing a lot more clothing than them."

"So what is our plan?" asked Jo.

They looked around the area for a place to take cover. It was decided: first they would move away from this location and if the men followed, they would have their answer. Their biggest problem was, they were not sure of their exact location in reference to their hotel. They hadn't seen any police in the area either.

"There is a door up ahead on the right side of the street I've that I have seen women go in and out of it while we've been in this area," said Marie, using her eyes and words to describe the direction they would take. "There doesn't appear to be a key or other security to get that door open. If we head there now, the men will just follow us inside. I think we should split up into two groups and do a fast walk around those two blocks before heading for that door. If we have enough of a head start, the men won't see us duck into that building."

"Sounds like a plan," Jill answered as their little group split up. "Angela and I'll take the block on the right. See you soon."

The woman started walking at a pace just short of running. The men were confused initially by the group of women splitting up, and this aided the escape plan. Each twosome had outdistanced the man following it sufficiently that they were out of view when they slid into the door that Marie had pointed out.

Breathing rapidly after the fast pace of the last five minutes, Jill surmised, "I think we escaped notice."

"Yes, but where are we? This looks like the hotel corridor, with numbered rooms touching the corridor."

Further down the hallway, one of the doors opened and a woman stepped into the corridor. She walked towards them while shouting Dutch words at them.

"Sorry, we don't speak Dutch," Jill responded.

"You need to leave this building," the woman spoke in English. "You are not permitted to be inside. Please leave."

"We had some scary men following us, so we ducked in here when they were not looking. We can't leave yet. Please, is there a place to hide inside this building in case they open the door and find us standing here?" asked Marie.

"Would you like me to call the constable?"

"They haven't done anything other than follow us, so I think we would have a hard time explaining that to the police," declared Jill. "Is there a place to hide in here?"

"Do you know what kind of building this is that you have walked into?"

"No, we just knew the door was unlocked," said Marie.

"This building is a house of prostitution. Each of these rooms that you see off this corridor faces the street. If you would like to strip to your bra and panties, then you could hide in plain sight as a member of the red-light district. Otherwise there is nowhere to hide in any of the prostitution rooms. Of course, you don't have a license, so you may not accept customers. I've got hats to cover your hair, and then you just need to keep your eyes down as that will not encourage men on the street to hire your services. I think if you stand in the window for thirty minutes, then the men will go away when they can't find you, right?"

"We can do that," observed Jo with her usual sense of adventure.

"My bra and panties are not matching; won't that look strange?" asked Jill.

"Yes it will look strange, but we don't have spare underwear for you to wear."

Jill looked at her three friends and said "we are running out of time, I say we implement the suggestion of our new Dutch friend and hang out in the window watching for the men to give up the search."

The woman directed them to empty rooms and provided them with hats. The hats would provide a disguise, as they were all versions of a cowgirl hat made of felt with varying degrees of bling on the wide rim.

Jo went first, stripping to her underwear wearing the hat. They left the room in shadows except for the black light inside the room, with the red light outside lit for business. The other three quickly followed suit in their own rooms. It was difficult to keep their eyes down because they were trying to watch for the two men to walk by.

They'd been at their posts for five minutes when each of the women separately noted the two men that had chased them walk down the street looking for them. They did not see the scantily clad women in the windows. The prostitute had been correct: they were hiding in plain sight.

The women stayed at their posts for another twenty-five minutes, but never again saw the two men. Their new friend from the red-light district had stayed behind to help them close down the four rooms, and then she took them on a series of quiet streets to a taxi stand.

Jill said to the young prostitute, "Thank you so much for your help. Would you be offended if we offered you a tip for your services?"

"It can be a hard life here, so I would just say thank you for the tip," said the young woman as she walked away with a smile. "And thank you for providing me some entertainment tonight."

Ten minutes later, they arrived at their hotel. Once they arrived into their suite, Angela made a call to the lobby reception.

"Hello, how may I help you?" said the lobby receptionist.

"We just had an unsettling experience while we were walking about the town. Two men followed us around until we evaded them. We just returned to our suite. We would appreciate if you would put a note on our account that if anyone inquires about us, to say we checked out of the hotel. Can you do this?"

"What a terrible experience. I'll make a note on your account that we are to state that you have checked out. We occasionally have celebrities staying here and that is how we protect their privacy, so this should work for you. Would you like us to tell you if someone inquires about your presence? Would you like to talk to our security?"

"Yes to both of your questions. As it is getting late, perhaps we could set up an early-morning appointment with your head of security for tomorrow. Can you confirm an appointment time for us and provide the person's name?"

"Yes madam. I'll call your room again in the next thirty minutes with an appointment time."

"Thank you. You have been very helpful. We will sleep better thanks to your assistance. Good night."

After the adrenaline rush of the last hour, none of them was ready to go sleep. They'd had an experience of a lifetime in the red-light district that would provide fodder for stories for years to come. They opened a bottle of wine that Marie had picked up at a shop near the train station and went to work on their respective areas of research. The hotel's business center was one floor down in a non-public area, so Jo and Angela felt secure setting up there with their glasses of wine to continue their research on Laura Peeters. The front desk had called and set up an eight in the morning meeting with their head of security. After that early meeting, they were planning to visit six different museums around the city of Amsterdam.

CHAPTER 7

*A*bout an hour after the women split up, they regrouped for an amazing conversation. Marie started things off, she'd pinpointed seven different aliases used by Laura Peeters. They were nowhere near finished given the time it took to investigate each alias, but a picture was forming.

"At an early age, Laura planned to make a career in the gemstone industry," Marie noted, beginning the conversation with the findings that they had dug up on Laura previously. "She sought and obtained the necessary education and certifications to pursue rating and polishing gemstones. Some two to three years later, after she was working for one of the major diamond houses in Antwerp, she came into contact with blood diamonds."

"Blood diamonds? Aren't those diamonds mined by slaves in Africa?" asked Angela.

"Yes. The mines were treacherous from an environmental perspective, and sometimes they used children or enslaved adults to retrieve the diamonds from the earth" responded Marie.

"How did she go from jeweler to diamond thief?" queried Jill.

"It is thought by the law enforcement's profiler that she confronted her employer about the blood diamonds. When the employer refused to decline shipments from rogue mines, Laura took the matter into her own hands. Her first diamond theft was from her employer and it was estimated to be worth twenty million euros."

"Why wasn't Laura arrested at the time of the theft?" asked Jo.

"Wise thief that she was, she quit her job four days before the theft was discovered and she disappeared off the face of the earth," Marie replied.

"Wow, and she eluded police for the next ten to fifteen years? She's pretty good at hiding," noted Angela.

"She apparently continued to steal gems during this time," said Jo, then asked, "Did she steal blood diamonds? Did you see any trends in her thefts?"

Marie continued, "The last Interpol Purple Notice listed Laura's modus operandi and gave a list of all the objects she is suspected of stealing. The total euro amount was over four-hundred million."

"Marie, what is a Purple Notice?" asked Jill.

"From what I can tell, Interpol issues a Purple Notice when it goes to all one-hundred-ninety or so countries that belong to Interpol," replied Marie. "They divide all of their alerts into one of seven colors based on their need to give or receive different types of information. So far this year, they have issued six Purple Notices."

"Wow, four-hundred million euros in jewelry. That is a lot of raw stones, necklaces, rings, and bracelets. Does the Purple Notice describe her preference for the type of diamonds she steals?" inquired Jill.

"She began by focusing her thefts on raw diamonds since she had seen them arrive in Antwerp while she was employed. Later she branched into stealing some substantial private collections in which she thought the source of the diamonds was mines in Botswana. She pulled off about four thefts a year," Marie explained. "She stayed out of the United States and Canada, but pretty much stole in every other country of the world. Interpol thought that she left Canada alone as they had their own diamond mines that were certified as ethical. It is thought she stayed out of the U.S. over fear of being caught."

"What did she do with the diamonds she stole?" Jill asked. "She likely stole more diamonds than she could wear in a lifetime, and it would seem to go against her code to keep and wear blood diamonds. It's not like she was invited to the major events around the world where she could have worn that many diamonds, anyway."

"I haven't found that out yet." Marie looked at Jo and said, "I was hoping you could help me with Laura's financials."

"The first couple hours of my investigation have been spent understanding where financial information can be found in Europe. What is their version of the IRS? What companies calculate credit scores for citizens in this part of the world? Where can I find public records with information like property purchases? I now have that figured out, and with Marie's help I'll start on Laura and her seven aliases tomorrow. I am a little jet-lagged and bug-eyed from staring at the computer too long. I'll be better in the morning."

"Jo, I'm with you there," agreed Angela. "The adrenaline rush that I had from our interaction with the strangers has dissipated and now I'm profoundly exhausted. I feel like we've made progress tonight, so I think we should all call it a night. Marie, if you'll bring your iPad with us, you could get some work done if there are any entrance lines at the six museums we're planning to visit. Just thinking of your desire to multi-task!"

They all said their good-nights, got ready for bed, and the lights were out twenty minutes later. For their peace of mind, the women had moved heavy furniture in front of the suite door and, as they headed to bed, their two bedroom doors. Paranoia might offer them protection going forward.

After a quiet night with no visitors to their hotel room, they were looking forward to meeting with the hotel's security person and then heading out for the museums.

They were planning on spending two additional nights in Amsterdam and then they would leave for Brussels. The hotel security person would be arriving at any moment and hopefully he or she had advice on staying safe.

The security person arrived and sat down with the four of them in their suite. He had served in the Netherlands municipal police and done a short stint with Interpol before branching off into private hotel security. His name was Nick Brouwer and he managed the security of at least ten hotels in Amsterdam. He was a charming fellow that appealed to Angela's eye. With his height at six-foot-two, she wouldn't have to worry about towering over him, and his Nordic features reflected in his dimples when he smiled, which was often.

After they performed introductions, Jill took the lead describing the group's background in crime-solving as well as the case of Laura Peeters. She'd pulled up an article from their last case in the spring so that Nick would know they were legitimate. When the women sheepishly described hiding in the red-light district window, he knew he was in for great entertainment mixed with some hair-raising moments, given their courage. Nick was tired of dealing with egocentric actors and musicians, the usual clients he met face-to-face. He was looking forward to assisting the American tourists.

"I can help you with your online search. I have a computer expert back in my office and I still have connections to both the Dutch police and Interpol. We'll look for information on Laura Peeters and whatever aliases you have discovered up to this point. I know that some buildings and streets have cameras aimed at the street, so if you can tell me where you hid last night, I'll see if there are security cameras in those areas and we might be able to track down the strangers. The red-light district has cameras due to the number of pick-pockets in that area. You will be relieved to know that none of the cameras were aimed at the red-light windows, so your appearance last night was likely not saved on camera. I will also have my office check the cameras around this hotel to see if we can find anyone that seemed to be stalking you."

"We aren't exactly sure of where we hid last night," replied Marie. "At least not the street name. We would have to visit it in daylight to figure it out. We're running late for our museum itinerary at the moment. If you're done at this hotel and have a car, perhaps we could go back to the scene of the crime right now and then you could drop us off at the Rijksmuseum?"

"Ladies, that sounds like a plan. Give me ten minutes to talk to my security staff at this hotel, and then I'll meet you at the hotel exit. Look for a silver Volvo."

Nick exited the suite and Angela closed the door. Leaning against it, she said, "Okay, he was most helpful."

The other three laughed out loud.

"What?"

"You liked him about five seconds after you met. Helpful seems like a mild term - like the hotel concierge. He was more than helpful, I got the feeling that our story might bring him the most entertainment he has seen in a month. Best of all for us and Dr. DeGroot, he's going to apply his resources to our research, which will help us solve the case quicker," said Jill.

"We better grab our stuff and head down to the lobby," said Marie with a smile. "Angela, you can have the front seat of his car to help direct him to where we hid last night."

The four of them arrived in the lobby. A man in a suit approached them, introducing himself as hotel security. He had them wait inside the hotel until he saw his boss's car out front. They headed outside and got into his car.

Angela directed Nick to the taxi stand that they'd used last night. From there they traced their steps to the ice-cream shop and then they weaved through the streets until they found the door with the corridor to the back entrance of the red-light windows. In the daylight, the area looked deserted and seedy. They were grateful that there would be no film record of their appearance in the windows. Nick wrote the address down and then proceeded to drop them off at the museum. He had the phone numbers of Marie and Jill as Jo and Angela had left their cell phones back in the States, and he promised to update them on any research that was relevant. They all agreed that they were safe on their museum tour, as the crowds would provide their own protection if someone was following them today.

They proceeded on their whirlwind tour and didn't notice anyone following them around. At the very least, if someone had followed them around they would be poorer for it after all the admission fees they'd paid at the various tourist sites. They'd been on the go all day, and were now relaxing in a pub close to their hotel. It was the first chance they'd to check their e-mail since that morning.

"Is there an e-mail from anyone concerned with this case?" asked Angela. "Did Nick or any of his people send us some information?"

"I see an e-mail from Dr. DeGroot and from Nick. I'll take the Dr. DeGroot email Marie, why don't you read Nick's e-mail," suggested Jill.

"Hmm, this is interesting from Dr. DeGroot. He did some more research on the diamonds in Laura's stomach. There is a strong possibility that they are conflict diamonds. He also did the DNA studies of the chocolate and was able to locate the chocolate store where Laura made her purchase. He had a conversation with the store's chocolate artist. The artist was aware of Laura and her nut allergy. He had been selling her chocolate for seven years, after she toured his kitchen. He's devastated to learn of her death and his store's role in it. He has pulled out of his display cases all of the chocolate that he advertises as having no nuts. He doesn't want another accident on his hands."

Jo asked, "Did he have an explanation as to why or how the nuts got in the chocolate?"

"Now that Dr. DeGroot has confirmed the origin of the nuts, it will be up to the police to question the chocolate artist. So we may not have that answer if it's not shared with Dr. DeGroot, since we have no legitimate authority in Belgium," said Jill.

"Perhaps Nick could find out that information if his connections stretch that far," suggested Marie.

"Let me read his email to you all. 'Ladies, hope you had a great day visiting our famous museums. I have a lot of interesting information about your case. We could either meet for dinner or I could meet you later at the hotel. Let me know your preference,'" read Marie.

"Well, that sounds like an intriguing email," said Jo. "I for one would like to do dinner with him. It would be nice to hang with a native. Plus we need to look out for Angela's interests. Ask him to give us a time and place for dinner."

Marie typed in the message. They ordered a second round of drinks and looked at the pictures Angela had snapped that day. Fifteen minutes later they had a response from Nick. He would meet them in their present location and they could go from there. They ordered their third round of beers and were having a great time conversing when Nick joined their table.

"Hello, ladies. It appears that you had a great day exploring my city."

"Hello, Nick," said a grinning Angela. "We had a splendid day. If anyone followed us, we are hopeful that we bankrupted them with admission fees for all the museums. We are re-hydrating after the thirsty work of the day."

"What was your favorite place?"

"Hmm, I didn't have a favorite place," said Jo and the other three nodded. "There was something I liked in every museum, and the collections we viewed at each were so different."

A waitress appeared and took Nick's order for a beer, as they all had nearly full glasses.

Tipping her mug to Nick's, Jill urged, "So tell us what you found out about this case. We were so busy sightseeing, we didn't do any research today."

"Let me talk about your safety first," Nick replied. "I was able to view some grainy footage of your incident last night. I could see the four of you on the street, although the picture was so bad, if I hadn't known it was you four I would have been unable to identify you. As you can imagine, your mystery men were also poor images. I couldn't identify their faces nor see if they were holding a knife or gun –it was that blurry. They walked by the windows you were appearing in at least three times, but didn't notice you under the red lights. They searched the area you hid in about five minutes after you exited the corridor with the prostitute, so good timing on your escape plan.

"I also looked at the footage around the hotel where we have better cameras, but I didn't see anyone hovering close to the hotel. Unfortunately, you can't see the entire street, so someone could have been located in a car."

"How about earlier in the day?" asked Jill. "We had someone follow us from the hotel to Anne Frank's house. When I confronted him he said we were mistaken, but I was sure he'd been on our train. He would have to have followed us from the train station to the hotel to Anne Frank's House."

Angela reached over with her camera and showed Nick the screen. "I took his picture while Jill was confronting him."

"You ladies scare me. You seem to disregard your own safety. I can't believe you confronted a complete stranger and accused him of following you."

"It was daylight, and there were other people on the street," explained Jill. "Why wouldn't we confront someone? I've found in other cities that confronting people that are following me deters pickpockets."

"Angela, can I borrow your camera to make a copy of this gentleman's picture? I have some databases I can match it against. Why don't I do that now? I'll walk you ladies back to the hotel. I will return in less than an hour and we'll head out for dinner. I didn't tell you the rest of the information I gathered on Laura Peeters."

They all finished their beer and exited the pub, strolling down the street toward the hotel. Nick kept an eye out for strangers on the street, but nothing looked out of the ordinary. Angela lingered behind while the other three women entered the hotel with the plan to meet up in about an hour.

Later, they joined Nick in his car and drove to a favorite restaurant of his. It was nice dining in an area not filled with tourists. With his help understanding the menu, they each tried a different Dutch entree.

Jill could wait no longer. "Nick, tell us what you learned about Laura Peeters. You've kept us in suspense long enough."

Nick leaned his blond head in and gazed at the women with his blue eyes, and he began softly speaking.

"I think you ladies have accidentally discovered the tip of a diamond industry conspiracy. With the potential size and scope of this conspiracy, I'm worried about your safety."

"In my most recent case, people at the heart of a political conspiracy combined with a powerful para-military corporation and threatened the lives at different times of Angela and I. We survive that and will survive this situation as well. Walking away from an investigation doesn't mean that the diamond conspiracy will go away," said Jill. "Nick, tell us everything."

After a pause he sighed, "Okay, this is the situation. I don't have all the facts yet, as the story is still unfolding. I think that there are some very bad people involved in this case who are anxious to make sure that Laura Peeters' killing goes unsolved. I believe that Laura was playing Robin Hood to the miners of conflict diamonds. A diamond merchant consortium, tired of her years of success in stealing diamonds from them, hired a contract killer to kill Laura. That person may now be after you four ladies."

"What? That is unbelievable! It all started with a random encounter in a restaurant. Could we really have the bad luck to fall into another case with contract killers?" commented Jill.

"Nick, please continue with the story. Where did you get your information and what more can you tell us?" asked Angela. She was torn between wanting to know more about him and learning what new information he had.

"Angela, it was your picture that opened up the case for me. A friend in the Rijkspolitie, which is our state police, ran the picture through his computer system and your stalker was identified as Jan Storms. He is wanted by Interpol for illegal trafficking of precious stones.

"That leads us to investigating Mr. Storms. He associates with three other men who are also wanted by Interpol for various crimes. My friend also did some research on Laura Peeters. As you know, she was wanted by Interpol for those diamond thefts. We thought they were associated, but it turns out they were on opposite sides. We believe the four men were hired by the diamond consortium, whereas Laura was stealing diamonds as a means to stop the diamond consortium from mistreating miners."

"Does your friend have access to financial information?" asked Jo.

"He has some access to financial information but the bigger problem is that he doesn't understand what he's looking at. He doesn't know how to interpret such information."

"Nick, if you don't mind, I'll give him a list of documents I need for the people involved in this case," offered Jo. "I'll serve as a free financial consultant to the Dutch state police. I've helped Jill with enough of these cases that I think I can be of real help here, especially if high-stakes financial transactions are at the heart of the case."

"Okay, I'll do that. I don't know how he will feel about sharing information with an American civilian, though."

"I could send him my standard contract that usually satisfies police departments in the United States. Can you ask him if that might allay his concerns?" Jill proposed.

"Good idea. Let me e-mail him and pose the question."

"Nick, do you have any other information on the players in this case and why they began following us?" asked Angela.

"I don't know how they got your names or why they are following you. Of course it's true that if they got Jill's name, then they probably know you are connected to her and are good investigators. Depending on what's at stake, the four of you may be targeted for some reason – I can't begin to speculate," Nick said. He added, "You could end your vacation now and return to America," added Nick.

He faced four resolute women staring him down for his suggestion.

"Sadly, if there are high-stakes behind the diamond consortium, America is not far enough away," said Jill. "Nick, would you provide us with the names of these consortium member companies and CEOs?"

"Yeah, okay, I'll do that. Let's talk about your protection and next steps."

"We leave Amsterdam the day after tomorrow and head to Brussels. We're staying at a boutique hotel, and I'm guessing they won't have security," said Jo.

"I think I mentioned that I manage several hotels in Amsterdam as well as Brussels. If your hotel would allow, I'll arrange coverage for you. Like I said earlier, you have a very interesting story and I would like to ensure that you stay alive. I'll make some calls tomorrow and let you know what happens with your hotel."

"Thanks Nick. We really appreciate your help and protection," said Angela.

"You're welcome. Let's talk about research on this case. I have some ideas and I'm sure you do as well. What are your plans for tomorrow?"

"We're going to Zaanse Schans in the morning to view the windmills. We're taking the train there and in the afternoon, we're going to shop. We will have somewhat of a leisurely day, so we'll have a little time to do research on the train," said Marie.

"I'm going to tail you ladies tomorrow to provide protection and see if I can observe anyone following you. I would like to build a case that you need police protection and assistance with this investigation. Right now it feels very circumstantial, and culturally we are a precise country. My friend in the state police thinks we need a little more evidence before they would get involved."

"Again, we appreciate your help. Personally I feel safer just talking to you, and it will be a relief to know we have back-up if we run into trouble. Let's talk about the investigation and where we need your help. I want to know more information about Laura Peeters. Can you get me access to Interpol's information," asked Jill?

"Wow, you don't start small with the information requests. I don't have access and I'll have to pull in a few favors to get the information. What else?"

"I'd like the names of the diamond consortium company members and their CEO names, which I believe, Nick, you were going to provide. I know where to search in the U.S. , but I am at a loss here so I expect to be slower in my discovery. Can you ask any of your friends how they or the state or local police search for such information for people suspected of crimes?" added Jo.

"I'd like the full names of the men believed to be following us. I'll use my contacts to research them on the Internet." said Marie.

"Nick, I won't ask for anything from your contact in the police since I'll be helping Jill, Marie, and Jo with their research," said

Angela with a smile. "My skills are best used in interviewing people, and they aren't being put to use much in this case."

The conversation had continued over dinner and they were contemplating dessert now. They agreed to share chocolate custard and a Rijstebrij, a cinnamon rice pudding. Afterwards, Nick dropped them off at their hotel promising to meet them in the morning before they traveled to Zaanse Schans. He asked Angela if she wanted a nightcap in the hotel bar and she accepted. Finally she would get to focus on the man rather than the case.

CHAPTER 8

The next morning, they awoke to rain and the weather forecasters said it would stay with them intermittently while they were at the windmills. The air and the clouds had an intriguing feel, as though something special would happen that day. It was either the electricity associated with approaching thunderstorms or anticipation of the case that fueled Jill's fanciful imagination.

Nick had phoned their suite to let them know he was in place and ready to tail them. Perhaps that was where the sense of anticipation came from: They might have an adventure beyond their planned sightseeing excursion. If someone other than Nick did choose to follow them, the women hoped they would get drenched in one of the forecasted downpours.

After a breakfast of chocolate croissants and coffee, they set off for Central train station on foot, armed with raincoats and umbrellas. They purchased round-trip tickets to Koog-Zaandijk to see the windmills. While they kept up their usual vacation conversation, they were all surreptitiously looking around to see if they noticed anyone familiar. They did not even see Nick in the crowd at the station, but they knew he was around. Relaxing, they boarded their train. It was a short thirty-minute train ride to their station.

When they got off the train, they looked around at everyone else getting off, again not recognizing anyone, including Nick. Angela asked for directions to the windmills and they followed the tunnel under the tracks to the street. Several other passengers were also walking down the street, presumably going to the same destination. The skies were dry but threatening rain at any moment. Once they put their umbrellas to use, it would limit their visibility. Marie was wearing a rain poncho, so she would see better than the rest, but they were all targets.

After a ten-minute walk, they arrived at a bridge over the river Zaan that afforded them a view of the Dutch village with its working windmills. Angela was taking pictures. They proceeded into the village and entered the Zaans Museum. It was there that Angela noticed a single man in a gray trench coat hovering close to the exhibits they were viewing. That struck her as unusual, as it had been all family groups walking from the train station. She decided she would initiate a conversation and see what happened.

"Hello. These exhibits are really good. What do you think?"

Jill, Jo, and Marie all turned to look at Angela as she addressed the stranger.

"I don't speak English," said the stranger in heavily accented English.

Angela wasn't deterred. She smiled and said in Dutch "Hello, my name is Angela. What is yours?" Angela was the best with languages among the friends and she often could speak a few polite phrases in any language.

The stranger just shook his head, and moved to leave. When he was gone, the four women discussed the stranger, deciding that his reaction was normal for a non-English speaker and they were just being paranoid.

They finished looking at the exhibits and moved on to the first windmill. A docent inside the windmill explained how it worked to grind spices and wheat. All four noticed the stranger was back and hovering behind them, not seeming to pay attention to the docent.

They left the windmill and moved on to the next one. The power generated by each windmill was used for a different purpose. Some had signs explaining what visitors were looking at; others had docents providing the explanation. It had started to rain, so the umbrellas were opened.

As the women were stepping out from the windmill, a dart came sailing their way and was deflected harmlessly off Angela's raincoat. Her coat was made from heavy waterproof vinyl that made it impenetrable to rain and, apparently, darts. No one saw the dart in the air; rather, Marie happened to be looking over her shoulder at Angela and she saw the dart fall to the ground.

"Hey, someone just fired a dart at Angela! Let's get back inside!" yelled Marie as she pointed to ground while they hurried back inside the windmill.

"That was a lucky move," said Jill.

"Whoever just fired at Angela went after the one person with the thick coat – the one person wearing a protective coat. I would have dropped to the ground with the dart sticking out of me, this rain poncho is so thin." said Marie.

Jo looked around the entrance and said "I don't like this situation at all. How do we protect ourselves? Can we shut the door?"

Unfortunately, they could see that the door was chained open with a lock holding it in place.

"I wonder where Nick is, we sure could use some help." said Jill.

"Does anyone have his cell phone number? Maybe we could call him," suggested Jo urgently.

"Duh, I have it programmed into my phone," said Jill locating him in her recent calls. "Let me call him."

As Jill dialed Nick, the four looked for places to hide inside the windmill. Each of them climbed up and hid behind beams, boards, and the windmill mechanism.

"Hello?"

"Nick, it's Jill and someone just shot a dart at Angela. We need your help now!"

"I'm following your dart shooter into the windmill. I'll be right there."

The four women were hiding but each kept an eye on the doorway. A stranger entered with a dart gun held at his side. He started looking around the building for his target, but no one was in sight. He began a methodical search getting closer to Marie. Meanwhile, a man quietly entered the building but he didn't look like Nick, although the man was the right height. He waited until he had a partition for protection, and then spoke in Dutch. They saw the dart shooter quickly turnaround and fire a dart where the man had been standing. The second stranger again spoke in Dutch and then they heard police sirens close by. The dart shooter ran out of the building and the second man stood in the doorway watching him go. Once he was satisfied he spoke in English.

"Ladies, you can come out of hiding. He's gone."

The four women dropped to the ground and approached Nick. It was his voice, but he was wearing a good disguise. His hair style and color and his clothes made him look twenty years older. He'd applied bushy eyebrows and yellowed his teeth, but when you looked at the bright blue eyes, they found the Nick they knew.

"Did the police arrive? We heard the sirens." asked Marie.

"Actually, that was a bit of trickery of my part. I have a ring tone on my cell phone that sounds like police sirens. I did call the police, but they aren't here yet. This is the second tight situation that ring tone has helped me avoid trouble."

"Nick, that was brilliant," said Angela. "Did you get his picture?"

"No, I was trying to avoid his dart gun."

"Let me check my camera - I might have his photo," said

Angela as she started reviewing her recent pictures. "I've started taking pictures of strange men..."

"Here we go, I thought I might have snapped a picture of him in the museum," said Angela as she showed her friends the camera screen. "I'm sure the dart shooter was the same man I tried to speak to in the museum. Do you guys agree?"

Her friends nodded their agreement as Nick viewed the man's picture. He'd briefly studied the man's face during the few seconds of confrontation inside the windmill.

"Yes, I agree, that's his picture. Can I borrow your camera again to get a copy of the picture?"

"Sure," said Angela handing over the camera.

"That's okay. Let me use my cell phone to take a picture of your camera screen. I think that will work." replied Nick as he aimed his cell phone at Angela's camera screen.

A moment later, the women were viewing the copy of the picture on the bigger screen of Nick's phone. They all looked up as police officers entered the windmill. On their heels was the supervisor for the site. They looked at each other and knew they were about to lose an hour of their vacation time. Of course, they could have lost their lives instead, so it was a fair trade-off.

Fortunately, in his haste to depart, the dart shooter didn't grab the dart so the police had it for evidence. The officers got copies of the pictures and a statement from the four women. They had a hard time believing their full story. Nick helped established their legitimacy as one of the other officers contacted the police in Amsterdam to provide a more complete description of the situation.

By the end of the conversation, the Belgian State Police and Interpol wanted to meet with the women. They set up an appointment for a meeting in Amsterdam in two hours. They would have time to finish their tour of the windmills and get the train back to city for the meeting.

They spent another hour at the site with Nick trailing them, then headed to the train station. Once they reached Central station, Nick escorted them to the State Police Office where Interpol was meeting them. Interpol's headquarters were in The Hague, which was an hour's drive away. The group's planned shopping excursion was going to get cut short.

CHAPTER 9

*N*ick and the women were shown into a conference room at the police station. It was their first visit to a European Police Station and they would later agree that it pretty much looked like its American counterpart. It would never be on their tourist must-see list for any city in the world.

After introductions, they were asked to recount their experience with Laura Peeters, the incident of the man following them two nights before, the pair of men in the red-light district, and the event that day at the windmill.

The police in turn provided them with the name of the assailant at the windmill. His name was Kenneth Lee Akselrod, a Belgian citizen, and he was wanted by Interpol for unlawful circulation of natural precious stones. The dart contained a substance used by veterinarians to subdue elephants in their natural habitat. The dose intended for the elephant would have rendered any of the four women unconscious. Mr. Akselrod had no history of violence, merely activities related to precious stones. It was disturbing that he was stepping up his criminal activities.

"So what are your next steps?" Jill asked the police and Interpol representatives.

"We have several problems. This is a crime that crosses borders. For unknown reasons, you are a target of this group and need protection. We need to understand more about this syndicate, and you're leaving the Netherlands tomorrow for Brussels for four days before returning to the United States. My first piece of advice would be for you to immediately arrange for your return to the United States rather than waiting four days," offered Inspector Berg.

"Our experience is that returning to the United States doesn't eliminate the problem, rather it just transfers it to another country. So we see no reason to cut short our vacation. Nick has agreed to help provide protection for us for the remainder of our vacation," replied Jill.

"How is Nick protecting you? Do you realize that he is not allowed to carry a gun in the Netherlands? He will be able to carry one in Belgium, if he has one registered in his name. This is not like the U.S., with every private citizen owning a gun," said Inspector Berg.

"In our last case in the United States, the only people using a gun on our behalf were the police, the FBI, and the Albania sniper who was after me, so I don't see that as different in this situation. My boyfriend, who also provided protection, has a black belt in hapkido, so again no guns. We would rather help you solve this case. We are really quite resourceful in solving crimes – it has been our team profession for the past five years," responded Jill.

"I have a black belt in kickboxing," said Nick, "so it sounds like you have the same level of protection as you would in the United States. I don't have a registered gun in Belgium, but my employees do, and so if there is a need for a gun, my company can legally meet that requirement."

"We agree," stated Marie, speaking for the group. "Let's talk about what's going on here and we'll share what we know about the players involved so far and what we think the motives are, and you can do likewise."

"Will you provide us with the names and dossiers from Interpol of the two men we have made contact with so far? We'll likely use different sources than you, so we may find different information. I can provide you with our standard contract, if that'll mitigate any legal worries that you have," said Jill.

Inspector Berg looked to Interpol for guidance. He'd not expected this outcome to the conversation. He'd thought he would be providing the women a police escort back to their hotel and on to the airport.

Interpol Criminal Intelligence Officer Graaf finally weighed in on the situation. Like Inspector Berg, he hadn't come into contact with aggressive Americans before, except as victims. The women were not behaving like victims.

"We have never had such a request before except from your government. Nothing you ask for is confidential, so I see no reason not to share with you. We have advised you to return to your country as we feel that is best for your safety, and we will pass that recommendation on to your embassy. Since you are ignoring our recommendation, you need to understand that we will be unable to provide you with the security you may need to stay alive. Please confirm that you understand your level of risk."

The four women, after looking at each other, nodded in unison that they understood the risk. They were all optimists, and with Nick's help, thought they could finish their vacation and help solve the Laura Peeters case. They would earn no income for their effort, but it might keep them alive.

"I'll contact our office in Brussels, and inform them of the direction of this case. They may wish to contact you further. I wish you the best of luck."

It was afternoon and they wanted to grab lunch, then shop. Nick planned to stay covertly in the background, meeting with them only in the privacy of their hotel room. He would change his disguise each day to reduce the likelihood that he would be recognized by any men tailing the women.

They stopped at a café featuring sandwiches and pastries. Jill checked her email and found that Inspector Graaf had indeed emailed them the information of the men that had tailed them, as well as the dart shooter. He also provided them with a name and contact number for the Interpol office in Brussels. The Inspector ended the email with another request that they return to the United States, which they planned to ignore.

She also had an email from Nathan, her boyfriend, that he would be joining them in Brussels. He would arrive there later that day. There were over seventy-five wineries in Belgium, and he had a few clients that he would meet with to discuss projects. He also planned to add his hapkido skills to Nick's protection measures, which would give the women additional security. He'd been learning over the past several months how negligent they could be about their own safety. He planned to work ten percent of the time and guard the women the other ninety percent of the time.

Nathan had even gone so far as to contact Nick since Jill had mentioned him in an email. He liked Nick so far, and they'd worked out a plan to keep the women safe. Jill and the others would hopefully remain ignorant of these actions. He didn't want their vacation wrecked with anxiety about their safety, but he was in love with Jill and would make sure he did everything in his power to keep her alive.

They finished their lunch, paid the bill and stepped out into sunshine. Their plan was to visit the main open-air market to view the flowers and other items for sale. Then they were moving on to an area called Nine Little Streets to aimlessly wander through the many Dutch stores. None of them needed anything; rather, it was more curiosity about what was for sale.

It was a relaxing afternoon, especially after the scare that morning at the windmills. They each found something small to take home for someone and had a fun time figuring out European sizing in women's clothes. They ended the afternoon with a quick stop at a purse museum. It seemed an appropriate way to end several hours of shopping.

They stopped in at a pub, ordered beer and sat back to watch every-day Dutch citizens going about their lives. Jo and Angela relaxed in the fading sun of the day. Marie, the multi-tasker, used the pub's wireless Internet connection to do some more research on the two gentlemen who had tried to harm them. Jill, likewise, was doing the same. Angela was playing a game with Jo, speculating which of the strangers in sight was Nick in disguise.

They pulled out a map to figure out where in the city they'd wandered to and how to get back to their hotel and began walking in that direction. They were planning to chill out in their hotel room for about an hour before heading out to a restaurant that Nick had recommended. He would join them in the suite and let them know if anyone had been following them throughout the afternoon.

They heard a knock on their door a few minutes after they returned to the suite. Nick had called from the lobby to let them know he was coming up.

"Hi Nick," said a smiling Angela. "Are you thoroughly bored from following us around all afternoon?"

"Actually, it takes a lot of energy to follow you guys, stay in my disguise, and observe everyone around you to see if anyone looks dangerous," said Nick with a sigh of relief as he sat down.

"So was anyone following us or otherwise acting suspicious towards us," asked Jo?

"I don't believe anyone was following you. After the incident at the windmills, and the time spent at the police station, you may have been hard to follow. I think you may be at risk for being followed to the restaurant. After you all entered the hotel, I observed the street, but saw no one watching the entrance," Nick replied.

"Not to question your professional abilities, but, did you pick up on the guy with the dart gun before he went after us this morning?" asked Jill.

"That's a fair question. I did find him suspicious and was closing the gap on the distance between us when I saw him pull out the dart gun. I'm very grateful that in addition to Angela's coat being water repellent, it is apparently dart repellent. Then Jill called me on the phone as I was running toward the windmill. I quickly found the police siren sound bite and got ready to play it upon entering the building. You know the rest of the story.

"You ladies walked all over Amsterdam this afternoon and I'm sure I would've noticed the same people at the different locations that you walked to. I also took some cell phone video of different groups of people that were near you, and I plan to review it this evening to see if anyone looks out of place," Nick explained.

"Nick, all of us are really appreciative of your surveillance today," said Jill. "Don't think by our questions that we're ungrateful. I got word that my boyfriend, Nathan, is landing in Brussels this evening, so we'll have a second guard in that city."

"What time does your train depart for Brussels tomorrow?" asked Nick.

"We don't have tickets," replied Jo. "We were planning to just show up at the station when we felt like it in the morning. I understand that trains depart hourly for Brussels, so if we have a little wait when we get there, it's no problem."

Nick thought these American women were very unpredictable. One moment they were aggressively asking for information from Interpol, and the next moment they couldn't be bothered picking a departure time from Amsterdam. Hopefully that unpredictability would help keep them alive.

"I am starving," announced Marie. "Are we ready to head out to the restaurant for dinner?"

Nick stood up, walking toward the door of the suite. "Ladies, give me ten minutes. I want to change my disguise, and check the hotel lobby and street for any suspicious characters."

Fifteen minutes later, the four women left the hotel to walk to the restaurant that was three blocks away. After the brief walk, they were seated on the second floor of the restaurant. They had a view of the street because the table next to them, immediately adjacent to the window, was empty. It was nice that they could see the activity on the street without being directly in view from the window.

A friend of Nick's owned the restaurant, and Nick was to be seated downstairs where he could monitor anyone approaching the second floor. Nick had helped his friend with the security for his restaurant, thus he knew the layout and entry and exit doors. Equally important, the food was excellent – a great example of Dutch cooking. Marie's hunger would be satiated by the end of the meal.

The meal was delicious and uneventful. Once they finished they proceeded downstairs to discover a lively bar. The plan to return to the hotel and do some more research on the diamond consortium went out the window in an instant, and they sidled up to the bar. Nick and Angela even found time to dance together motivated by other patrons taking to the dance floor.

Two hours later, doubtful they could have passed a sobriety test, they weaved their way back to their hotel. It was only three blocks, and they didn't think anything could happen in such a short distance. They hadn't been bothered since that morning's incident.

Nick had been wondering when the women would give up and return to the hotel. It was a long day and he had been hyper-alert since the morning all day. His restaurant owner friend was tending bar that night, and enjoyed the company of the women. Additionally, regular patrons had also been engaged talking to them. This was not a restaurant that catered to tourism so generally it was mostly all Dutch patrons. The women were attractive, amusing, and fun to talk to so he couldn't blame his fellow man for enjoying the moment. To make matters worse, two of the patrons followed American football and so there was a long conversation about the Green Bay Packers. Finally, the women looked ready to leave.

Nick approached the bar and asked his friend, "Max, do you want to join me in escorting the ladies back to their hotel?"

Max did a quick assessment and determined that his bar could survive without him for thirty minutes. He had two other bartenders working, who seemed more than capable of keeping up with his patrons.

"Sure, just let me grab my cell phone."

The men left the bar, following the women about half a block back. Nick had briefed Max on the situation with the women before he had booked the dinner reservation.

When they started down the second block, an industrial van turned onto their street and seemed to pace the woman.

Nick had a bad feeling and said to Max, "That van looks suspicious; let's get closer to them."

The two men took off jogging as Nick yelled, "Angela! Jill! Jo! Marie! Run!"

The woman had a slow reaction to the words, but when they looked over their shoulders and saw the van with its door open and Nick and Max, running toward them, they took off in a sprint. Three of the four women routinely ran five-kilometer races and the fourth quickly realized she might be running for her life.

Nick and Max had quickly closed the gap and reached the women at the same time as two men who had jumped out of the moving van. Nick saw the first assailant pull out a gun from the back of his waistband. Before the kidnappers could take aim, Nick executed a roundhouse kick, knocking the gun to the street, and followed that with a sweeping kick, which sent the man to the ground.

The four women had the other man surrounded and were swinging their purses at the man's head. He was so busy ducking the constant purse swings making contact with his head that it interfered with him reaching for his gun. Max pulled the gun out of the assailant's pants while the women kept him occupied. He got a few punches in at the second man and he toppled to the ground.

It appeared that the third man in the van wasn't going to come to the aid of his buddies. He was waiting for them to get up and run for the van, but they stayed on the ground, so he sped away as sirens in the distance got closer. Angela took a picture of the van, including its license plate, just in case it would be helpful later. Nick and Max detained the two men until the police arrived to take them into custody.

Shortly, Inspector Graaf from Interpol arrived to join the party. "If you ladies had done as I asked and left the country, you wouldn't have been attacked tonight."

"If we had left, perhaps you would not have gotten these two men who I suspect are on your most wanted list," replied Marie to the inspector.

"Look, do you want a license plate number for the van or not? There's still a third suspect out there," said Jill.

Jo was quietly watching the scene with a kind of detached feeling about her." How did the men know we would be on this street at this time? They came from another street. They didn't follow us from the restaurant."

"I'll check your purses for a tracker," said Nick. "I didn't see these two gentlemen at the restaurant or bar so I think you are right that they have another way to keep tabs on you."

"Ask the police to question them about surveillance during their interview." Jo would have asked them herself but the men were already in the back seat of the police car, so she couldn't speak to them.

Jo was usually the most laid-back of the group. She was excellent at forensic financial research, but she stayed on the sidelines in any case they had thus far. This was the first time she and

Marie had been put in harm's way, thanks to this Laura Peeters case. With her friends and her own life at risk, she was taking a very active role in the case. It was a side of Jo that Jill had rarely seen.

About forty-five minutes after they left the restaurant, the women were able to enter their hotel, completely sober after their experience. Nick escorted them up to their suite and he made a call to his office to get some laptops sent over.

Later the women sat in a circle in the suite's living room with Nick, computers in hand. They divided up their research, with Nick helping Jo with any translations of the financial information in Europe and South Africa. Nick could read the language of the data, and Jo knew how to interpret it once it was in English. Jill went back to studying Laura Peeters. Marie and Angela split up the diamond consortium members. Once Jo got the hang of the reports' translations and what column headings meant, then it was all about the numbers. Nick began his own search on the two men in custody. The plan was that everyone would do research for half an hour, taking notes on relevant information, with the plan to share it at the end of that time period.

After the half-hour had passed, Jill spoke. "Let's start sharing what we found. I'd like to do this in an organized fashion. How about if we start with a brief bio on the person followed by whatever we found on social media, and the financials of all of these persons of interest. Does that sound like a plan?"

Everyone nodded approval.

"Nick, why don't you start with our two men who were arrested tonight?"

"Sure. The man that you took down with those mean swings of your purses is named Kenneth Lee Akselrod and he is also the man that fired the dart at Angela earlier today. The other man was Jan Storms – the same guy that followed you two days ago. They are both on Interpol's list of most wanted, so even if they aren't charged with trying to abduct you ladies, they'll have to answer to other charges."

"Did you find anything more about them? Did Interpol share their information with you?" asked Angela.

"Yes, Officer Graaf did email a list of all the crimes they are wanted for and descriptions of those events. They've been on the most-wanted list for at least a decade. They're what I believe you call in your country 'guns for hire', or in this case, burglars for hire. They aren't connected to any murder or kidnapping attempts up to this point. Their prior alleged crimes are connected to moving precious stones, and burglary. Interpol attributes a total of thirty crimes between the two of them."

"I wonder if they were trying to kidnap us or do some greater harm in their actions tonight?" Marie said.

"Hopefully we'll know more after the police interview the two gentlemen. Let's move on to the diamond consortium," said Jill.

"I investigated the individual companies, while Marie looked at the consortium as a whole. I'll do some more research on the members, but nothing really stands out so far," Angela reported.

"The diamond consortium is composed of six companies, each with an equal stake. Diamond thievery is a common problem costing the companies millions. About forty percent of the stolen diamonds were stolen by the workers themselves. The other sixty percent was attributed to Laura Peeters," said Marie.

"Wow!" exclaimed Jill.

"How could one person steal so many diamonds?" questioned Jo.

"I think I might have the answer to that, or at least the beginnings of the answer to that question, but let's continue with the consortium," responded Jill.

"Five of the six consortium members were South African companies and the sixth was Russian. They have mines in South Africa, Botswana, Tanzania, Russia, and Democratic Republic of the Congo and produce two-thirds of the world's diamonds. The consortium was formed almost twenty years ago when diamond mining began in Canada and Australia as they were worried about competition in new parts of the world. Between these new sites and routine losses in the mines, their profits were flat.

"At first they focused on marketing strategies to keep their diamonds as the most coveted. They worked with the diamond institute in Antwerp to assure their diamonds were given the highest rating of clarity. Diamonds are diamonds and there's no such thing as one part of the world having more clarity than another, but as a strategy it worked for a decade, before independent gemologists outside of Antwerp began questioning the claims in journals like *Science* and *National Geographic* magazines. As near as I can tell, this clarity rating allowed the consortium to demand prices that were twenty-five percent higher," explained Marie.

"Was this falsely high rating of diamonds occurring when Laura Peeters worked in Antwerp?" asked Angela.

"We'll need to compare the dates, but it's possible that she was one of the gemologists that marked up the clarity during part of that decade. After the clarity characteristic was clarified, no pun intended, the consortium again face declining profits as they'd lost the twenty-five percent mark-up that they'd been enjoying, so they next turned to reducing losses at the mines themselves. Remember that the mines were losing some of their diamonds to the workers, so they installed cameras and x-ray machines, which helped reduced theft. Labor was plentiful and cheap, so as they discovered miners that stole, they would fire them and replace them with someone new. My research doesn't say anything about if they collect the workers' excrement to recover the diamonds."

"Yuck," the three women said simultaneously.

"The clarity scandal was followed by the problem with conflict diamonds. The mere thought that any diamond coming from Russia or South Africa could be a conflict diamond made some consumers look more favorably on Canadian and

Australian diamonds. The consortium suffered losses, as they were either paying warlords off or had reduced demand from consumers for fear of where the stones were mined. So the consortium worked to create a United Nations agreement, called the Kimberley Process, which was mostly window dressing for the problem," said Marie finished with her synopsis of the consortium.

"So what don't we know?" asked Angela.

"What is Laura Peeters' role in all of this?" Jo asked.

"Did the consortium hire the men who attacked us, and if so, why are we the target? What do they think we know? Why do they want to kill us?" Marie added.

"With the two men in the custody of the Dutch police, are we safe to travel to Brussels and revert to being tourists?" Jo asked

"What is the money, power, or sex motive in this case? How does that motive lead to us being a target?" Jill asked

"How did Laura Peeters manage to be such a skilled diamond thief?" Marie asked. "I like to understand how people develop their talents."

"What is the consortium up to financially? What are the actions they are presently pursuing?" said Jo.

After they exhausted themselves posing questions they did not have answers to, they gave up on that fruitless effort to return to discussing the results of their research. Everyone had reported out except Jill. It was time to look at Laura Peeters.

"I've been working on her seven aliases. Laura Peeters was her real name. She seemed to use three names at a time, eventually killing off an alias after about five years. Laura was born in Mechelen, which is fifteen miles outside of Antwerp. Both her father and grandfather were certified gemologists, so it's probably natural that she went in to that occupation. Her parents were killed in a bicycle accident when she was ten or so and then she was raised by her grandparents. Her grandparents have since passed and she seems to have had no siblings, aunts and uncles, ex-spouses, or children. She killed off her original name nearly fifteen years ago, but wanted us to know it."

"Had she become a diamond thief while her grandparents were still alive?" asked Angela.

"Good question. Give me a moment to look that up," Jill replied.

After a brief pause and a little keyboard typing, Jill had her answer.

"Her first theft was two months after her grandfather died. Interesting timeline - perhaps after her grandfather's passing she no longer felt any loyalty to her profession.

"Interpol has the most detail on her first crime. It seems likely that she'd been planning it for at least six months prior to that first theft. That guess on my part is based on when she set up her first alias."

"So her first theft wasn't a single raw diamond? You would think it would be very tempting to start small," Marie commented.

"Actually, Interpol commented on that theory as well. The steal-a-raw-diamond-one-at-a-time theory seems to be the way most thieves are caught, including another woman working at the same gem house as Laura. So she had good reason to know that technique would quickly fail. I think that when she made the decision to steal, she went for the whole enchilada - or safe, in this case."

"So how did she pull the theft off?" asked Jo.

"She replaced the raw diamonds with cubic zirconia for a week. She had a vacation scheduled for the following Monday which was also the start of a national holiday. When the first jewelers called irate that they'd been sent CZ instead of diamonds, the switch was discovered the following Tuesday. Meanwhile, she had successfully switched the diamonds for CZ for a week thus walking away with a large loot of diamonds estimated at the time as twenty million Euros. The CZ stones had the exact weight as the raw diamonds. Her desk where she examined, rated, and certified diamonds was on camera. She was so skilled with sleight-of-hand that the police had to have a computer study the film to pinpoint when she switched diamonds each time. She actually lasered a serial number on the CZ stone. Meanwhile, her stolen diamonds were certified and easily dumped them on the wholesale market."

"So why didn't she just quit there? Twenty million euros is more than the average person needs in a lifetime," commented Angela. "She could've retired to the Australian Outback and enjoyed her earnings."

"Her motivation seemed to be mission-driven. Since she couldn't stop the mining and sale of blood diamonds, she turned her attention to making the lives of those miners better. Don't get me wrong, she lived an elegant life; she didn't give every penny back to the miners. Interpol speculates that she got plastic surgery immediately after the first heist. The pathology report states that she changed her nose, cheeks, and jawline. She was a natural brunette, made blonde, and she was wearing brown contact lenses that covered up her blue eyes. She hid in plain sight, perhaps even staying in Antwerp. Certainly staying in that city would keep her close to the diamond business. It was the best way to monitor how well the mines were producing, what the consortium was doing, and keep current with the new technology gemologists were using."

"It seems like the first theft was somewhat easy," said Jo. "Laura just had to master the hand motions and find the perfect weight of CZ to replace real with fake. How did she carry out the second theft?"

"She pretty much used the same methodology all the time. She copied information from her employer before she left. Specifically, she had a list of some two-thousand diamond wholesalers worldwide. She visited their showrooms and asked, as many customers do, to see raw diamonds, where she would proceed to substitute CZ stones for the diamonds. She would ask for a particular carat and carry that same carat on her so she could make the substitution."

"This sounds like it hurt the diamond stores rather than the consortium members," commented Jo. "I also recall you said that her calling card was piece of chocolate left at the scene of the crime. Where does that come into this story?"

"It has taken me a while to run down that Interpol statement about Laura as I couldn't figure out the chocolate thing either. Laura did steal from some private diamond owners. The other piece of information she took from her employer was a list of fifteen to twenty wealthy individuals who had commissioned special diamond settings directly from the consortium members. These were things like chandeliers, ball gowns, tiaras, etc. Again, these diamonds could be resold since as a gemologist, she could verify their provenance and make changes if necessary. In the case of these small items, she did one theft a year, which gave her a lot of time to plan. She clearly knew where the item was located, and had to know what the security system was as she always managed to keep any image of herself off cameras. It was these private residences where she left a piece of chocolate, and that was the only way the theft could be attributed to her."

"Perhaps anyone who owns a ball gown with real diamonds deserves to have it stolen. What a waste of money," said Jo. "I guess that is what happens to your judgment when you have too much money to blow through in this life. I am liking Laura's style more and more. Is there any proof that she stole from the diamond shops, or is that just speculation?

"Believe it or not, Interpol didn't know what she looked like all these years. If you look at their website, the picture posted is not what Laura looks like. A headshot taken of her at the mortuary was shared with a few diamond shops that suffered thefts. Even though the thefts were as long as a decade ago, there was still video surveillance that the shops had kept for insurance purposes in which they were able to match by facial recognition software.

Once Interpol found the match in three stores, according to Inspector Graaf, they sent out notification worldwide over the last day, so they're just beginning to compile fifteen years of crimes potentially."

"To think a nut allergy brought this incredible career to an end. Someone really wanted her dead," said Marie thinking about Laura's astounding run of thefts." If she hadn't revealed her name, she might have died under one of her aliases. What a break that she gave her real name in the restaurant, especially since her ID had someone else's name on it. Someone knew who she was and what she did for a living. So, how are we connected?"

"I think that whoever killed Laura believed she told us something in the restaurant," suggested Jill.

"I would think that before someone chased us through two cities, they would have asked at the restaurant if we engaged in conversation and anyone who was there at the time could've told them that Laura had been too sick from the start," said Angela.

"Are they worried that she gave you something in the restaurant?" said Jo. "If she was so good at this sleight-of-hand thing, she might have slipped something to the two of you in the restaurant. She was unconscious when she left in the ambulance and you didn't speak to her at the hospital. However, while you guys knew she didn't recover consciousness in the ambulance, whoever is after us doesn't have that same knowledge. Have both of you gone through your clothing that you had on that night? Man, has my imagination taken off with this case. Usually I'm two thousand miles away from your cases, Jill. My imagination is much more active when people start trying to kidnap me."

"Good suggestion, Jo. Let's go look in our purses," said Jill to Marie.

They left the room to go find their purses and returned to the suite's living room.

"What are we looking for? Diamonds in a side pocket?" queried Marie.

"I have no idea. Perhaps a piece of paper, or maybe some diamonds, that were not in your purse when you left the United States," suggested a laughing Jo.

The two women proceeded to search every nook and cranny of their purses looking for something out of place. Five minutes later, they gave up disappointed not to find diamonds or anything unusual.

Angela added, "Look at the bright side, if you had found diamonds, you would have had to turn them over to the police lest you end up on Interpol's most wanted list. Maybe the next time someone tries to kidnap one of us we can yell that Laura neither said anything to us nor gave us anything, then these perpetrators would just have to believe us and go away."

"I have not had enough beer to believe that'll work, but let's try it next time, since you know there'll be a next time. Shouting that statement should at least provide us with a laugh. Until everything comes out on this case, I think we'll remain targets," Marie said.

Nick had been sitting quietly typing away while they discussed the case and their research when an email arrived from the Dutch police.

"Hey, I just received an email from the Dutch police. Unfortunately, there's little new information. The two men were already on the most-wanted list so they were aware of their crimes. During the interview, they let slip that they'd been hired, but not by whom or for what purpose. I think it was safe to assume that the men were operating on someone else's direction before they admitted that during the interview."

"Will they be questioned again?" asked Angela. "I would really love an opportunity to question them."

"Wow, you people don't give up," said Nick with exasperation. "No you can't question them. It's against police procedure rules, and the Geneva Convention rules. Once the Dutch police are done with them, Interpol will want to interview them and assume custody, and likely transport them to their headquarters in Lyon, France, since they are wanted by so many countries."

All four women turned and looked at him with indignation.

"Uh, Nick, how do think we solve cases? By waiting for information to drop in our lap? Of course we would like to speak to the two gentlemen, if for no other reason than to tell them off for trying to kill us, if that is one of the men in custody," said Jill.

Nick threw his hands up in surrender as he said "Are all Americans like you four? You're rather terrifying in your desire to pursue this case!"

"You forget the huge incentive we have - we want to take many more vacations together and we can only do that if we stay alive," Marie said.

"OK, we have gotten off track," Jill redirected the conversation, as she was the one who always kept them on task. "So we have a lot more information about Laura's criminal behavior. We don't know what she did with diamonds, or presumably the money she earned as a thief. We also don't know what she did to make someone want to kill her, or how they knew who she was if neither Interpol, nor anyone else did. She wasn't a random murder; it was very deliberate and it was planned so that it wouldn't be obvious. Is a millionaire upset with her chandelier being stolen also a murderer, or is it someone from the consortium, or is it one of the retail store merchants? It seems a little extreme for it to be one of the merchants. I think we have to focus on the diamond consortium or a millionaire in a rage."

"I don't know about you guys, but I'm dead tired," said Jo as she stood up to head to her bedroom. "A contact lens is irritating my eye, so I'm heading for bed. I'll see you in the morning."

"I have to agree with Jo," said Marie, "except for the contact lens. I've crashed after the adrenaline rush of running away from those guys."

Jill stood up, preparing to head to bed, and paused at the door frame, "Nick, thanks for your help. We'll call you in the morning before we head for the train station. How about thirty minutes' notice - will that work for you?"

"Jill, that will work for me. What's your best guess of when you'll leave?"

"Angela, would you agree that we'll be ready to leave around 10a.m.?"

"Yes, that sounds reasonable. See you in the morning, I'll see Nick out."

"Goodnight."

The room had emptied fast. Angela was left alone with Nick.

"Unlike my friends, I'm not sleepy. How are you holding up, Nick? We seem to be a new experience for you."

"It's never a dull moment around you ladies. I like the way your minds work. I like your confidence and the way you have managed to still have fun on your vacation despite the seriousness of this situation. You have me thinking about what I want to do with my life. It now seems pretty dull and I'm enjoying the intellectual work of this case. So I've a lot to think about."

Nick stood to leave and Angela followed him to the door. As she approached he wrapped her in his arms for a first kiss. Exactly what Angela had wanted to do since she met Nick two days before - explore Nick's kissing ability.

CHAPTER 10

*T*he night had been quiet. In the morning they packed and then ate breakfast at the hotel. Angela took some ribbing for making the most of her opportunity with Nick the night before. Afterward, they called Nick to tell him they were ready to leave for the train station. They'd debated simply driving to Brussels, but five adults and their baggage simply wouldn't fit in Nick's car. Instead, Nick had arranged for a friend to accompany him carrying the baggage in his car as they drove to the airport. At the airport, the two cars entered long-term parking and departed fifteen minutes later from that lot and then returned to the train station. They might still be followed, but at least they would make it difficult.

After they were dropped off at the train station, they purchased tickets for the train to Brussels. It was a three-hour ride and they had wireless Internet on the train to continue their research. Nick was close by in disguise and they had his loaned laptops so they all could continue their research. Nathan was meeting them at the station to help with their luggage. They didn't see anyone suspicious, so perhaps their airport ploy had worked. But, they didn't know if there were new hired thugs that they wouldn't recognize trying to chase them down, as there appeared to be no criminal activity around them.

As the women were in an open compartment, with strangers around them, they kept any discussion about the case to a minimum, with their voices low. They spent the first thirty minutes loosely planning their tourism itinerary for the three nights in Brussels.

Since Jill and Marie were the early-risers, they'd spent a little time organizing the next round of research while waiting for Angela and Jo to finish their preparations and pack their luggage. They wanted to do more research on the diamond consortium, as well as on Laura's financials.

Jo would study Laura's finances using Angela to follow any loose threads once Jo spotted them. Marie had three consortium members and Jill the other three members. Nick was keeping an eye on passengers and new arrivals and departures at the few stops they had along the way. Natives had a habit of getting on one rail car and walking to another car. Nick would tense after each stop and then relax once all the passengers settled into seats or left for the next car. In the end, it was an uneventful ride. Nick had informed them that they could safely discuss their research in the final twenty minutes of the ride, as none of the seats were occupied.

"Marie, what did you find in researching the consortium members," asked Jill?

"So I took two of the South African companies and the one Russian mine. The Russian mine is interesting. They announced a huge find of carats in an asteroid crater in Siberia. Apparently, asteroid craters are a known source of the minerals that create diamonds. On closer examination, the diamonds turned out to be industrial grade rather than jewelry grade, so its stock declined upon the diamond quality clarification."

"What does industrial grade mean?" Jo asked.

"You know, I'm learning a lot about diamonds with this case.

Apparently, diamonds are divided into two grades: those used for cutting and those used for jewelry. I'd heard of diamonds used for cutting, but had assumed they were the same type of diamonds used for jewelry. It must have something to do with mineral content because they can now grow diamonds in the lab that are destined to be used for cutting. Isn't that a weird idea, growing a diamond in a lab?

"So this Russian company discovers a huge crater and is riding high on the diamond discovery, and then their company stock plunges when the diamonds are discovered to be industrial grade only. Since that announcement, they've had a smaller diamond mine discovery in an area close by, but it's nowhere near the size of the industrial mine. So the company recovered their fortunes somewhat. It has been a couple of years of rapid changes in both directions. They seem to be the most creative among the three members I looked at as far as advancing ideas to promote profitability."

"What did you find out about your two South African companies?" Jill asked.

"My two companies are the oldest mines in the world. There is some talk that they will run out of diamonds within seven and ten years respectively. Neither company has located any additional mineral resources so in theory they'll be out of business. They've paid for exploration in other parts of the world, but it hasn't come to fruition. Based on what I read, these two members will drop out of the consortium when their reserves are depleted and they cease to exist. I wouldn't concentrate any more attention on them. Instead I would focus on my Russian company and perhaps all three of Jill's companies depending on what she says," Marie suggested.

"OK, I guess that means we are moving on to you, Jill." Angela said while taking notes of their conversation.

"Thanks. My three companies are South African-based with mines in Namibia, Rwanda, and the Democratic Republic of the

Congo. A significant number of their diamonds come from mines where the workers are paid poorly and they're laundering conflict diamonds through a few shell companies to put them into the wholesale market. In summary, I found few redeeming qualities about them. They seem to be behind every strategy that treats the workers poorly or forces higher prices for their diamonds. If I were to guess who hired our kidnappers, I would bet it would be these three companies," Jill speculated.

"I began looking into their finances. Fortunately they are traded on foreign stock exchanges, so there are European regulations that require company reporting similar to the United States. All have revenues above a billion dollars and no shortage of diamonds in their mines. They funded a resolution several years ago that created regulations around conflict diamonds, but with enough loopholes that it has done little to improve the lives of the miners. Their profits have grown in seventeen of the last twenty years," Jo said while reading from the financial reports that she had located.

"So I am back to my two recurring questions," Jill said. "What was their relationship to Laura and why are they after us?"

"In reviewing Laura's finances, I found a charity she operated and I passed that on to Angela to investigate. Angela, what have you found on this charity that Laura ran?" asked Jo.

"Good idea on the strategy for locating her foundation. I tried companies set up in her aliases. Nothing. Organizations that serve this part of Africa and there are too many. Let me research this some more based on deposits to a foundation. Of course, it could be a private foundation rather than a non-profit charity or whatever they call it outside of the U.S. Jill, why don't you talk about Laura while I do one more round of searching to see if I can find the name of this organization."

"Thanks, Angela, and good luck locating Laura's charity or whatever it is. Like Angela I tried to find any financial reporting for Laura and her aliases and came up with nothing. So then I tried her father and grandfather's names and struck gold on the grandfather's name. Someone is filing taxes and operating a checking account in her grandfather's name even though he has been dead for fifteen years. The account seems to always contain around twenty-thousand euros. The account is paying mundane things like health premiums, insurance, and hotels bills in cities around Europe. Whenever money goes out, a deposit is made from a Swiss bank account. So I bet that the majority of her assets are held in accounts in Switzerland.

"I was going to pass this information on to Interpol as they should be able to access her account since she is a criminal and she is dead. Maybe we can trace her organization from there, as well as figure out the consortium's role in her life," Jill said.

She continued. "More information was sent to us by Inspector Berg and Interpol. They have a timeline developing that lists each of the diamond heists that have been attributable to Laura. They also have a running dollar total on the value of those thefts. It is more than they originally thought might be credited to her. We don't know the name of the organization she created to provide services to the miners, so perhaps we could figure it out by cash deposits to organizations that fund services in those African countries that mirror a short time period after the heist. How did she dispose of the diamonds she stole? Wouldn't she have to sell them somewhere in order to get cash?"

"Do you think Interpol will share that kind of information?" asked Jo.

"I don't know. I thought we could feel them out on their level of cooperation," suggested Jill. "After all, the U.S. is a member so they should be responsive to us. If they don't seem cooperative, I'll give Special Agent Ortiz from the FBI a call since she was helpful with our last case. As a final effort, we could withhold the name on the bank account unless they give us the information from the Swiss bank account. Let's not share our strategy with Nick. He might give the name away to Interpol just to keep us safe and out of the case."

"He has continued to help us even though he clearly thinks we should give it up. Besides I think he has respect for you, Jill, since he read up on the Graeme St. Louis case. Let's feel him out by telling him our strategy. If he's against us, then we don't reveal the grandfather's name to him. I would like to give him a chance. We could also wait to have this discussion after Nathan meets us in Brussels. I'm sure he would have an opinion on our argument," Angela said.

"I like your suggestion about Nathan. Let's do that," Marie concurred.

"OK, we'll give that a try," agreed Jill.

"So our next steps are to finish this train ride and meet up with Nathan. Introduce the guys, settle into our hotel. Then share our latest information with them. Then I think we should start playing tourist in Brussels," Jo suggested.

They all nodded in agreement and returned to the conversation about what to see and do in Brussels. The train slowed into the station and everyone removed their luggage, preparing to exit. Nathan was supposed to meet them at the arrivals hall.

They hauled their luggage down the steps at the station. Nick was in the vicinity but wouldn't be introduced to Nathan until later at the hotel. Instead, he was watching the crowd to make sure that no one presented a threat to the women.

Jill was happy to see Nathan and gave him a hug and a kiss in the arrivals hall. Jo, Marie, and Angela had already met him during their visits to California, and they were happy to each get a hug from him. He had a van waiting outside to transport them to the hotel.

Nathan had visited two clients since his arrival and had two more clients to schedule. The wine industry in Belgium clearly took a back seat to the beer industry. It was an old industry, likely dating back to the ninth century in the regions of Wallonia and

Flanders. Ninety percent of the wine was the white varietal. All of Nathan's customers were in Flanders, which had Brussels as its political seat. When he designed labels for his clients in Belgium, he had the added complexity of language. Nearly all wines used French, which he spoke, on their labels. Artistically, he needed his clients' help to think in French in order to develop the perfect design. He enjoyed the challenge of creating wonderful labels in another language, and so far his labels had been well received. He'd planned to stay two days beyond when Jill was due to depart as he thought he might not get any of his work done if his first priority was to provide protection. This was a last-minute trip;he'd booked it when Jill mentioned the street chase in Amsterdam in an email.

As they exited, Jill felt like someone was watching her and she turned around to look. No one seemed to be watching them. Maybe it was Nick that she was sensing. She climbed into the van while the driver stored their luggage. She stared out the window, but again saw nothing. Fifteen minutes later, they arrived at their hotel. Again they had a suite with a common living room and separate bedrooms. Nathan's luggage was already in the room he would share with Jill. Nick had been able to book a room in the same hotel, so they could meet together in the suite.

Once inside the suite, introductions were made between Nick and Nathan. The two of them sat in the living room chatting while the woman unpacked their bags and freshened up.

After organizing their clothes, they headed out to the city's central square, the Grand Place. Nick brought along two guards from the properties he had hotel contracts with in Brussels. He was very concerned about their safety as the diamond consortium had a lot to lose if Jill and her team continued exploring their connections. They seemed to have millions of euros on the line, as well as a centuries-old reputation. The guards were in plain clothes like Nick, just keeping a watch on the group.

The Grote Market square was full of people and chocolate

shops. They decided they wanted to try a Belgian waffle since they missed lunch on the train. Each of the women tried something different for a topping since one could get a waffle with bananas, strawberries, whipped cream, chocolate, and nuts.

Following the commentary in a popular walking tour guidebook they viewed the historic buildings of the square where seven streets intersect. The Old Town Hall, the Palace Hotel, and the many buildings of the square, some dating to the fifteenth century were amazing. They also knew that the entire square had been covered in a flower rug in August which must have been an awesome sight. After exploring the square and some of the surrounding streets, it started to rain, so they took shelter in a pub.

The group was directed to an upstairs dining area and they were quickly served their beer of choice.

"Nathan, since you have clients here in Belgium, I assume you have been to this city before?" asked Angela.

"Yes, I've been here three times previously. I've acquired my clients one at a time, but they've all been with me for at least five years. So while I may not have journeyed here at the start of design work, I've visited them all at some point. It helps me to design a better label if I can visit their vineyard and speak with the client in-person. I try to include in my label design what makes the vineyard or its owners unique."

"What is your favorite part of Brussels?" Marie probed.

"I discover something new with each visit, but mostly I like the ambiance. It feels very old world in this city, yet modern when you view the people and the businesses. Of course, I also like exploring the beer. The beer glasses that pair with the beer are unique in my experience, and I like the artistry of that pairing."

The group must have been getting a little too jovial for the pub as a waiter came by to quiet them down. It was hard to tell if the increase in voice volume came from the beer or the sugar high of the Belgian waffle.

"Looks like the rain stopped. Let's go back out on the square and visit the City Museum, then maybe do some window shopping on all those cute streets afterwards," suggested Marie as she looked out the pub window.

They paid their tab and exited the pub, likely to the relief of the waiters. They'd never before been asked to keep their voices down. They headed towards the museum housed in King's House.

The City Museum contained a fascinating scale representation of the town in the Middle Ages. Additional paintings tracked the history of the city. By far the biggest square footage was devoted to the costumes, some eight hundred in quantity, of the Manneken Pis Fountain. Embassies, businesses, and artists had contributed to the collection over the past century. The women had not seen the fountain yet, but the costumes contained a life-like model of the little boy inside each costume. There were so many costumes that some were lying flat in glass covered drawers. Amazing that one little fountain has drawn so much attention worldwide.

They finished viewing other parts of the collection and decided they would browse the area. Everyone bought chocolate to take home as gifts. They headed toward an indoor shopping mall. Nathan and Jill decided to sit on the bench while the others shopped. Marie and Angela were in a chocolate store and Jo was browsing in a shoe store. Nick hadn't been sighted since they left the hotel.

While chatting on the bench, Jill was leaning against Nathan's shoulder watching the chocolate store. Nathan was keeping an eye on Jo. Suddenly he stood up and walked toward the store Jo was in.

"Nathan, what did you see? Is someone threatening Jo?"

"I think I just saw a large knife in the hand of the man who entered the store behind her. I'm going in."

"I'm right on your heels."

"Good. I don't want to be distracted as I protect Jo because I'm worrying about you."

Jill looked through the chocolate store window, hoping to catch a glance of Angela and Marie. She wanted them close for their safety and to help her and Nathan protect Jo, but they were tucked in the back of the store looking at the chocolate display.

She and Nathan entered the shoe store. Jo was in the back looking over her shoulder toward the two of them, as a man was attempting to drag her out the back of the store. The man held a knife in view of Jo to ensure her cooperation. Scattered around the floor were the shoes she had been thinking of trying-on, but had dropped once the man showed her the knife.

"Let go of that woman!" Nathan commanded as he approached the two of them.

"Call the police!" said Jill to the store employee as she stood staring at the man wielding the knife.

Jo, aware of how close the big knife was to her body, cooperated with the man, just trying to stay relaxed, while letting him drag her backwards. It helped to have Nathan and Jill in the shop with her. Their presence reduced her panic a little and made it easier to think.

Jill had no idea what Jo was thinking beyond a panic she surely must be feeling. Nathan approached the man, thinking about how he could make use of his hapkido skills.

"Sir, let the woman go," and he repeated the order in French.

"Do not call the police," yelled the man in English at the woman who had been dialing the phone. She dropped the phone on the floor in shock. Jill could only hope that, like in the U.S., an emergency operator would trace the call if it had gone through before she dropped the phone, or that she left the line open.

The man with the knife was watching all of them, looking less confident than a minute ago. Meanwhile, Angela, Marie, and a disguised Nick all entered the store. The man with the knife was considering his escape, whether he could drag the woman with him, or if he should let her go and run. He wouldn't get paid for the job, but he wouldn't be caught either. He heard the sirens in the distance and decided he'd best abandon kidnapping Jo and escape the store and the growing crowd. Suddenly he shoved Jo at Nathan, and then took off out the back door.

"Are you okay? Did he cut you?" Nathan questioned Jo, examining her for any injuries.

"No, you got here in time. Thanks for coming to my rescue. I need a hug right now."

The four women gathered in a group hug while a few tears were shed. Nathan gave Nick a look and took off after the man. The assailant had a head start on him, but Nathan was younger and likely in better shape, given the size of the man's beer belly.

Jill looked up and around, asking, "Where's Nathan?"

"He took off after Jo's kidnapper," declared Nick. "I stayed behind to make sure there wasn't another kidnapper waiting in the wings."

"Go after Nathan; he may need some help. Besides we've each other and the police will be arriving momentarily."

Nick did a quick assessment of the timing of the police's arrival and the crowd now forming, and decided that he could safely take off after Nathan and the knife-wielder.

Jill asked Angela, "Did you get a picture of the man?"

"Does the sun rise and set each day? Of course, I have about four pictures of the man. I think when he saw me aiming my camera at him, he made the decision to flee. He could not harm all of us before the police arrived. Here, look at the pictures."

The four women gathered, focused on the camera screen, just as the Police Locale entered the store. Introductions were made and a short conversation took place between the shopkeeper and the police in Dutch. They heard the word "Amerikaanse" and assumed that she was telling the officers that they were Americans. One officer continued with his interview of the terrified shopkeeper, who had been fairly quiet through the whole altercation. The other officer approached the women and switched to English.

"I am Inspector Willems, what are your names?"

"I'm Jill Quint."

"I'm Jo Pringle. I'm the one that the man with the knife was holding hostage."

"I'm Angela Weber. I have a picture of the man in my camera."

"I'm Marie Simon."

"Thank you. Can you tell me what happened?"

"Before we start with that, two men took off after the knife-wielding creep. Would you send an officer to assist them, or maybe we can all exit the store and try to help them?" reasoned Jill.

"No, I would like a report of what happened here first."

"Sorry, you'll have to get that report from the shopkeeper. We're going to go help our friends," said Jill and the women exited the store's back door in pursuit of their men.

"Let's split up and send two to the left and two to the right since we don't know which way Nathan and Nick went," suggested Marie, as they scanned the empty alley.

Inspector Willems departed the store behind the woman with the second officer joining him. They likewise split up and followed the women who were jogging to the end of the alley. When they reached the street, they looked up and down the intersecting street for Nathan or Nick. Marie and Angela shouted down the alley at Jill and Jo. They were too far away to hear what they were saying, but they were gesturing for Jill and Jo to join them. They must have sighted Nick and Nathan. Jill and Jo ran to catch up with Angela and Marie. They soon joined a developing crowd down the street. They found the police putting handcuffs on the knife-wielding man as he lay on the ground. Until the handcuffs were secured, Nathan and Nick had a foot each in the center of the man's back.

"Nathan, Nick, are you injured?" asked Jill.

Both men viewed her with a 'what a stupid question' look,' eyebrows raised.

"Okay then, I'll take that as a no."

The police hauled the man upright, preparing to take him to the station for questioning. They'd seen Angela's photo of the man holding a knife to Jo's body, so it would be an easy conviction. Inspector Willems was finally able to circle back to the women and ask them what this past thirty minutes had been about.

"Can you tell me the full story here? Why did the man pull a knife on one of you and why did you chase after him?"

"Let me start with an explanation of who we are. As you might have guessed, we're American tourists here on vacation. By the way, this is Nathan Conroy and this is Nick Brouwer", said Jill as she introduced the two men to the inspector.

"We became accidentally involved with a Belgian citizen in Antwerp who needed medical assistance in a restaurant shortly after we arrived in this country. That was six days ago. We have been in contact with the Dutch police and Interpol as it seems that the citizen we provided assistance to was the best diamond thief in the world and held a place on Interpol's most-wanted list. Somehow a diamond consortium has been trying to kidnap or harm one or more of the four of us since the original event in the restaurant." Marie explained, summarizing for the inspector.

Angela picked up the story. "We don't know why people are after us. We have pretty much been spending every waking moment pondering the answer to that question. Interpol in the Netherlands assured us that Interpol Brussels would be informed of our arrival and be prepared to assist us. It seems that they now have their proof that we need protection and they need to help us solve this case."

"All four of us hid in a dark courtyard while a man with a gun hunted for us. Angela was shot at with a poison dart gun and we hid in a windmill in Zaanse Schans, then there was an attempted kidnapping last night in Amsterdam. Other than that, we have been enjoying our vacation." Jill said, adding her two cents to the story.

"I love to shop and if I hadn't been so fascinated with a pair of shoes, I would have noticed the man before he got so close. He didn't say anything to me before you arrived. He showed me the huge knife and motioned that we would be exiting through the back door," Jo explained. "Perhaps he knew that I didn't speak Dutch or French or maybe he didn't speak English. Regardless I understood in a universal language that he wanted me to leave with him out the back door."

Inspector Willems had been scribbling many notes while the women spewed their descriptions of everything that had happened in the past several days. Ordinarily, he would have assumed that he needed to transport them to a mental health center, but they seemed otherwise normal and the gentlemen also agreed with their descriptions. He was simply nonplussed by them.

"We are going to continue with our vacation, starting with a stop at a pub for a beer or two to relax after this altercation," stated Jill. "If you'll arrange a meeting with Interpol and us and yourselves then we will take a taxi to whatever meeting location you specify. Nick and Nathan will stay with us as protection. They've done a great job keeping us safe so far."

Jo was looking a little worse for wear and Jill was convinced that one to two beers would go a long way to restore her to good health.

With that statement, the four women turned and began walking toward a pub down the street, the two men, providing escort. Inspector Willems and his partner stood there, completely dumbfounded by the women just walking away from them.

"Nathan, how did you get the knife-wielder flat on the cement?" asked Jill.

"I used a bi-directional kick from hapkido to knock the knife to the ground with one foot and the other foot made contact with his head. He just dropped. Nick and I each put a foot on his back to keep him safely on the ground."

"Why, Nathan, I sense you enjoyed yourself assisting this guy to the ground," remarked a grinning Angela.

"Seriously, I always wanted to test my martial arts skills in real life, and I wish my Songseang-nim was here to see this. I'm sure he'd give me some feedback that would bring me back down to earth," Nathan said with a laugh.

"After watching you in action, I would hire you in a heartbeat," said Nick with some awe in his voice. "I'm going to start searching for new employees in the various martial arts gyms in Belgium and the Netherlands. Jill, you need to stop worrying about whether Nathan can defend himself. I've never seen anyone better able to take down the common criminal."

"Nick, the problem is that no matter how great a master black belt Nathan is, he's not faster than a speeding bullet, which is the weapon of choice in the United States. I'll, however, stop worrying about him while in Brussels."

With that comment, they settled into a pub, taking the edge off the adrenaline rushes with a pint of beer. Thirty minutes later and into their second beer, Jill received a call from Inspector Willems that a meeting had been arranged in an hour at Interpol head-quarters. He provided Jill with the address and disconnected the call.

"Jo, we have a little time. Do you want to go back to the shoe store and try those shoes on? They were cool and unique. Given some time, I'm sure I would find some shoes that interested me," suggested Marie.

"They were great shoes, but I don't think I want them in my closet reminding me of when a man pulled a knife on me and I had my life flash in front of me. However, if you ladies would like to spend a few minutes shopping, I'm fine providing an opinion on your choices."

"Nick, do you have an idea how long it will take us to get from here to the meeting's location?" asked Angela.

"I would guess ten minutes by cab, thirty minutes walking."

"Since we have a little time and we're in the neighborhood, how about if we look for the Manneken Pis fountain and his sister, the Jeanneke Pis fountain, and we can cross that off our list of things to see in Brussels. When we're done, we can take two cabs to our meeting," Angela suggested.

The group had taken Angela's advice and viewed the fountains, which were located on opposite sides of the Grand Place. Rather than wait for two taxis, Nick had two of his employees drive them to their appointment at Interpol. They presented themselves to a reception desk and were escorted to a meeting room on the seventh floor. When they arrived, Inspector Willems and three other people were seated around a conference table and introductions were performed.

"Dr. Quint, we contacted our colleagues in The Hague and your American FBI. You have quite a reputation for crime solving in the U.S.," announced Criminal Intelligence Officer Dubois.

"It's actually the reputation of my team, rather than me. This case has nothing to do with my occupation. We're here on vacation. It was dumb luck that we were seated next to Interpol's most famous diamond thief. Now we're involved just trying to save our own lives. These guys are getting bolder and more violent and we need your help."

"I would advise you to return to America."

"You think that will be the end of this? These men will just hop a plane and follow us there. We cut short our vacation, and we still have these men trying to harm us. Why can't you get information out of the men you have in custody so far? There're two from Amsterdam and one this afternoon in Brussels. What new information do you have from those three? Will you allow Angela to question them? She's the best on our team at questioning people."

"I do not think that would be a good idea, nor do our laws

permit civilians to question people in custody," replied Inspector Willems.

"Can we view a tape of your questioning of the men in custody in Amsterdam? We have questions we would have liked asked of them. If they were not asked of the first two men, perhaps you could do so as and ask the man you have in custody now." asserted Angela.

"What other information have you collected on this case? What do you know about Laura Peeters and the diamond consortium? Can you tell me what your laws are regarding the review of financial information? Do you have an expert in financial documents that I could sit down with to better understand the financial records of Peeters and the consortium?" queried Jo.

Faced with so many questions from the women, Officer Dubois, his staff from Interpol and Inspector Willems excused themselves and left the room to discuss the case. Given Nick's experience as a Dutch police officer, he wasn't surprised by the move. Nor was he surprised by the questions of the women, since he had grown to know them over the past several days. He admitted to himself that life would not be nearly as exciting once they returned to the United States. He contemplated how he could spend time with Angela, or perhaps play a role in Jill's company. He would have to give it some thought.

"I'm hoping they will call their FBI colleagues in the U.S. to find out how helpful we can be to them in solving a major crime." Jill said.

"After we get done here, where do you want to go next?" asked Marie.

"I think that depends on what they decide to do," responded Nathan. "If they allow you to participate in this case, we may be occupied here for several hours. If they do not allow us to participate, I think we'll be subject to perhaps thirty minutes of questioning and then we'll be free to go. We're within walking distance of the Royal Palace of Art, so we could go there when we're done here."

Nick observed how Nathan related to the women and thought he needed to copy his behavior as the women obviously held respect and affection for Jill's boyfriend.

Just then the conference room door opened and the men resumed their seats at the table.

"We have had a discussion with our peers in Amsterdam, Interpol, and your FBI. It seems that they all agree that you can be of more help than harm to this case. Furthermore, your FBI would like this case solved on Belgian soil before you return to the United States as they have recent memory of your last case, Dr. Quint. They think that our criminals are less likely to have helicopters with black ops people fully armed. The FBI is correct in this assumption. We are prepared to consult with all of you," said Officer Dubois with a distinct lack of enthusiasm.

"Awesome," said the women.

"Let's start with the report of what happened today at the shoe store. Madame Pringle left the scene before Officer Willems and his men had a full report. We would then like a quick recap of all the events that have happened since you began this holiday. Then we will share with you a tape of the man that was arrested in Amsterdam. We will consider any questions you would like asked of the man in custody presently. We would then like to discuss your theories on the diamond consortium. Have I left anything out?" asked Officer Dubois, looking at the assembled group.

"If you have a forensic accountant, I would like to work with him or her while you guys watch the tape," replied Jo. "My expertise is in money matters and I'm struggling with accessing financial data in Europe."

"We do not have such a person in this office. We do have someone with those skills in our headquarters in Lyon, France. Let me make a call before we start to see if I can arrange that."

Inspector Dubois left the room, phone in hand, to make the call.

Marie looked at the other Interpol representatives and requested computers be brought into the room.

"I can multitask. When you give us the names, including their aliases, of the men you have in custody, I'll begin my search of their backgrounds."

"How many computers do you need?"

"I think maybe two or three," replied Jill. "Angela will be observing the tapes and everyone in this room, so she won't need a computer. Nathan also will not need a computer. Nick, I'll leave you to make your own decision."

As Officer Dubois reentered the room, one of his officers left to retrieve three computers. They all assumed that Jo would be moved to another part of the building, if Officer Dubois could arrange the conversation with the forensic accountant in France.

"I was able to reach our headquarters in France. Madame Barnard will be available to consult with Madame Pringle in thirty minutes. I've arranged for you to use a phone and a computer to speak with her."

"Does she speak English?" inquired Jo.

"Yes."

The second Interpol officer returned with another gentleman carrying three laptop computers. They were set in front of Jill, Marie, and Nick.

"Good, let's get started. Madame Pringle, would you begin by giving us a description of the event in the shoe store a few hours ago?"

"We were doing a walking tour of the Grand Place. We went inside the City Museum and then settled in for a drink at a pub afterwards. When we were done, we wanted to browse the streets around the square. Angela and Marie entered a chocolate shop. Jill and Nathan were parked on a bench watching the world go by. Nick was in the area, tailing us in disguise, to provide protection after the close calls in Amsterdam. I saw a shoe shop two doors down and entered. My friends here would tell you that I'm not one to pay attention to my surroundings normally. I admit that I was distracted by the array of shoes, so I dropped what little guard I had while I shopped.

"I had two shoes in my hand and I was about to ask the shopkeeper to find them in my size. When I turned around to speak to her, the man seemed to have appeared out of nowhere with a massive switchblade in hand. He could have sliced me with the knife, but he seemed more interested in taking me somewhere. He held the knife up and pointed to the back door and gestured that 'I should walk toward it,' which I started to do when Nathan and Jill entered the store. I'll let them describe what happened next as I was so relieved by their arrival that I shut out the situation."

With that last sentence, Angela had to lean over and give Jo a hug. After a few moments, Nathan carried on with the story.

"Jill and I were sitting on the bench. I was glancing occasionally into the two storefronts where the women were shopping. I noticed a man looking first into the chocolate store and then moving on to the shoe store. I saw him enter the store, pushing the door open with his left hand while pulling something out of his pocket with the right hand. It was then that I saw the trigger release and a blade appeared. Jill and I stood up and went quickly towards the store. Jill gave a quick look inside the chocolate store, but Angela and Marie had their heads turned away from the shop window so we continued into the shoe store. Jill gestured as we went towards the shoe store, not expecting anyone to see her hand movement through the chocolate shop window.

"We entered the store and confronted the man. He did indeed have a knife. He was pushing Jo toward the back door, but when we entered he switched positions so that Jo was in front of him, presumably with his knife aimed at her back. Jo was blocking my view of the knife. I told the man 'Let Jo go.' Jill yelled to the shopkeeper, 'to call the police,' and she started dialing the phone.

"The man spoke up at that point, holding the knife closer to Jo. He told the shopkeeper, 'Do not call the police,' and she dropped the phone. At the same time Angela and Marie entered the shoe store. Angela, always camera in hand, took a picture of the man holding the knife to Jo's back. It was my impression that the man made the decision to run when he realized we had his picture.

"He departed through the back door of the store. We all gathered around Jo to make sure she was okay. When I could see that she had not been injured, I left through the back door to chase the man down. Fortunately he was not in good physical shape and I reached him two blocks later. Nick was a minute behind me. When I caught up to the man, I yelled for him to stop as I placed a hand on his shoulder. He spun around and flipped out the switchblade. I then made a decision to use my martial arts skills. I levered a bi-directional kick, knocking the blade out of his hand with one foot while the other foot connected with his head. He dropped to the ground, and Nick and I held him in place until Officer Willems and his men arrived to take custody. Can anyone else think of something to add?"

"Madame Weber, we need a copy of the photo you took for legal proceedings. I will take you over to a technician to download the picture."

"Would you also like a picture of the man that followed us in Amsterdam? I don't know if he's in custody in Amsterdam. If he's not, then Nick can tell you about him."

"Thank you for being so good with your camera. It is very helpful. If you have any other pictures of suspicious people, we would appreciate you downloading them."

"You're welcome. One other comment - when we were paying for our chocolate, one salesperson said to the other, 'Did you see that woman walk by our front window gesturing down the mall corridor?' I asked her if it was a woman with long blonde hair and she said 'yes'. Marie and I hurried out thinking Jill might need our help. That was why we entered the store so soon after you did. I pulled my camera out thinking that if there was a problem, I wanted a picture of it."

"An excellent plan on your part, having a picture of a man holding a knife to someone makes it so much easier to prosecute. Is there anything else, any other detail that we should add to the narrative about today's event?" said Inspector Willems.

After a moment in thought, the assembled group collectively shook their heads "no".

"Let's start at the beginning then," directed Office Dubois. "I took the opportunity to read the reports prepared by my colleagues at The Hague, and by the Dutch police. I am most puzzled by why anyone is after you. What is the purpose of harming or kidnapping you? What do you know, or what do you have that is of interest to someone else? And who is that someone else? You all seem convinced that it's the diamond consortium. How do you know it's not a long-lost relative of Laura Peeters? Perhaps the gentleman that followed you on the streets of Amsterdam simply wanted to speak to four beautiful women. I am interested in your thoughts on these questions."

"Those are all very good questions; in fact we've been puzzling over them for the past six or so days," agreed Jill. "Let me pick off two of your questions for which we may have answers. We don't believe that there is a mad relative of Laura Peeters after us because we got her to the hospital alive. She was completely under the control of the hospital when she was killed. As to the man in Amsterdam, if he was keen on meeting us, why did he run off once we confronted him? We gave him the perfect opening to introduce himself and instead he walked away, and not out of shyness. His posture and mannerisms did not indicate shyness."

"So we're back to the question of what do we know, or what do we have that is of interest to someone else," surmised Marie. "And is that someone else the diamond consortium? We dumped our purses out a day or so ago looking for something of interest to someone. We found nothing beyond our own possessions in our purses."

Officer Dubois pointed to their purses and asked "Are those the purses you had on you at the time you met Laura Peeters?"

Marie answered, "We each only brought one purse with us on this trip, so yes, these are the two purses involved."

"Who was sitting where in the restaurant, when you provided assistance to Laura?" Inspector Willems inquired.

"Marie was sitting closest to Laura. I was facing Marie which allowed me to look at Laura and see she was in distress. Jo was next to Marie, and Angela was seated on my right."

"How long had you been seated in the restaurant before you noticed Laura?" asked the inspector.

The four women conferred and agreed that it was in the range of seven to ten minutes.

"Madame Simon, may we take your purse to our lab for examination? You're under no legal obligation to comply with this request," remarked Officer Dubois.

"Let me keep my passport, my wallet, and my iPhone, and you can take the purse to your lab," said Marie as she removed the items from her purse and handed it to an officer.

The officer stepped out of the conference room to hand the purse off to a staff member, who would take it to the lab.

"Dr. Quint, we should really have a look at your purse as well. Remember, Laura Peeters was a master at sleight-of-hand movements. From a seated position, could she have reached your purse by bending forward, or by reaching under the table? Was it possible for her to reach her purse?" questioned Willems.

Again the women conferred and agreed with Inspector Willems that it would have been possible for Laura to reach her purse. Jill silently removed the same three items that Marie had from her purse and handed it over to an officer.

"Please call us by our first names. I think we can speak faster without the formality," requested Angela.

"Thank you. Jill and Marie, were you wearing outer garments, like a raincoat?" asked inspector Willems.

"I had on a leather jacket with no pockets, resting over the back of my chair," replied Jill.

"I had a short jacket with side pockets. It was also resting over the back of my chair."

"Where is that jacket now?"

"In our hotel room. It's much warmer in Brussels than it was in Antwerp when we arrived."

"Did you search those pockets in your jacket, the day you searched your purses?"

"No, we didn't think of that."

"Marie, if you remember where the jacket is at this moment, and if you don't mind one of my men retrieving it from your hotel room, I could have it brought here for you," offered Nick.

"I could do that. My hotel room key went with my purse down to the lab. Angela or Jo, would you give your room key to Nick?"

"Nick, my jacket is in the closet of the second bedroom from the entry door in our suite. It is sort of an aqua green-colored coat with a Nike swish on it."

Nick stepped out of the room to handle the matter.

"I think after we examine your purses and the jacket, we'll have our answer as to whether it is something you have, rather than something you know," observed Willems.

CHAPTER 11

"Officer Dubois, if you would connect me with your accountant in Nice, I'll tell her what I'm looking for to give her a start on pulling that information for us," Jo requested.

Dubois called Lyon and, in another room, put Jo on the phone with a Ms. Bernard. After a short conversation, Jo returned to the conference table.

"Will you share any and all information you have obtained from the men in custody? I'd like to noodle on the case while we chat, and I feel like that missing piece of information is somewhat blocking my thought processes about this case," said Jill.

"Yes, we can do that," replied Dubois as he retrieved some computer files on his laptop.

"These reports are written in Dutch and French. Can any of you read those languages?"

They shook their heads no.

"Nick is likely literate in those languages, and Nathan, you can read French, but the rest of us may know about fifty words in any language beyond English," lamented Jill. "So I guess you'll need to translate for us, unfortunately."

"There is a lot of information on this report that you probably would not find useful. Why don't I read the names of the men, including any aliases that are in the report, a description of any previous crimes that they're wanted for, and the questions and answers during the interview with the police?"

"Thank you, that would be satisfactory."

"In Amsterdam, the first man arrested was Kenneth Lee Akselrod. His aliases are versions of his own name – Kenneth Lee, Lee Akselrod, and Lee Dorleska, which is Akselrod spelled backwards. The second man is Jan Storms and he has no aliases. They are both wanted for crimes in connection with precious stones. Neither has a history of violence. They were interviewed separately, but told the same story.

"They were hired in Antwerp two days after Laura Peeters's death. They were offered fifty-thousand euros each to capture the four of you. Once you were captured, they were to contact the person that hired them and give her your location."

"A woman hired these thugs?" Angela exclaimed.

"Did the men know we were traveling to Amsterdam and then Brussels?" asked Jo.

"Yes, they knew your itinerary including the hotel name in each city. They said they followed you from the time you left the lecture hall until they were arrested. The information was provided by the woman who hired them."

"Were the men able to provide a description of this woman?" Marie asked.

"We had a police artist do a sketch based upon their description and there was no match to her in any database, so perhaps she was in disguise. Whether her disguise was through make-up or plastic surgery, we cannot determine. We have links to all passport agencies as well as driver's licenses for most of the world. They did say she spoke with an accent that could have been Dutch or German or one of the other countries in this region. She was

Caucasian, about five foot six, slender, perhaps thirty-five to forty-five in age and a brunette. She had a tattoo on one wrist, but neither man could describe it."

"Did she pay them up front? Has she been in contact with them since the initial meeting? How would they contact her, once we were captured?" asked Jo.

"They were given ten-thousand euros upfront. They were told that they would be watched and she would know when you were captured."

"That suggests that she has been in the neighborhood of our various encounters with these men," Angela mused. "Are there any videos in those areas that might be analyzed to find a common woman in the background?"

"We need to question our suspect from today's attempted kidnapping. We have a list of routine questions, as well as some additional questions based on what we know from the first two men. There is room for two of you to observe the questioning, but it is going to be in French. I understand that you wanted Angela to observe, but given the language barrier, I would recommend the gentlemen."

Angela looked disappointed with that piece of information, but she had to agree that she couldn't overcome the language barrier. Nick's French was better than Nathan's, and he had expe-rience in law enforcement, but it was good to have Nathan observe as well. The women gave him a list of questions that they wanted asked and the two left the room.

"Did you find anything in our purses or Marie's jacket? I know you've only had the items for about an hour, but I would think that would be enough time to examine them," remarked Jill.

"I was just about to check on our lab," replied Dubois as he picked up the phone. While they did not speak French, the women could tell by the conversation that something had been found.

After hanging up the phone, Dubois returned to the table and said, "They found something in the jacket. It appears to be a small computer component that was placed in the inside pocket of the jacket. The lab is trying to access the chip as it is not a normal flash drive. Would you like to accompany me to the lab to see the component?"

"Yes, and can we retrieve our purses at the same time? I feel naked without it on my shoulder," said Marie as the group left the conference room.

Brussels had one of the largest Interpol locations in the world and the criminal science lab occupied an entire floor. Jill and Marie located their purses next to a technician with a sigh of a relief. They were in a police building, but still had trouble trusting strangers with their personal belongings.

Dubois greeted a technician with what looked like a disassembled computer in front of her. When they got closer they noticed that she had a series of computer components and cords as she was examining what looked like a watch battery. Dubois performed introductions.

"Have you ever seen such a chip or whatever it is before?" asked Jill.

"Yes, if you look inside this computer, you'll see similar components. The difficulty is finding which component to put this chip in and I've located that just now. Let's see what's on the disk when we power it up."

"Accès refuse" was the response by the computer.

Marie commented, "I'm thinking that is French for 'access denied.'"

The technician nodded without looking up. She spent the next twenty minutes using various software programs.

The technician's first goal was to get to a login page and the second was to figure out a username and password. A few minutes later, she was able to hack into the disk. They all leaned closer to read the screen. Again, it was French, so they leaned back and waited for the technician to translate.

"There is a lot of information here. Why don't I use translation software? It will give you about a ninety percent accurate translation."

The women nodded and a few minutes later had a paper copy of the files with the content translated into English. They left the lab, following Dubois back to the conference room. Coming out of the elevator on the seventh floor, they were met by Nick and Nathan exiting an adjoining elevator car. They entered the conference room along with Willems and Dubois.

"Inspector Willems, why don't you start with what you learned in the interview of our suspect, beginning with his identity?" began Dubois.

"His name is Lloyd Judson Benjamin; he is a dual Belgian and South African resident. He is wanted for illegal trading of precious stones, and thought to be connected to jewelry thefts in several European cities. He has no history of violence. He appears to be hired by the same woman as the other two, although she seems to have had a different disguise when she met with him. We don't think he had a partner, but he does know the other two men in custody. He was offered the same payment as the others fifty-thousand euros."

"How did one man think he could capture four women?" Jo said, puzzled, ever the strategic thinker.

"Mr. Benjamin isn't a violent person by nature – he was looking at the situation as capture and release. He would kidnap each of you one at a time; take you to an apartment to hold you for questioning by the woman that hired him, then release you."

"He didn't think we would object to his scheme, perhaps tell the police about the apartment location?" Marie asked.

"Let's just say he wasn't the sharpest criminal we have interviewed here in Brussels. Would you gentlemen agree?" asked Willems.

Nathan, of course, had no experience with the criminal element, but even he thought that Mr. Benjamin was likely to have a short tenure in his life as a criminal.

"He is about the dumbest and most naïve criminal I have ever seen interviewed by law enforcement," affirmed Nick. "He really believed kidnapping you ladies, one at a time would work. The woman that hired him must not be very insightful about people's skills."

"When asked how he would contact the woman once he had you in custody, he responded that he'd been provided with a disposable cell phone to use to contact her. It's interesting that she didn't tell the man she would be watching for your capture like she told the first two men.

"We checked the records on the phone, but it had never been used so that was a dead end. When questioned about what she wanted you for, he indicated that she just wanted to talk to you. He really wasn't very helpful. Now he will go through the legal process as this is such a clear case of attempted kidnapping. We have too many witnesses and the picture of him holding a knife on Madame Pringle."

"Thank you, Inspector Willems. Is there anything else that anyone wants to add about the interview of Monsieur Benjamin?" asked Dubois, looking at Nathan and Nick. They both indicated they had nothing to add to Inspector Willems' report.

"Now, let's move on to discuss the contents of the disk that Laura Peeters dropped into Marie's jacket. Our lab technician ran the file through translation software and that's the report that Jill is holding. I have additional copies here in French for Inspector Willems as well as Nick and Nathan. Let's all take a moment to review the information."

There was silence in the conference room while they all examined the report of the disk contents. Dubois waited until everyone appeared to have finished reading the report.

"This disk appears to contain an extensive list of precious

stone thefts over a fifteen-year period. My assumption is that we may attribute these thefts to Laura Peeters. I don't know how else she would have these records unless she was involved in the crimes," asserted Dubois.

"This also seems to be a general ledger of sorts," proclaimed Jo. "She has the estimated value of the theft, what she received for those stones when she sold them, deposits to what I assume is a Swiss bank account, and deposits to the charity that she operated for the miners. What's odd to me is it appears that she received income from the diamond consortium. If she was stealing from them, why was she getting income from them? It appears to be a direct sale back to the consortium?"

"I don't understand this ledger that you speak of - can you walk me through how you arrived at your conclusions," Dubois requested.

Jo proceeded to walk Dubois through the financial transactions of Laura Peeters. Angela was researching the charity that Laura operated and Marie was doing an extensive search on the names in the ledger. Inspector Willems had gone to a whiteboard in the conference room and was creating a timeline of Laura's activities over the past fifteen years or so and added pictures of her, the three men in custody, the unknown woman who had hired the men, and the known heads of the consortium. Jill closed her eyes and reviewed what she knew about Laura.

Obviously, the unidentified woman guessed that Laura had given the disk to one of the four women. So that meant that Laura had informed the woman of the existence of the information. Was the woman a friend or a foe of Laura's? Was she trying to recover the information to protect Laura or to protect something else? Was the woman related to the consortium? Jill decided she would focus on identifying the woman who was organizing the kidnapping attempts.

Jill opened her eyes and asked Willems for the artist's sketch of the woman.

Sketch in hand, she said to Nathan "Would you be able to make a few adjustments to the sketch? This isn't your usual wine label, but I figure you've an artist's eye."

"Yes, what do you need me to change?"

"The facial recognition software was unable to identify her picture. With all the access that Interpol has to passport and driver's license pictures, I can't believe there is no match for her picture. What could she do on a temporary basis to confuse our facial recognition of her? I think she could change the shape of her eyes with sufficient makeup. She can't do anything temporary with her chin or nose. She could change her teeth and her cheeks with some temporary dentures and padding, but that might get in the way of her speaking abilities. She could also plump her lips. So let's make subtle changes to her picture and see if we get any matches. Make her eyes a little more rounded, narrow her lips, and thin her cheeks."

Jill watched Nathan sketch in the features she was suggesting.

"How is this?" said Nathan holding the sketch up for her to view.

"Perfect! Inspector Willems would you run this picture again through your facial recognition software?"

He left the room with the sketch. Jill continued to think, but was unable to come up with any new ideas. The inspector returned to the conference room after a brief time.

"We have a match! Her name is Chloe Martin, and she's Laura Peeters' cousin - And like her cousin, she has several aliases. Jill, altering the sketch was a brilliant suggestion."

"How do you know they are cousins when we didn't think Laura had any family?"

"Yes, younger by two years, from Laura's mother's side of the family. When we got a match it listed family members. Laura's mother's maiden name was Wouters, which was different from Chloe's mother's maiden name. As the two mothers were step-siblings, there wasn't a match for family. We didn't make the family connection between the two women until we dug a little further into the marriage records of the city of Mechelen, where they were both raised."

"What do you know about her? Since she has aliases, I'm guessing that she is known to the Belgian police?" speculated Marie as she started a new search on Chloe.

"Yes, she is known to both the Belgian police and Interpol. She left DNA behind on a jewelry heist some ten years ago and has been wanted ever since. Officer Dubois, is the diamond heist at the Palace Hotel on the list?"

"If it occurred in 2003, then yes, it's on Laura's list."

"Have the police installed surveillance cameras around the city?" asked Jill.

"Yes."

"Can your information technology people set-up the facial recognition software to examine your cameras across the city for a match to Chloe's sketch?" Jill suggested, "We would at least be able to identify which sectors of the city she travels in when she is not wearing the full disguise."

"Is that a technique you used in your last case in San Francisco?"

"Yes, and it worked very well. The San Francisco Police Department was able to make an arrest within an hour of sighting a suspect on-camera. We were amazed at how close he was to the building in which the FBI was keeping me in protective custody."

"Let me call my chief inspector so that he can have a technician evaluate our ability to do that," said Willems. "I also think he'll want to be brought into this conversation, as what began as a simple kidnapping attempt is evolving into a much larger case."

"Inspector Willems is correct; we likely need to inform both of our superiors as we'll want to set up a joint task force. Why don't we plan to reconvene in our Command Center on the fifth floor in four hours? That will allow us time to invite our colleagues in

Antwerp and Amsterdam, as well as to notify the U. S. Consulate here in Brussels of your situation and give them sufficient time to travel. Ladies and gentlemen, I would be happy to show you to a cafeteria we have in this building to wait while we assemble a larger group." Inspector Dubois said.

"Thank you for that offer, but we would rather walk over to the Royal Palace area and explore the treasures of Brussels. I think if you alert the officers in that sector of our possible need for assistance, then we'll be fine," replied Jill. "We've two excellent bodyguards. After the museum, we'll get dinner and then return to this building at the designated time. You have our mobile phone numbers if you need to contact us. We might come up with some fresh ideas about this mystery away from this conference room."

The group departed the building, heading toward the Royal Museum. They appreciated how nice it was to be outside and act as tourists for a few hours and they agreed that food and beer was definitely in their near future. Keeping an eye out for anyone paying too much attention to them, they were still managing to enjoy the friendship of one another.

From the grounds of the Royal Palace, they could look out on the entire city and the view was incredible. In the distance was the Atomium, built for the World's Fair in 1958. It looked like a giant molecule. They ducked into the Church of Notre Dame, followed by a visit to the Cinquantenaire Museum. There was a chamber quartet concert being conducted in one of the rooms there that they were able to enjoy for a brief time.

They left the Royal Palace square and followed Nick to a restaurant that served French pub food and, of course, beer. Not wanting to appear intoxicated in front of Interpol and the Belgian police, Jill, the alcohol lightweight of group limited her consumption to one beer. She retrieved the print-out of the materials on the disk that had been found in Marie's jacket pocket and spread it out on the table in front of everyone. They all took a moment to study the information.

"It looks like there is a detailed listing of each theft," concluded Nick. "She records the carats of the diamonds, the quantity, setting if relevant, any other stones, and where she delivered or otherwise disposed of the stones. Those are the column headings in French."

"It also looks like she records her estimated value of the theft and what she was able to resell them at," Jo said guessing at the french words.

"What do think the initials are for in this column?" asked Marie, pointing to the second column on the paper.

"I have no idea," Angela said. "She labels the column heading 'job' and it looks like there are repeating initials."

"It appears that there are six sets of initials," Marie declared. "Do you think that corresponds to the six diamond consortium members?"

"Good catch, Marie. Do the initials compare to the company name, or the CEO, or the family name?"

"Here is the list of the company names let's compare," Jill suggested, and they all leaned forward to compare the two lists.

"I don't see any correlation," remarked Nathan.

"No, I don't either," replied Jill. "Where's our list with their CEO names or any other information we have on the members? I wouldn't think she would deal directly with the CEO on the thefts. It's too coincidental to have six sets of initials and six consortium members. We just haven't found the legend to these initial sets."

"Leave that to me to figure out, since I love puzzles like this little mystery," said Nathan. He took the list and moved to another table.

The other five returned to the print-out to discuss what other information was contained therein.

"There's an interesting trend on the estimated value of the theft and the resale value," Jo mused. "She seems to have been able to keep a stable eighty to eighty-five percent. I wonder how she did that over the course of the fifteen years. It seems improbable to me that you would always have the exact same percentage. It almost suggests she had a contract to always guarantee a certain return. If I could see the original spreadsheet, I could determine if there are any formulas in use in any of the columns. That would imply either an estimate or a contractual obligation in some of the columns."

"She appears to be an exact person in her record-keeping so, Jo, I would concur with your explanation of a contractual obliga- tion," Marie agreed.

"What other information is available?" Angela asked "Is this all of the files of the disk? Is it just this spreadsheet?"

"When the technician opened the disk, there were three files," replied Jill. "Do we have that many files worth of information in this print-out?"

"It looks like there are two files," verified Nick. "We'll have to ask about the third file. I don't think they purposely are keeping something from you - maybe it was just the disk directory."

"Okay, we won't worry about missing information. Rather, let's review the second file," directed Jill as they all leaned over to examine the second set of pages.

"It appears to be an accounting of her charity perhaps," Angela observed. "These expenses are wide ranging from health care to clothing to education. The quantity noted suggests her charity was supporting hundreds of people. This is an impressive operation."

"How many years of accounting does there appear to be on all these sheets?" Jo asked.

"At least ten years. In the beginning, it looks like she started with just education. Over time she added healthcare, clothing, and perhaps some micro-loans. It's a very sophisticated operation. She's a thief, but I like what she did with her money. She makes me have conflicted feelings since she did so much good with her earnings from thievery," said Angela, wavering in her impression of Laura. "She is a modern-day Robin Hood stealing from wealthy diamond mine-owners and retail stores that sell conflict diamonds. Then she turned around and gave the proceeds to a miners' fund. Jo, what is the total size of this charity? Can you perform your accounting magic and summarize this charity for us?"

"I'll go and join Nathan at the other table so we can both work in silence," announced Jo. With papers in hand, she stood to join Nathan at the other table. "Why don't you all have another beer; give me and Nathan a few minutes to puzzle over our respective documents, then hopefully we'll have the answers to discuss over dinner."

"Okay, what else can we work on? Nathan and Jo have their assignments," Jill noted. "What else don't we know?"

"We don't know much about the cousin, Chloe Martin."

"We don't know why she wanted to speak with us. We don't know the significance of the flat reimbursement rate for Laura's heists; we don't know who sat Laura up in the hospital or how they knew that would kill her."

"We don't know why she was receiving payments from the consortium; we don't know who poisoned her or who she was meeting for dinner that night."

Angela and Nick tossed out questions that Jill wrote on a napkin.

Marie had been mulling over thoughts and added, "Somehow, all roads lead back to the consortium and Laura. I really wish we could have spoken to Chloe to get her take on the situation. Did she want the disk back because of the data on it or because she thought there was something on the disk that would involve her?"

Just then Nathan reclaimed his seat at the table. As he sat

down he said, "I think we should order dinner to make sure we have enough time to eat before we have to return to Interpol."

"Did you break the code around the initials?" asked Jill.

"Of course. I'll explain after we order dinner. I want to make sure we have enough time to eat," Nathan gently but firmly repeated.

Jill understood that Nathan wasn't going to reveal his information until they'd all ordered. She recognized that he knew from past experience that when she was deep in thought on a case, she did a poor job accounting for meal-times. If he didn't override her, they would all starve.

She glanced over at Jo, who was making notations on a napkin. Jill did not want to interrupt her train of thought, but perhaps if they handed her a menu, she could order her meal, then go back to her analysis. Nathan translated the French menu for Jo and she made her choice. She indicated that she needed another few minutes and she would be done. With a little help from Nathan and Nick, the other three made their choices as well. None of the women had much experience with French food, so dinner promised to be an adventure.

"Okay, Nathan, my curiosity is killing me." Jill demanded, "What is the meaning of the initials?"

"It was actually very simple. The initials represent the first letter of the diamond company name, and the first letter of the CEO's last name. So the set of six initials either represents the six members of the diamond consortium, or it is a huge coincidence."

"So she attributed each job to a consortium CEO," Marie mused. "Did that reflect who she stole from or who ordered the theft?"

"I would've thought the initials represented who she stole from. It really taints her legacy if she was stealing at the direction of the consortium members," Angela remarked. "Forget her label of Robin Hood."

"We need to find out more about some of these thefts," Marie said. "We know that the thefts occurred in many retail jewelry stores. I wonder if they were company-owned stores? We also know from Interpol that some of the thefts were from private owners – are they on the list with initials assigned to them? Did they have the same flat percentage for the sale?"

"I want to know how you steal a chandelier or a ball gown," Angela announced. "No matter how good a thief is with sleight-of-hand, you can't fit either of those items inside your pocket, or even in a large purse. What was her strategy in those thefts?"

Jo appeared to have finished her analysis of the charity since she rejoined the group, her note-filled sheet of paper in hand. Overhearing Angela's questions, she added her own curiosity about stealing those large items.

"Good question, Angela. I didn't learn the answer to that question during my analysis, but I did learn that she had a well-run charity. These statements are in euros and I don't have a sense of how far a euro goes in the regions of these diamond mines. From what I can see, the administrative costs are minimal. I've looked at the accounting records of several U.S. charities over the years, so I have some experience in this area. Laura has paid staff in these mine regions that operate her programs. Given the size of the mines, each mine is treated as a separate service area. She started with one mine and expanded to the additional five mines within five years.

"Like we noted earlier, she began with education and expanded to healthcare and housing. In the last couple of years, she started providing micro-loans to miners with a desire to start a small business. About seventy percent of those loans have been paid back. I think that's a pretty good payback scheme in less than three years. She's supporting some great entrepreneurs. In each of the five mines, she provided about seventy-five percent of the funding to the charity, the other twenty-five percent coming from sources around the world. The charity fund has been growing at about ten percent a year, due to increased funding from Laura as well as worldwide donations, and through its investment strategies. Like I said, it was a very successful operation. I want to look at the public website for those charities and take a look at their annual reports. I would also like to know if Laura has a trust that will disburse whatever remaining money she has to those charities. They aren't likely to survive without her patronage going forward. That's the trouble with such a disproportionately large source of funding of a charity."

"Does she support the miners in Russia with her charity?" asked Angela. "I thought there were six mines?"

"I can't find any record of support for the Russian miners," replied Jo, and then she speculated, "Perhaps it was because she knew their supply of diamonds would dry up thus eliminating the work for the miners, or maybe it was too hard to operate a charity in Russia."

"Let's add that to our list for our discussion later with Interpol – the location of a will or trust for Laura," Jill asserted. "I can't imagine that the charity is the cause of Laura's demise. She was their golden goose. I'm back to our speculation about how you steal a chandelier or a ball gown. Nick, do you think that Interpol will have the answer to that question?"

"Yes, it should be part of any crime-scene description – theories of how the crime was committed."

"So we have a few more answers to our questions, but really a lot more questions than answers at this point," Nathan pointed out. "I think we should move the conversation to the wonderful French food that's about to grace this table. Since I recommended what dishes to order, I feel responsible that you enjoy your food."

Picking up their beer mugs, the women and Nick toasted Nathan on his fine suggestion as their food arrived at the table. Nick and Nathan had wide experience with French food. Jill was an extreme conservative in exploring new foods and spices. Jo,

Angela, and Marie couldn't wait to try something new. Outside of weird stuff like bugs, or fish with their eyes looking at the diner, they were willing to try anything.

"Jill, as our resident expert in boring food, how do you like your beef bourguignon?" Marie asked.

"Go ahead and make fun of my limited palate! I'm very happy with my choice. The beef is delicious and tender, as are the carrots and pasta. It's nicely soaking up the alcohol content of the beer I've had, so my mind is losing it fuzziness. I would order this again, and my thanks to Nathan for knowing my taste."

Marie moved on to Nathan's menu choice, "Nathan how's your confit of duck?"

"Like Jill's dish, confit is a traditional French recipe. The difficulty is having the proper preparation and a mixture of spices for the duck. If the chef is a poor to average cook, the duck will have some degree of greasiness to it and the flavor will be bland. This pub has an excellent cook as this might be one of the best duck entrees I've ever had."

"Wow, that's high praise. My gambos sauvage is very good," pronounced Marie. "I wasn't sure what the difference would be between wild French prawns and prawns that I've in the U.S. I had a vision of a prawn in a bikini living the high life in Nice before it was captured and thrown into a cooking pot."

"Ugh, a vision like that is driving me towards becoming a vegetarian," Angela said cringing.

"Wouldn't you rather have your prawn living the high life than swimming around in a boring fishery tank?" observed Marie.

"I can honestly say I've never given it any thought," replied Angela. "My tarte de jour is splendid. I love the variety of vegetables, and since my mushrooms were also wild, perhaps they lived the high life with your prawn before they were roasted on this tarte."

"How many beers have you two had?" remarked Jill. "Do you realize you're infusing the food with personality?"

"I think it's more stereotyping," Angela declared. "Growing up, anything French was larger than life and I'm just applying lessons from those cartoons onto my food. I've only had two beers, which is way below my limit."

"Nick, Jo, any comments about your food?"

"I don't think I can top Marie's and Angela's vivid descriptions, so I'll just say that my meal is delicious," said Nick.

"I concur. Since my plate is empty of food, you know I enjoyed the taste," said Jo.

"Dessert anyone? I would be happy to translate anything from the dessert menu," offered Nick.

Angela suggested, "Why don't you just order six spoons and four desserts for the table and we'll taste them all."

"That sounds like a great idea. I like this American idea of sharing dessert."

Over fondant au chocolate, tarte tatin, sorbet, and crème brûlée, they savored the incredible desserts that ended a perfect meal. The women declared it the best French meal ever.

With an eye on the time, Jill said with a sigh, "I guess all good things must come to an end. We're supposed to be back at Interpol headquarters in twenty minutes. Time enough to pay our bill, use the restroom, and walk back to their building."

Nick signaled the waiter for the bill. When she returned with the change, Jill asked how many stalls were in the ladies room. The waitress looked a little puzzled by the question, but shrugged and said, "Two."

"Anyone else need to visit the restroom?" The other three women nodded in agreement which was no surprise, given the quantity of beer they had.

Angela and Jill left the table, walking in the direction the waitress had pointed. They opened the door and found a woman washing her hands at the sink and two toilet stalls on their right. They proceeded into the stalls.

Jill had noticed something familiar about the woman as she

entered the stall, and now she thought she knew why. She quickly pulled a scrap a paper from her purse and wrote a note to Angela, which she quietly passed under the wall between the two stalls to Angela. Jill was grateful that there were not floor-to-ceiling walls in this bathroom. The note quickly came back under the stall wall from Angela.

Jill had written, "Is the woman washing her hands, Laura's cousin, Chloe Martin?"

And Angela had returned the note with, "Yes! What now??"

Jill passed the note back one more time with, "Let's confront her."

Angela passed the note back with, "Okay, I will."

Jill and Angela flushed the toilets and left their stalls at the same time to take up position on either side of Chloe.

"Are you Chloe Martin?" asked Angela.

The woman jerked and tried to move away from Angela, only to find her exit blocked. They could see indecision in her eyes. After a few moments, she nodded "yes".

"Why are you here? And why did you hire those men to kidnap us?" challenged Angela.

"I heard you say to your friends that you were heading here before returning to Interpol. I wanted to speak with you."

"Why" asked Jill. She was worried about how much time they would have alone with Chloe.

"I know you tried to save Laura and I wanted to hear about that. I was running late that day and arrived at the restaurant just as the ambulance was leaving."

"Why didn't you try to contact us in a normal manner rather than trying to have us kidnapped for conversation?" demanded Jill, unable to keep the sarcasm out of her voice.

"I didn't know if you had any relationship with the diamond consortium. I needed to discover what relationship, if any, existed before I could understand your actions."

"Why would we have a relationship with the diamond consortium?" Angela asked, puzzled.

"It's a long story. I don't have time to discuss this now as you are supposed to return to Interpol shortly. I'll contact you later," announced Chloe as she rapidly slipped away from the women and quickly disappeared from the pub out to the street.

Jill and Angela took a few steps to chase after her and then rethought that idea. They returned to the table, and they all got up to leave. The others knew something was up but noted a silent signal from Jill and Angela that they would explain outside of the pub. They'd no idea who else was listening to their conversations.

Once out on the street, Jill and Angela looked around for Chloe Martin, but they didn't see her in the vicinity. Looking around, they saw that there were no pedestrians within hearing range. They began walking toward the Interpol building.

Angela started the discussion with, "We met Chloe Martin in the ladies' room."

Nathan, rather used to Jill's adventures by now, said nothing, while Nick exclaimed, "What?" while giving them a look like he thought maybe he hadn't heard right.

"You heard correctly," confirmed Jill. "We met Chloe in the bathroom."

Marie peppered them with a quick volley of questions, "How did she find you there? Did you recognize her? Did you approach her? What was she doing in there? Did she know that you knew who she was?"

"Okay, don't laugh, but Angela and I passed a note under the stall's wall to each other, just like in junior high! We both recognized Chloe Martin standing at the sink touching up her make-up when we walked in."

Jo burst out laughing so hard that she had to lean against a building, while she fought to regain her breath and stop laughing. The others just grinned after the stressful day.

Catching her voice, Jo restated, "You mean you passed paper

under the stall walls like teenagers do in middle school?" and she went off in another paroxysm of laughter.

A little chagrined, Jill declared with some dignity, "I wasn't sure what else to do and, with a few notes back and forth, Angela and I solidified our game plan."

They all had to smile at that vision of an amateur hour of sleuthing. Marie advised "Don't let the FBI know about your technique, Jill; they might not take you seriously the next time."

"When you're all done laughing, perhaps we can tell you about our actual discussion," said Angela, trying to bring them back to the point of the conversation.

"Go ahead, Angela, and tell us about your conversation," encouraged Nathan. "That should sober us all up."

"Actually, it wasn't much of a conversation since she left the restroom in a hurry. We confirmed her identity and then asked her why she had been attempting to kidnap us. She said she had been on her way to meet Laura for dinner but had been running late. She wanted to talk to us about Laura, but first she wanted to determine our relationship with the consortium. I told her we didn't have a relationship and then she took off, saying that she knew we had an upcoming appointment with Interpol and she would be in touch."

"So the guy holding a knife to me earlier really meant me no harm?" Jo asked. "Good to know in case another one of Chloe's minions tries to kidnap us."

"I think we're over the kidnap attempts from Chloe based on her behavior in the ladies restroom," concluded Marie. "Of course, that's not to say that someone else isn't after us. Did she ask you about the computer chip?"

"She did not," answered Jill. "I don't know if that is because she didn't know about it or she didn't have time, or she didn't trust us because of an alleged relationship to the consortium."

"This vacation and this murder investigation continue to get more and more curious!" Marie said. "So what do we say to Interpol? ' Hey guys, we met our kidnapper in the restroom and she is really quite nice so we don't need your help anymore'?"

"There's still the chip, the consortium, and the charity in Africa. So you still have lots of unanswered questions," Nick reminded them, and they all nodded in agreement. He worried about their safety, but Nick was also having the time of his life and wouldn't give up his seat at the table of this mystery.

Nathan held the door as they entered the Interpol building. They were a few minutes late, but it had really been a wild day. A lot had happened, yet they'd still enjoyed the museums, and had some great beer and food. They took the elevator upstairs with an escort from the front desk and were shown into a different conference room than earlier. It was larger and filled with many new faces. Apparently, they were the last to arrive.

"Let's begin with the introductions of our visitors to Belgium," said Dubois.

The six friends introduced themselves and their role thus far in the mysterious death of Laura Peeters. This was followed by introductions of the law enforcement personnel. There were Belgian police officers from Antwerp and Brussels, Dutch police officers from Amsterdam, and Interpol officials from Brussels and, The Hague, and the accountant that Jo had conversed with initially on the phone. She'd arrived from Lyon, along with a vice president for Interpol, Europe. Rounding out the group was a representative from the U. S. Consulate. In order to ensure that everyone in the room had equal knowledge about the death of Laura Peeters and the subsequent events and findings, Officer Dubois provided a detailed explanation of the events that began the night the women arrived in Belgium. When he finished, Angela raised her hand.

"We have one more piece of information to add to the story. While everyone was assembling for this meeting, we decided we would visit the museums and palace that are close to this building. We then walked to an excellent French pub for food and drink.

While Jill and I were in the ladies room, we encountered Chloe Martin and spoke with her."

"Excusez-moi!" exclaimed Dubois, clearly so surprised by this latest development that he lapsed into French.

There were other murmurs in the room. Privately, Angela loved a little drama, as that was when people's true personalities often came out of hiding.

"Officer Dubois before you get too excited by this information, we ended up with more questions than answers. Jill and I noticed Chloe in the mirror as we walked into the ladies' room. We verified her identity with each other and then confronted her."

"Why didn't you just call us for assistance?" challenged Willems. "Weren't you worried that she would harm you?"

Looking abashed, Angela shrugged and replied "We didn't think of that. We just knew that she had no weapons in plain sight."

Jill decided to rescue Angela from the conversation and interjected, "We asked her if she was Chloe Martin and she responded affirmatively. We asked her why she had been trying to kidnap us, and she responded that she wanted to ask us questions. We asked her why she didn't simply ask us questions by walking up to us and she responded that she didn't know if we had a relationship with the diamond consortium. She then added that since we had a meeting with Interpol in ten minutes, she would make contact with us later, and then she dashed out of the ladies room, exited the pub and disappeared."

"You have no contact information for her?" probed Nick for the benefit of the others in the room.

"No. She'll contact us when she is ready, which will hopefully be soon. We return to the United States in two days."

"Two days?" asked Willems with a worried look.

"Yes, we have tomorrow and the day after in Belgium, then we leave on a flight that next day," Marie explained. "So we're down to about our last fifty hours to solve this murder."

"Are you able to stay longer to assist the Belgian police and Interpol? The U.S. Embassy will assist you with travel and hotel accommodations as well as any fees for changing your flights," the embassy representative offered.

"We will have to discuss our schedules and get back to you tomorrow. However, a day or so ago, people in this room advised us to cut short our vacation and return to the U.S. as soon as possible," Jill said. "Officer Dubois and Inspector Willems, have you changed your minds?"

"If you are able to do so, we would appreciate your assistance until this murder is solved," replied Dubois with evident sincerity.

"Why did you have the change of heart?"

"We had a lengthy discussion with your San Francisco FBI office while you were out of this building. They said many complimentary things about the four of you, and most specifically, 'that we would be fools to pass up your help.' They attributed the resolution of a huge ten-year political conspiracy to you, Jill, and your team. You were an asset in solving the case and you didn't add to their burden or otherwise slow them down. Those are very complimentary words from your FBI. I have dealt with them previously and they usually have nothing good to say about any seemingly helpful U.S. citizens. Their usual response is that they want you sent home to the U.S. We would appreciate your assistance on our team for as long as you have the time."

"Nice to know we get good recommendations!" exclaimed Angela.

"Yes, okay, let's move back to this case. Based on Chloe Martin's comments to you, she seemed fearful of a relationship between you and the consortium. I wonder why she feels that way when it seems that she and her cousin had an ongoing business relationship with them. Was that your impression Jill and Angela?" Dubois asked, clearly pondering Chloe Martin's words.

"I've been wondering about that too. She went to some real extremes in hiring those men just out of a need to talk to us," Jill remarked. "She must have the impression that Laura said something or gave us something relevant to her future."

"Or relevant to the consortium's future," Angela added.

There was quiet in the conference room as everyone gave thought to the potential angles of the relationship between Chloe, Laura, and the consortium.

CHAPTER 12

*J*o broke the brief silence, "I spent time earlier in the pub analyzing the financial records of Laura's charity and what we could learn of her finances. I would like to spend some time with Ms. Bernard and see if we can find any new financial records on Laura, Chloe, or the consortium. I'm not much help otherwise for this portion of the conversation."

Ms. Barnard stood up and they moved to another room to chat and review financial records. They were two accountants looking for the cause of a murder, and an understanding of the world through numbers.

After they exited the room, the conversation returned to the relationship of the two women and the consortium.

"I think we have to assume from what Chloe said that they did not have the best relationship with the consortium, which is strange given the money and diamonds flowing back and forth," Jill pointed out.

"Let me see if I can describe the history between these parties. Let's all start from the same page. Laura Peeters' first theft was some fifteen years ago and her younger cousin, Chloe Martin, was involved beginning around ten years ago. Laura started by

155

stealing from her employer in one large heist and then managed independently for several years. I've put a timeline on the wall that describes the jewelry thefts we think are her work."

Everyone stared at the wall examining Dubois's timeline of diamond thefts.

"Which thefts are also attributed to Chloe?" asked Marie.

"She doesn't have a signature style that we are aware of. We are tracking back again to jewelry store owners to see if Chloe is caught on camera for any of those thefts. As to the private residences, I don't think we will ever know unless Chloe confesses to those thefts as there's no evidence that she was involved. There may also be additional thefts, but the owner is still not aware that cubic zirconia has been substituted. We don't even know if all of the private residences with the chocolate calling card have been discovered. Just because you discover a piece of chocolate in your home, doesn't mean you immediately notice the CZ sparkling in your chandelier instead of your diamonds."

"True enough," affirmed Angela. "How about the relationship with the consortium? Did she sell the diamonds she stole from private residences to the consortium or did she sell them through her own network?"

"Interesting question," Dubois considered. "I'll ask Mademoi-selles Pringle and Bernard to trace that for us since you discov-ered that financial arrangement."

The conference room door opened, and an officer stepped in and passed a note to Willems. After reading it, he muttered, "Damn".

"Bad news, Inspector Willems?" asked Angela.

"Unfortunately I have received word that Chloe Martin was found dead thirty minutes ago. She had ligature marks around her neck. Her body was leaning against a trash container in a small alley close to the Church of Notre Dame. Whoever killed her wanted her body found quickly since she was placed in such a public area. Our investigators are on the scene and gathering evidence."

"That's indeed bad news," murmured Angela. "I wish we would've stopped her from leaving the ladies' room; perhaps she would still be alive."

"We started with a triangle of players - Laura Peeters, Chloe Martin, and the diamond consortium. We're down to just one player. It sure points this investigation toward the consortium," Jill concluded.

"Actually, we've seven players whose roles are still not understood – the six individual members and the consortium as an entity. We should check in with Jo and Ms. Bernard to see if they've uncovered anything in the financial data," Marie suggested.

"Good idea," replied Dubois. "Why don't I check to see if they are ready to rejoin us? After their report, we may want to end this meeting pending new information from the crime scene and additional information that we can uncover on the consortium members. I'll have my data experts work on this overnight."

After checking in with the two accountants, the pair agreed to rejoin the bigger group and share some new information with them.

Jo and Ms. Bernard re-entered the room and took their original places at the table. They'd been briefed on Chloe's death on the way back to the conference room.

Jo had chills running up her arms thinking about her own experience of being held at knife point, and now to know that Chloe had been murdered by strangulation made the world feel dark. Of the four women, she was the most inclined to shrug things off and go with the flow, but she had never been this close to the criminal world before. She'd not even been inside a police station prior to this vacation. She took a deep breath searching for that quiet place in her mind. Then she opened her eyes and smiled.

"We found a couple of unusual circumstances to investigate further within the documents we examined. Ms. Bernard is able to navigate European databases much like I can do with U.S. databases. It seems to be very clear that funds flowed from the consortium to both Laura's bank account and to her charitable foundation. We think there's enough evidence to have your attorneys evaluate criminal charges as co-conspirators in the thefts. There were additional payments as well to Laura that look potentially like extortion. We think she was blackmailing the consortium with the knowledge that she had been paid to steal from the jewelry shop owners. Those payments were going to her charitable foundation and had been increasing every year for the past several years by one million each year," said Jo.

"How do you know it was blackmail rather than just a straight donation to the charity?" Willems asked.

"It was the code used to describe the payment," Ms. Bernard replied. "Remember those six sets of initials? Nathan identified them as belonging to the first letter of the company name and the first letter of the CEO's last name. As idiotic as this sounds, the initials spell out f-a-i-r-e-c-h-a-n-t-e-r which is a French word that translates to blackmail in English. She had an interesting sense of humor and we didn't see the initials forming the word at first, or maybe it is pure coincidence. Laura must have worked hard to come up with the right set of initials to get the letters. Trouble is I don't know how you use something like that in court. I would think a judge or jury would laugh at you for that weak proof."

"Ms. Bernard and I wondered if you could find her personal residence and tap into her computer. There has to be some documentation somewhere given the regularity of payments. Maybe she had a Swiss bank safe deposit box that contains her important documents."

"We've asked Swiss authorities for their assistance in locating her bank records and boxes," Dubois said. "I'll need to contact them now for Chloe Martin's account since I would suspect that she also had an account and box. Have you seen any transfer of money from Laura to Chloe in these accounts?"

"It is hard to say. There are no checks or ledger adjustments with Chloe's name or initials," suggested Ms. Bernard. "She could have paid her in cash, or again one or both of them could have used an alias or a business name."

"I think we need to look at the Swiss documents," Dubois asserted. "Hopefully, there will be something that is relevant to this case. I also think it is time to arrange to interview these consortium CEOs. Given the large flows of money, I don't see how they could not know."

"Ms. Bernard and I need to review the financial statements for the consortium members so we can determine how they were accounting for these payments to Laura. I assume that Laura's charity would just appear as a corporate contribution to a worthy cause. Do you have jurisdiction to get the private financial statements of the CEOs?"

"We'll have to explore that as I don't know each CEO's country of residence, or the laws of those countries. Interpol's legal department will have to do some research for me tonight so I can determine our options."

Jill was exhausted and noticed that her friends were also fading and so she said, "I think we're ready to return to our hotel. Given Chloe's murder, would it be possible for a policeman to accompany us to our hotel just to make sure there are no surprises awaiting us?"

Willems nodded his agreement and the six friends stood up to exit the room. They agreed they would meet in the same place at nine in the morning. Depending on what was discovered overnight, the women would either be spending their day being tourists or continuing the conversation with law enforcement.

The Belgian police provided two officers and a paddy wagon to transport the group back to their hotel. It was the most unique transportation that they'd been in worldwide. Nick noticed no one appearing suspicious in the lobby. Their rooms appeared safe, quiet, and untouched. Nick wished he had thought of placing a temporary camera in the hotel hallway to catch any suspicious activity.

They grabbed a beer from the hotel bar so they could unwind, reviewing the events of the day. Jo had her Brussels tourist book out and they planned their next day of sightseeing. Whether they would have the opportunity to fulfill their itinerary remained to be seen. They would know more in the morning. Again they shared a suite with bedrooms surrounding a common lounge. Nick joined them for the conversation before retiring to his own room in a different area of the hotel - he didn't need a large suite, which was all that was available on their hotel floor.

They each also needed to review whether they could extend their stay in Belgium. Angela had a photo shoot that she had to return for, much to Nick's disappointment. Marie sent a note to her assistant back in the States to determine her availability, but she didn't think she could alter her stay. Jill was available for at least a week. Jo would normally not sacrifice critical meetings at work for a delayed return from her vacation, but this was a unique situation. She was beginning to believe that a return to the U.S. without the case being solved would endanger her life back in Wisconsin. She was also convinced that her financial acumen was critical to solving this case. They would see what happened overnight, but it looked like Jill, Nathan, Nick, and Jo would be extending their vacation in Brussels. All of them were exhausted, both physically and emotionally, from the day's adventures and sleep came quickly.

Angela was dreaming of her favorite chocolate store. In the dream, the confectioner was trying to get Angela to try his smoky chocolate-covered cherry, which sounded disgusting to her. She tossed and turned and awoke with a start, - wondering why anyone would make a smoky chocolate-covered cherry?

Suddenly, she realized there was real smoke in her bedroom! She leapt off the bed and ran to the door. She was trying to remember how you were supposed to handle fires. She felt the door and it was not hot. She took a scarf, soaked it in bottled water and got down on her belly near the door.

Reaching up, she slowly opened the door. The suite lounge was filled with smoke, but Angela could not see any flames. Moving quickly on her hands and knees she banged on the other bedroom doors to wake everyone up. The smoke alarm began sounding, but the old hotel did not have a sprinkler system.

"Wake up! There's smoke in our suite, but I haven't found the source of the fire. Go find something to cover your face; and I've a bottle of water to wet it."

Her friends were unable to hear her words at this point as the fire alarm was so loud. So she motioned grabbing something to put over their faces to help prevent smoke inhalation. While the smoke was thick, they could not see nor feel the heat of the fire. Just then someone banged on the suite door.

"This is hotel security! We have a report of a fire alarm. We're entering this suite!" The statement was repeated in French.

While Nathan approached the door, the women turned on every light switch they could find in the dark smoky suite. It was then that they noticed a device on the carpet.

"What's that?" asked Marie.

"It appears to be a smoke grenade," said hotel security. "The police use it to smoke out suspects. It should be harmless once the smoke dissipates."

The Brussels Fire Brigade appeared in the doorway, axes and fire extinguishers in hand. Behind them stood a disheveled Nick, who must have run up the stairs from his room.

"I don't believe that anything is on fire. It appears that the smoke has come from that grenade," hotel security proclaimed, pointing to the object lying on the carpet.

Members of the fire brigade checked the hotel suite and

returned a few minutes later with the same conclusion as hotel security. Occupants from other suites on the floor had begun to gather around the entrance to the Americans' suite.

The grenade had nearly run out of smoke. The air was beginning to clear and the smell of phosphorus was dissipating. The fire brigade gave them a look as if they were wondering whether the crazy Americans had set off the grenade.

Nick quickly took over and explained the circumstances. He called Willems to advise him of the situation. Hotel security comforted the occupants of the other suites, and the fire brigade prepared to leave. One fireman reached for the grenade to dispose of it, but Nick stopped him.

"There may be fingerprints on that grenade. We need to leave it here for the police to take as evidence."

The firemen and hotel security departed. The friends changed out of their night clothes while waiting for Willems' officers to arrive on the scene. The smell had completely dissipated, so there was no need to find a new room.

"This is just weird", declared Marie, saying out loud what they were all thinking. "Clearly the grenade was not intended to harm us. Whoever broke into the room could have thrown a real grenade if that was the case. Were we supposed to evacuate and then we would have been taken hostage? Was it just a threat trying to warn us off this case?"

"Nick, are there any cameras in this hotel in the hallways or stairwells? How did you know there was trouble in our suite?" Angela probed.

"It's funny you ask that question. I had thought I should have a hallway camera installed and was planning to follow up with hotel management in the morning. I know there is nothing in your hallway, but whether there are other cameras in the hotel, I won't know until that discussion. I'm sure that the assistance of Inspector Willems will render a quicker answer on those questions. As to how I knew there was trouble in your suite, I heard the fire brigade sirens, and that was followed by the smoke alarms and I thought it likely that your suite was the source of trouble."

"Are you implying that we are the source of any trouble in the city of Brussels?"

"I'm not implying it; I'm just looking at the evidence. I've had more adventures with you Americans in five days than I think I had during my year of service as a policeman," disclosed Nick with a grin, "and I have loved the entertainment and mystery of this entire episode."

They heard a knock on the door and Willems entered, followed by Dubois, each with a crime scene investigator. The women had the look of someone pulled out of a deep sleep, with creases still on their cheeks from the pillows..

"Ladies, what happened here tonight?" asked Inspector Willems. "I spoke with my counterpart in the fire brigade and he said they responded to a smoke grenade in your room. Can you give me the details?"

Angela took the lead. "I was dreaming about smoky chocolate, when I awoke out of the dreams and realized the smoke was real."

Since the men looked dumbfounded, Jo took pity on them, "Angela always has very vivid dreams, and she typically shares the details with us. Fortunately, most of them do not come true! What did you do when you realized the smoke was real, Angela?"

"I jumped out of bed, went to my bedroom door and felt the door for heat. Since it wasn't hot, I figured it was safe to open. I grabbed a scarf and wet it and put it over my face and then crawled on my hands and knees into this lounge. Frankly, I didn't know how to call the fire department here in Belgium but I knew there was a phone out here that I could call the front desk. I couldn't see any flames so I went and banged on everyone's door, getting them out of their rooms. Then the smoke detectors went off. A guy from hotel security arrived, followed by the fire brigade and then we discovered the source, which hotel security identified as a smoke grenade. We asked the firemen to leave it here in case there were fingerprints or other means of identification.

"Can you guys think of anything else to add to my description of the smoke?" Angela asked.

After a few seconds' thought, the group all shook their heads no.

"I would like to talk to the hotel security person. Let me call the front desk," Willems said as he walked over to the suite's phone, which was sitting on a desk.

Nick said to Dubois, "I had hoped to talk to management in the morning about putting temporary cameras in the hallway outside of this suite and to understand where they might have cameras in this hotel."

Inspector Willems returned to the suite with a puzzled look on his face. "I just spoke with the front desk and they indicated that the hotel does not have security staff here at night. They have no idea who the person masquerading as security was."

The three friends looked expectantly at Angela and asked, "Did you get his picture?" nearly simultaneously. Then they laughed at how well they knew each other.

"For once, I did not have my camera in hand, so no pictures." Angela glanced over at the desk, where she had left her camera charging overnight. The cord was plugged in but the camera was gone. "I think my camera is missing. Let me go check my room for it, but I think I left it there last night," she said, pointing to where the plug was sitting on the desk.

They heard Angela searching her room for her camera, and a few minutes later she returned to the lounge. "It is not in my room, and I'm certain I left it charging on the desk last night."

"Perhaps that was the point of this elaborate ruse with the smoke grenade?" Jill hypothesized. "Was it to allow time for the fake security guard to search this room for a camera? Is anyone missing anything else?"

They each returned to their bedrooms looking through their

belongings. They found their purses, cash, iPad, and passports all in place. Jill's cellphone and Marie's camera were also missing. Jo and Nathan had left their phones in their coats and thus they were still in place.

"It seems like everything they took had the potential to have taken photos while out and about," said Nathan. "Otherwise it doesn't make sense that the iPads were left untouched. You can take photos with a tablet but you wouldn't walk around as a tourist snapping photos with such a big item."

"Yeah, but they didn't get all of our photos. I changed my memory card while we were at the Royal Museum. I had over four-hundred pictures by then. My original memory card is still safe inside a pocket of my suitcase. I looked for it when I searched my room for my camera."

"So this smoke grenade event was to give cover to a fake security guard while he lifted all of your smaller electronics?" Officer Dubois asked incredulously. "What is possibly among your photos that has anything to do with this case? It seems very far-fetched. Angela, we would like a copy of all of your photos on the memory card. We cannot compel you to turn those photos over to Interpol, but we'd appreciate your cooperation.

"If you agree to share your photos with us, I would like to see you meet with our expert in facial recognition software. I'll ask him to go through the photos with you one by one, focusing on any people in the background of any of the photos. I can't think of another reason to steal your cameras."

"Of course I'll turn my memory card over to Interpol, as long as I get it back – there are a lot of good memories on that card. Whoever our suspect is, he must have thought we would immediately run out of the suite for the stairs. He didn't know we were not easily frightened. I bet he was standing in the hallway waiting for our exit and when we didn't leave, he thought the noise and confusion of the fire brigade would be enough cover for him to take care of business, and he was right. And he got our cameras.

I'm glad he used a smoke grenade rather then something that could have done real damage to us."

"He also had a master pass key which is concerning. Nick, how hard is that to get from a hotel?" Nathan asked.

"That depends on the hotel. Hackers with sophisticated software have been known to be able to develop their own master key. When I acquire a new hotel client, evaluating hotel key security is one of the first assessments I do. In the morning, I'll have a conversation with management about their key system and that will tell us if the criminal was sophisticated, or if a lousy lock system made it easy. Inspector Willems and Officer Dubois, I'll follow up on the hotel security and the hallway camera situation in the morning since that is my area of expertise. If I need your authority behind me, I may call you to vouch for me with management."

"Not a problem. It is getting close to two in the morning. Let's all return to our beds. Again, we appreciate your ongoing assistance and we would like you to join our meeting at nine. Maybe we can figure out how you can sight-see tomorrow, and still provide assistance to us," Dubois said standing up and preparing to leave. "Good night, ladies and gentlemen."

The two officers left and closed the door behind them. Nick turned to the group and said, "I could sleep on this sofa tonight if you want additional security."

"I think we're good, and you deserve some solid sleep for whatever is remaining of this night. The fake security guard will be back once he or his superior notices the lack of pictures on the camera, but I don't think it will be while we are here. I would wait until we leave and then do a thorough search of every nook and cranny of every piece of luggage. Thanks for coming to our aid," said Jill with a huge yawn. She stood up and headed toward her room with a "goodnight all" thrown over her shoulder at the group.

CHAPTER 13

$\mathcal{I}$n the morning, they were all dragging with a lack of energy after their adventures in the middle of the night. After Jill left for her bedroom, everyone had soon retired, but it was hard to shut down their thoughts. Jo, Angela, and Nathan were still in bed. As usual Jill was up first followed by Marie. They left a note for the others planning on visiting a café across the street from the hotel. They watched the street for a while before crossing it, but saw no suspicious people. They then sprinted across the street quickly entering the cafe's doors and sitting in the back of the table space.

Jill was reading the menu and divulged to Marie, "I could eat breakfast for every meal in this country. I love the croissants and strong coffee."

"Me too, but I might alternate the croissants with a Belgian waffle and strawberries."

"I suppose I should be looking around for anyone suspicious entering this cafe."

"You do live an interesting life. So far it has been fun. My kids would be appalled if they knew about the red-light-district appearance. Think I'll wait until I'm really old to scare them with that adventure. Seems to me, though, that this is far less scary than the helicopters and gun battles of your last case. Jo has been in the greatest danger of any of us. I'm sorry I can't stay longer to see what happens as I don't think we are going to solve the case before we're scheduled to go home."

"So far I have been able to keep calm. I am not scared, just high on adrenaline. Thankfully, Nathan is also calm and supportive. I couldn't ask for more," Jill said.

She continued, "As for the case, in some ways I feel we've made almost no progress since you and I were doing CPR on Laura. Sure, we know a lot more about diamonds, but the motives are still fuzzy. It feels like Laura and later Chloe were thieves for themselves and for the consortium. Then there was some interaction that made the consortium want to kill Laura. Chloe muddied up the picture by dying before we could have a real conversation. Now I am puzzled by the theft of our cameras. If we're lucky, maybe we'll find the answer in Angela's pictures from the beginning of our trip.

"I had a hard time falling asleep last night because I was retracing in my head where we've been and snapped pictures. I don't think the consortium CEOs are wandering around in the background of our vacation photos or anything. I'm tempted to sit with Angela and the facial recognition expert since I can't think of what to add to solve this case. Jo may have more on the financial side once they retrieve information from the Swiss banks. What are we missing here?"

"My expertise is in people, so I have been thinking about who the possible players could be in this case beyond the ones that we have met so far. Is it truly the business reputation of the six diamond companies? It would seem like some regulatory body would find them guilty of criminal behavior. I don't think their reputations or their businesses will recover once the public knows about their paying Laura to steal, and that is probably enough to kill for – millions of dollars and hundred-year-old companies. However, I think someone could have harmed us last night with either a real grenade or just in the chaos that followed. So is the problem that, even if we are all dead, we have some evidence on us that the police would continue to investigate?"

"Do you think they were looking for a picture of the information that was on Laura's chip?" speculated Jill, sipping her steaming coffee. "That doesn't ring true for me as it would not be a likely vacation picture. If we had asked, the police would have sent us an email with an attachment, not have us take a picture with the camera. In fact, they'll allow our review of the paper copy anytime we want."

Looking through the café windows from the back of the room, they could see Angela and Nick crossing the street to join them. They made a good-looking couple – tall and seemingly in-concert with each other this morning. That was especially remarkable as Angela's charm, while always evident, tended to be less powerful in the morning.

Jill greeted the two as they approached. "Good morning. This is a delightful café for breakfast. Marie and I've been discussing the events of last night. Maybe we should switch the conversation to what we should do if we have some tourist time in the city. Nick, you've been here many times. What's your favorite part of Brussels?"

"Good morning, ladies. That's a nice change of topic. My favorite place depends on my mood to some degree. Sometimes I enjoy watching the world go by sitting in a perfect café on a perfect street. There are concerts here that I've traveled to see – like U2, or the Stones, and Gotye. What might be a different experience for you ladies today is the Foret des Soignes, or the Sonian Forest translated into English.

"As it's fall, the oak and beech trees are changing color, so it's spectacular this time of year. There are also a few art museums if you would like to be indoors. From a security perspective, a museum is safer than a wide-open forest."

"I think that sounds like a perfect idea as we've been cooped up in too many police conference rooms," affirmed Angela. "The spirit of a beautiful forest will clear our minds. Too bad I don't have a camera to take pictures with."

"I always keep a camera with me as I never know when I might need a picture related to a job. It's digital, so you could take the memory card with you back to the States," offered Nick knowing that a camera was one of the paths to Angela's heart.

"Thanks Nick. I'll take you up on your offer whether we go to the forest or not. I feel naked without my camera. If it's not a bother, I would like to borrow it for the reminder of our stay in Belgium."

"It is not a problem and the camera will be happy in the hands of a true professional."

"Okay, we've the fun part of the day planned. Jill wanted to join you, Angela, to review the photos on your card with the facial recognition expert. I'm leaning toward that also as I can't think where else I can contribute to this case at the moment."

"Let's see if Nathan and Jo are awake and alert yet. We should be heading over to the Interpol building in about twenty-five minutes," said Jill as she stood up from the café table and approached the cashier to pay. "Should we grab something for Jo, to take back to the room? I'm selecting a pastry for Nathan and coffee to go."

"Let's get Jo the cheese, fruit and bread combo, and some coffee," suggested Angela. "I'll help you carry it."

They left with their purchases, scanning the street before stepping off the curb. Nick was also keeping an eye on any pedestrians that were getting close to the women. There were no mishaps and shortly they entered their hotel suite. Jo and Nathan were in the lounge dressed and ready to go, but looking pitiful since they hadn't had their morning cup of coffee. Both were pleased with the items from the café. Nick left to grab his camera for Angela from his room. They caught two taxis and traveled to their nine o'clock meeting.

Arriving at the conference room, the women saw the committee seemed to be growing in attendees. Dubois had Angela describe the events of the previous night, including the theft of the cameras. No one had a picture of the fake hotel security man and the smoke grenade had prints that had been traced to the manufacturer, so that was a dead end.

Jo and Ms. Bernard, along with one of the new faces, left for a smaller conference room to discuss finances. Nick and Nathan stayed in the conference room. Both were at a loss as to how they could contribute to the investigation.

Angela, Jill, and Marie joined up with the Interpol facial recognition expert, Josef, and walked to his lab. Soon Angela's pictures were on a big screen. They agreed to set aside all pictures that contained no faces. This took the four-hundred pictures down to two-hundred. Then they slowly went through each picture starting at Austin Straubel International Airport in Green Bay, Wisconsin. From there they magnified each picture to assure that no face other than one of women was in the picture. This further reduced the number of pictures under review to about forty.

"Let's enlarge and focus on each face and give some thought as to why the person is in our picture and whether anything about the person looks odd," suggested Marie. "Or really I guess we should ask you, Josef, how we should sort through some forty pictures?"

"Ladies, I think that is an excellent idea. I was trying to remember the last time I was asked to view so many pictures that may or may not contain a clue, and I can't think of another case like this one. I like your suggestion and would agree that we proceed."

In the end, they narrowed it down to about twelve pictures, which gave Josef thirty-two faces to look up. He entered each face into his system and by the end of about an hour, they'd names to go with all but two of the faces.

"I think we should return to the larger conference room and flash these pictures up on the screen with their faces tagged with names," said Jill. "Josef, can you connect to the conference room and see if we can break into their meeting?"

Josef checked in with Dubois and permission was granted. Josef downloaded the pictures onto a memory stick and they returned to the conference room.

When they entered the conference room, Jill noticed that Jo and Ms. Bernard were not present. She hoped that was a sign of them finding some good information in the financials.

"We have narrowed the original four-hundred plus pictures down to twelve and we have labeled them with thirty-two faces," said Josef. "Shall we start by taking a quick look at each picture? Then we can return for a longer view on a second pass?" The pictures started moving across the screen, and no one said anything at first, so they went back for the second longer view of the pictures.

On the third slide, there was a call out from one of the Belgian police officials to stop on the third photo. It was a picture of Jill staring into a jewelry store window with an amazing array of diamonds sparkling in the background. Also in the picture, three storefronts away was a group of three men seemingly speaking with each other. "One of the men in that picture is the owner of the chocolate store where Laura Peeters purchased the chocolate that caused her nut allergy. His name was Andre Jacobs. I remember that name from the police report. Who are the others in that photo?"

Names and brief descriptions were called out as someone had searched some databases. None of the men had criminal records so it was a matter of their physical characteristics. Marie went to work using her informal information gathering sources to begin framing the facts about each of the men.

"Mr. Jacobs has been in business twenty years. After nearly losing his business in the worldwide recession five years ago, his business is doing better, and in fact, he recently opened a second location. He is married with grown children. His wife was very ill, but she is doing much better after getting treatment for a rare cancer in Paris. We might want Jo and Ms. Bernard to probe his finances."

"I now understand why my American counterparts gave you such glowing references," Dubois observed. "I am impressed with the speed at which you have found details on this man. Would you like a job with Interpol?"

As the laughter died down, Marie moved on to the second person. "The second person is related to the Russian diamond company consortium member. He's a nasty customer rumored by the Russian police to have killed miners who complained about working conditions in Mirny, Siberia, the location of their largest mine.

"The final gentleman is employed by Interpol, Russia. I don't know what his role is there, but he lives in Russia, and I can't comment on why he was on a street in Antwerp."

Marie was looking at Dubois while she spoke, and watched a look of sad resignation cross his face.

"Let's get all three names to Jo and Ms. Bernard, so they can focus on their financials," said Jill, skidding to a halt in her speech. "Excuse me Officer Dubois and Inspector Willems for trying to take over your operation, and I'll apologize now for any future transgressions of taking command of your investigation."

The Russian Interpol agent identification was the elephant in the room. It was like a bad case of indigestion, where no one wanted to be the first to burp. They all wanted Dubois or his superior to comment first.

"Apology accepted. And this is not a problem, I will just attribute it to the reputation you Americans have of being pushy. It also happens that I agree with your direction. Let's pull them back into this room for a few minutes to brief them. After that I would like to research the Russian Interpol agent," said Dubois, making eye contact with his superior from Lyon.

Jo, Ms. Bernard, and a third accountant returned to the conference room and were briefed on the men in the picture.

Jo pondered, "What are the odds that we would capture that meeting in a vacation picture? Equally intriguing is how our fake security man knew we had the picture, especially since we ourselves didn't know the picture was relevant. Of course, this could all be speculation on our part. Maybe the answer is in one of the other twelve pictures. If this is the important, do you think our Russian agent in the Interpol office informed one of the three men of the investigation into Laura's death, and he remembered seeing us on the street in Antwerp? Angela, did you recognize the fake hotel security guy in any of your pictures?"

"That is good question. I'm going to study the pictures again, but none of us had a sense of familiarity when we looked through the pictures the first time. Then again, we weren't looking for him, either."

Again they looked through the photos, but none of them could visualize any of the faces as belonging to that man.

"I'm anxious to find the financials on Mr. Jacobs," Jill said. "If there's anything there, perhaps the police could bring him in for questioning?" She couldn't seem to stop herself from telling the police how to manage their case. At least she managed to zip her lips before giving them suggestions on how to handle the rogue Russian Interpol agent.

"If you folks can avoid asking too many questions that distract our train of thought," said Jo, thinking aloud, "I believe Ms. Bernard and I could sit in this room and run through the documents while everyone listens to our conversation, and views the documents on screen. If you understand how we're looking at the numbers, it might cause you to think of some other thread to follow in this case."

Dubois had put a trace on the Russian Interpol agent and Mr. Jacobs. If they had decent information in the next hour, they could make a move on both men. Since there were potential leaks in his organization, he was trying to avoid alerting any more Belgian police or Interpol agents other than the ones in this room. Because of the work of his secret committee, he had requested and individually received affirmations that they would keep their findings confidential. They could reach Antwerp in under an hour if it became necessary to round up the men. Regardless, his agency would do further review of the Russian agent. He nodded to Jo and Ms. Bernard to proceed.

The two women huddled over a laptop, swiftly bringing up records. The tax return for Mr. Jacobs showed the increase in property taxes for the second store. Health care costs were not a line item, so they could not view the cost of the special care in Paris. Both the current and prior tax year showed a significant increase in revenues related to sales. A quick glance at the prior five years showed sales had increased 1 to 3 percent each year, yet in the past two years, sales had increased 30 percent. Something very unusual was going on with the chocolate store's sales. It was odd enough that they could bring him in for questioning. As Jo and Ms. Bernard were having their conversation in front of the group, law enforcement would be better prepared to question their suspect.

"Does everyone have time to talk about the finances of Laura, Chloe, and one of the six consortium members?" asked Ms. Bernard. "Unfortunately, we didn't start with the Russian company – it's one of the African companies. Jo has been very helpful in analyzing what the tax statements are really saying, beyond just the straight numbers."

"Yes, please proceed with your explanations," responded Officer Dubois.

"As you know, both Laura and Chloe operated under a variety of aliases. Laura actually filed tax returns under three of her aliases, and no return was found under the name Laura Peeters. One of the names, Julie DuPont, was the one found in her purse at the time of her death. It seems to be the most active name, with tax returns going back over a decade and a home address of Antwerp. Her other two aliases had addresses in Brussels and Mechelen. She went to considerable effort to keep all of the identities active, though some of the documents must be forged as the finger-prints would have identified her, and indeed, that confirmed her identity in the morgue, according to the autopsy report.

"Each of the identities was related to diamond industry occupations, as one of the tax returns listed appraiser, another had her owning a jewelry store, and the final alias said she sold diamond-cutting tools to businesses. Perhaps the extensiveness of these identities is what allowed her to remain free during her many years of thievery. As for the Laura Peeters identity, she filed a death certificate shortly after that first heist, so the tax collector shows her as deceased. She used the aliases to buy property, among other things. Her driver's license and passports had to be forgeries since fingerprints are required for those documents and she could not provide unique prints. She was entitled to pensions and had different medical records for each identity.

"We correlated the documents left by Laura on the chip to the thefts and the tax documents. It appears that her private thefts were laundered through her own jewelry store rather than the consortium. She poured profits from her jewelry store into her charity.

"What we can tell is she worked for the consortium for over a decade. We think she offered her services to them rather than them seeking her out. We don't believe the consortium members knew of her identity as Laura Peeters until recently."

"Why do you believe that they didn't know her real identity?" Willems asked.

"In looking at Laura's documents with the consortium, there's not a single mention of Laura Peeters. You might guess that is because her name is dead, but there was use of the other aliases including names that she killed off in the beginning. If they found out her birth name recently, that might have angered the original employer that she stole diamonds from, but none of the consortium members would have been impacted.

Jill interjected, interrupting everyone's train of thought on the names. "In thinking about this case from the beginning, one of the facts that mystified me is why she had swallowed diamonds hours before her murder. The other mystery is who sat her up in the hospital, ending her recovery from anaphylactic shock. Those features of her death have puzzled me, so is there any connection to the Russian consortium member or Laura's original employer, and do we know how recently she was in her own retail shop before her death?"

"Dr. Quint, I'm also puzzled by those questions," replied Willems. "With this new information from the financial review, I agree we should search her shop – she should have video surveillance, which may provide some clues. I would also like to know if Chloe Martin had a role in the shop. Have you located anything about her financial records yet?"

"My brain needs a break from looking at numbers," said Jo while rubbing her temples. "I believe Ms. Bernard can follow up on Chloe's records, and it sounds like Interpol and the Belgian police are going to make a visit to Laura's diamond shop and Mr. Jacobs in Antwerp, which will take several hours. I think that my friends and I should stop at a shop for picnic food and head out to explore the Sonian Forest. Should we meet back here this evening to review the findings?"

The Belgians had still not gotten used to the Americans' ability to shift so quickly from vacation mode to crime-solving mode and back to vacation mode. They'd barely moved from contemplating the various names and occupations that Laura had functioned under, and their connection to the Russians.

"Excellent idea, Jo," said Jill, standing up and gathering her belongings. "Inspector Willems, Officer Dubois, what time would you like to reconvene today? I assume you'll lose time commuting back and forth to Antwerp. We can set a time now, or you can text me once you're done in that city."

"I don't like the idea of you wandering around in a forest. It offers plenty of places for bad people to do you harm," warned Willems.

"We don't seem to be safe anywhere in this city except in this office building and we aren't going to stay here until we depart," Jo countered. "We have Nick and Nathan, and if you would agree to again take us out of here in a paddy wagon, and make sure that no one follows us, what are the chances that they'll find us in the forest? Slim, and that's good enough for me."

Just like that the meeting broke up. The six friends were escorted to the same garage as the previous night to catch a ride courtesy of Interpol. After driving around a bit, just to insure that no one was following them, the driver stopped at his favorite café where they purchased food and wine for the picnic ahead. They got back in the vehicle and headed for the forest.

"Let's eat first, then Nick, perhaps you can direct us to your favorite parts of this forest," said Angela. "And of course, I want to try your camera for some pictures of this glorious fall foliage."

Nick led them to a picnic area and they set out their supplies on a table. Nathan had chosen the wine and proceeded to uncork the bottles. It was the perfect spot, exactly where they all wanted to be at in this moment. There was something magical about Mother Nature's majesty in the form of the vivid colors and blue skies that surrounded their flawless setting.

"Wow. Thanks, Nick, for telling us about this beautiful spot." Jo said. "My headache has evaporated and my mind is being cleansed. I'll have fresh eyes when we get back to the conference room. Tell us about this forest. It has something to do with

Napoleon. Did it belong to France at that time, or was it just occupied?"

The afternoon evolved into lazy friendship, lots of pictures, a few history lessons, and casual strolling through the many pathways among the trees. There had been no discussion of the two murders or diamonds all afternoon. A nearby small chapel that through the ages belonged to monks was so peaceful. It was no wonder that they called the forest, "The Lungs of Brussels."

Sooner than anyone expected, Jill received a text from Officer Dubois with a meeting time in two hours. "They must have quickly found new information from their excursion to Antwerp."

"It would be nice to wrap up the case before we leave tomorrow," said Marie. "Let's hope they have new information on both the consortium and on Laura's jewelry shop."

"Should we head back into the city now and stop at a pub near the Interpol building?" Angela suggested. "I'm always looking for opportunities to try more Belgian beer."

"We could do that, but I'll have to substitute a diet cola for the beer," Jill said. "After the interruption to our sleep last night, this fabulous afternoon in the forest with the fresh air, great food and wine, and most of all, friendship, I'm afraid I might fall asleep after drinking any quantity of beer."

"You're always such a lightweight with beer!" exclaimed Jo. "Let's go find two taxis and head back to the Interpol building. We can find a pub to relax in close-by."

"Ladies, let's have the taxis drop us off about three blocks from the Interpol building," Nick recommended. "If anyone is watching the building for you, let's not make it easy. While you're having a drink, I'm going to do a quick reconnaissance of that building just to make sure it is not being watched. If it is, then we'll call for the paddy wagon to make it safely inside."

Nick's comment jarred everyone. For a few hours in the forest, the women had forgotten that a murderer might be looking for them.

The group piled into two taxis and Nick gave both drivers an address three blocks from the Interpol building. Shortly thereafter, they arrived at their destination and noted a pub down the street. Nick saw them inside the pub and then left to begin surveying the area around the Interpol building. When he'd left the hotel that morning, he didn't know what the day would bring so he had chosen a reversible jacket and hat in case he needed to alter his appearance at some point. He made those switches in appearance before setting off for Interpol.

Nick started with a view of the street directly in front of the entrance to Interpol. He then backed up and examined each of the feeder streets to that main street. He was fairly alarmed with what he saw – men on each of the feeder streets loitering, with frequent glances as though they were doing their own surveillance. Nick's changed appearance and that fact he was a party of one rather than with a party of four women allowed him to go undetected.

He pulled out his mobile phone and called Dubois. "This is Nick Brouwer. We're back in the city and the women are at a pub about three blocks from your building. I left them there to survey the area to be sure they would be safe entering the building. I believe I have found a surveillance man on each feeder street to Avenue de Cortenbergh. Can you send a paddy wagon for the women? Second, I would be pleased to identify the men to your staff, if you would like to send them to me."

"Nick, that was good thinking on your part. I'm in traffic returning from Antwerp. Give me the name and address of the pub that the women are at and I'll send an armed escort for them. Inspector Willems has a tactical group that will work with you on these men let's see who we can round up."

Nick texted Jill to tell her they should remain in the pub and expect an escort from Interpol.

Back in the pub, Jill shared the news with the others that the building entrance was being watched, but they would be safe as

Dubois was sending a vehicle for them. They all toasted Nick's wisdom in surveying the street.

Nick met the tactical team two blocks away from the surveillance men. He had snapped a picture with his cell phone camera of each man he found suspicious and proceeded to show the pictures to the team. The team would capture the men and bring them in for questioning. A separate part of the tactical team would survey the surrounding buildings, looking for anyone conducting surveillance.

A little over an hour later, seven men were in custody, and likely two had slipped away before capture. All seven were from Europe – Belgium, The Netherlands, France, and Germany. They all spoke English and were being questioned by the team.

The larger group reconvened in the conference room. They'd gained significant new information thanks to their interviews in Antwerp.

"Let's start with Laura's store," said Dubois. "It's being operated by her staff. After Laura's death, Chloe stepped in to keep the store operating. The staff hadn't been notified that Chloe was killed last evening. They were unaware of who would inherit the store in the future and gave the name of Laura's attorney and accountant, whom we are interviewing by phone as we speak. We've no way of knowing if the goods that are presently in the store are stolen or were purchased. The staff loved working for Laura and it looked like the shop was prosperous, which of course it should be if you do not have to pay for all of the stones that are in these dazzling settings.

"Interestingly, the staff was told by Chloe that Laura died from her nut allergy. They were shocked to learn she was murdered. We closed the store for now until we can learn who inherits it and whether it's fencing any stolen jewels. The chocolate store was on the next block from Laura's store.

"Mr. Jacobs was very interesting and he broke down very quickly. In the end, I don't believe he'll end up serving time given the great duress he was under. He was approached by a man with a Russian accent about a year ago. His wife had just been diagnosed with a rare cancer. Soon after her diagnosis he did some research and found a hospital in France that had experience with her cancer. He corresponded with the hospital, but knew he could not afford to take his wife there. The Russian man entered his store with an offer he could not refuse. He wanted Mr. Jacobs to bake some special chocolate for Laura with nuts in it. He refused. The Russian's next offer was that he would add nuts, and Mr. Jacobs was just expected to sell the pieces to Laura. He refused a second time. Then the Russian described his wife's routine for the past two weeks. He threatened to kidnap her and withhold the cancer medicines that she was taking. If he would cooperate, not only would his wife be safe, but they would have the funds to send her to Paris. He quickly succumbed to the threat but required that his wife complete her treatment in Paris first before he would sell chocolate to Laura that would kill her if she did not get treated in time. He knew of the allergy and the EpiPen she carried. He thought in the end she would have uncomfortable moments, but she would survive, as she had told him about prior allergic reactions she'd had."

"He was a smart man to require that his wife get her treatment first," observed Nathan. "That delayed Laura's death by a good nine months. I wonder why the Russian didn't approach another chocolatier?"

"Maybe it was due to the unique situation of this particular merchant," remarked Jill, taking up the question from Nathan. "This Russian guy had to figure out which chocolate stores Laura felt safe purchasing chocolate from and then research each of the owners to see if he would have leverage. I suspect that this owner's compliance only came about with the impact on his wife's life from two different angles – he could accelerate her death by withholding medication, or he could prevent her death by getting her to a top hospital. So the next question is why he went to such lengths to want to hide Laura's death. It likely would have been less chance of discovery and quicker if he took her out with the dart gun like someone used on us at the windmill park."

"Did the Russian guy ever explain to the chocolatier why Laura needed to be dead," Angela asked. "The Russian was insanely angry with Laura yet was willing to wait over nine months to kill her?"

"Ladies, sometimes it's hard to get the full story out before you start peppering me with questions and theories!" exclaimed an exasperated Dubois. "The Russian visited Mr. Jacobs about four times while his wife was receiving treatment in Paris. The purpose of those meetings was to keep the heat on the shop owner by informing him of how his wife was doing. When they would move beyond this part of the conversation to the diamond industry, little bits and pieces would leak out.

"The Russian was in the most desperate circumstances as far as a continued supply of diamonds. His mine of over forty years was running out of diamonds. It was a huge hole in the ground over five hundred meters deep and over twelve hundred meters wide. They'd discovered the mining pit created by an asteroid in the 1950s. Close to the surface, mining operations yielded ten million carats a year. As they dug deeper, the diamond supply decreased eventually to four million carats and would soon decrease to two million carats and then none. Laura had begun siphoning profits out of the consortium just as the man's mine was seeing strong declines in production. He suspected his fellow consortium members were delighted that they would be reduced to five members in the future as they all had plenty of supply.

"So at the root of this was the demise of a family business due to the natural geology of the earth, but as the company was dying, he also had to pay Laura. It was like poking an old dying bear."

"Isn't that irrational? Laura's thefts were creating greater demand for the diamond supply," Marie said.

"In the last three years, they were more a nuisance than a help to the industry," explained Dubois. "As diamonds from Canada and Australia were capturing a bigger part of the market, Laura's total haul of stolen diamonds was equal to one to three percent of the African members of the consortium, and after they paid her eighty percent of the diamond value and redid the serial numbers, they were making the tiniest profit, if any. For the Russian, her thefts represented more like ten to fifteen percent of his business, resulting in no break-even point.

"The consortium had tried to end the arrangement, but she loved her charity and threatened to expose the consortium theft arrangement to the public. They knew they would never recover from the bad publicity and criminal sanctions if the information got out. Our chocolatier said the Russian had lost his mind when it came to Laura. He had contemplated just hiring a sniper to take her out, but he began to relish the idea of killing her with her favorite pleasure, chocolate, and thus his plan was formed."

"What was Chloe's role in this plan? When we met her in the ladies room, she seemed fearful of the consortium," Angela noted. "Why would she feel that way?"

"Good question. We didn't think to ask Mr. Jacobs that question, but we released him on his own reconnaissance with the promise that we would be following up with more questions in the morning."

"Is he safe at home, or will the Russian kill him too?" Jill asked.

"Inspector Willems and I discussed that scenario with Mr. Jacobs. He thought it unlikely, but he took an immediate vacation with his wife and left his mobile number so that we could check on him as well as ask further questions."

"When Mr. Jacobs made that decision to take a vacation, was he aware that Chloe had been murdered?" questioned Jill. "He might rethink his decision if he knows that there have been two murders and not just Laura."

"Good point. Inspector Willems, would you like to call him

and see if he would like police protection while we search for this Russian?"

Willems stepped out of the room with his mobile phone and made the call. Since he had Mr. Jacobs on the phone, he would ask him what he knew about Chloe Martin.

"So what doesn't fit for me is Chloe's fear of the consortium," Jill pointed out. "She didn't mention the Russian rather, she named the whole consortium. Where or why was she or Laura threatened by the consortium, and why didn't she tell the staff that Laura had been murdered?"

"There's also the unanswered question of why Laura swallowed diamonds shortly before her death," prompted Marie. "That question still puzzles me."

"Yes I can't fit the swallowed diamonds into this scheme so far," Jo agreed. "Why don't Ms. Bernard and I investigate the Russian consortium's financial records? Maybe the answers are there."

Inspector Willems re-entered the room. "Mr. Jacobs has agreed to police protection. You were correct, Jill once he knew that Chloe was dead, he was immediately worried for his wife's safety. While I had him on the phone, I asked him about what he knew of Chloe Martin.

"He had met her several times over the course of a decade usually in the company of Laura, but occasionally on her own. His sense was that the two were close and had the common bond of the diamond industry. He had most recently seen the two of them together within the last month and he had asked them if everything was okay. They assured him things were fine and asked after his wife. He remembers the conversation because he felt so conflicted and guilty, offering words of caring and concern when he planned to allow her to eat nuts hidden in chocolate from his store within the month. He didn't know when he would be asked to give Laura chocolate; he just knew it would be soon, as his wife had successfully completed her treatment in Paris. I probed him with a few other questions, but he provided no other new information.

"I have word from my men that they have completed the interrogations of the seven men we captured earlier this evening. I will have them join us in this room as it's the fastest way for all of us to be informed." Inspector Willems had no sooner finished that statement than there was a knock on the door and his men entered.

Each man proceeded to give brief highlights of their interviews of the suspects, and the story was consistent throughout all seven men, even though they'd been interviewed separately. Each person was individually hired, but they each described a different Russian as doing their hiring. Their assignment was to capture the four women – they were to kidnap them, not hurt them. There were no weapons found on any of the seven men. The captured men were working with a police artist to create a drawing for the person that hired them. All seven failed to identify the Russian diamond company CEO as being involved. They were paid a quarter of their hundred-thousand euros fee up front with the remaining seventy-five percent to be paid upon the completion of the job.

Willems excused himself to put in one more call to Mr. Jacobs. He wanted to e-mail the photograph to him to confirm if he was the Russian who demanded Mr. Jacobs sell Laura chocolate tainted with nuts.

Dubois's men departed having completed their report. Willems returned to the room and said, "Mr. Jacobs stated that the diamond company CEO matching the picture on screen is not the man who asked him to provide Laura with the nut-contaminated chocolate. However, he indicated that the tray with the tainted chocolate that we confiscated at his store had the Russian's fingerprints on it, as he'd handed the tray to Monsieur Jacobs."

Many of the participants in the conference room were dragging from the lack of sleep the previous night. They decided to let the crime lab process the fingerprints on the chocolate tray and reconvene early the next morning. While Jo and Ms. Bernard had about half of the financial information they needed on the Russian CEO, they were both grateful for the overnight break from staring at financial reports. Jo would leave it to Ms. Bernard and her staff to pull the data and she would need less than ten minutes in the morning to review it.

They received a ride in another Interpol vehicle, and before they entered their hotel, it was searched by Willems' men for weapons, explosives, and listening bugs, but everything came up clean. Since they'd a late lunch and no dinner, Nick was elected to find food. He returned thirty minutes later with Chinese take-out and bottled water. It was actually the perfect meal to end the long, strange day.

"Hey Angela, how are you going to describe today's pictures in your scrapbook?" asked Marie.

"What do you mean how am I going to describe today? I think every day of this vacation has resulted in good pictures, but we have managed to do a good job playing tourist and then flipping the switch and playing Sherlock Holmes with more technology. I'll just leave out the picture of the Interpol building I'm not sure I could find the scrapbooking decals to describe that photo."

"I am hopeful that the case will get solved tomorrow so we can all leave on schedule, and Nathan can get back to visiting with his clients in this region," said Jill, looking over at Nathan. "And just how would you begin to describe yesterday and today to those clients?"

"You know, I don't even try," Nathan replied. "You ladies lead such a weird existence that I can't begin to describe it for acquaintances, so I don't. My excuse for canceling earlier meetings is that this is your first trip to Belgium and you are running all over the region and need my language skills to better enjoy Belgium. That's my story and I'm sticking to it."

"Good cover story! I'm tired after this long day, so I am

heading to bed," mumbled Jill, a yawn interrupting her speech. "I think we should slide a dresser over in front of the door once Nick leaves for added protection tonight. Call me paranoid, but I just want a good night's sleep."

The others, equally tired, soon went to their respective rooms. Before Nick left, he helped Nathan move a heavy piece of furniture over close to the door. Nathan would slide it in front of the door once Nick left.

Shortly thereafter Nathan joined Jill in bed, but she was already deeply asleep. With a quick kiss to her brow, he settled down for some sleep himself.

CHAPTER 14

*A*fter an uneventful night, the group had an early meeting at Interpol. A vehicle was sent for them after the surveillance problem yesterday. Coffee, tea, and pastries were provided, and they enjoyed this breakfast as they reviewed the night's new evidence.

Dubois started the conversation with, "We got fingerprint identification from the chocolate tray back and it's our CEO – Alexei Bok of the Russian diamond firm. Sometime in the last five years he's had extensive plastic surgery, but his prints don't lie. Thankfully Mr. Jacobs kept the tray in a plastic bag in his store-room in case it would be useful someday.

"We are attempting to locate Mr. Bok with the plan to bring him in for questioning. We checked passport control and he has not left Belgium by any of the airports. He could have taken a train or car across the border, but we hope he is still in Belgium. His company owns an apartment in Antwerp, so naturally we are looking for him there. We have also begun looking for family members or company employees to help us ID who hired the seven men who were supposed to kidnap you yesterday."

"That is indeed good news," said Jill. "It sounds like the case

189

will be resolved today. What new information have you gathered in the financial records?"

Dubois turned to look at Ms. Bernard and she replied, "Sir, we have significantly more information on the financial transactions of Laura, Chloe, and now Mr. Bok. I would like a few minutes to discuss these transactions with Jo before we explain them to a larger group."

"Go ahead and use the room next door and come back here when you are ready," said Dubois. "I have just received word that the Belgian police have Mr. Bok in custody in Antwerp. He is being transported here and should arrive in about an hour."

Unable to resist asking, Jill requested Dubois and Willems get two questions answered for her "I know I can't be in on the questioning, but I would love to have these questions answered by Mr. Bok. First, did he know why Laura swallowed diamonds on the day of her death, and second, what's the consortium's relationship with Chloe? I know you have far more questions for him to answer, but I hope you could work my two in."

Dubois and Willems shared an amused expression with each other, but nodded to Jill that her questions would get asked. Nearly everyone in the room was catching up on their e-mail during the lull provided by the wait for the financial analysis and Mr. Bok's arrival. Marie and Angela were hard at work planning their last day in Brussels with the assistance of one of the Belgian police officers. They didn't know how much free time they would have today, but they didn't want to waste a moment of it.

Jo and Ms. Bernard reentered the room and, after securing everyone's attention, Jo began the narrative. "We have some fascinating financial data collected by your people, Officer Dubois. With the help of the Swiss Bank, we have a more complete picture of Laura and Chloe's finances. Let's start with the consortium members, then focus on Mr. Bok, and finally on Laura and Chloe.

"These are old companies in business a minimum of three decades. There have been billions of euros worth of diamonds dug out of the ground and sold during this period. Profit margins have ranged from a low of seventy-five percent to a high of one hundred-fifty percent. Four of the six are privately owned and operated and thus have far fewer public records. However, no matter where you live on earth, there's a tax authority that knows your business and this is where we acquired most of the data.

"All of the consortium members except the Russian company are doing well with no financial worries. Their executives are well-paid and their profit margins are stable. During the time they initially hired Laura to steal for them, their profit margins had dipped low, but that was a reflection of a global recession. Margins recovered two years later, but by then Laura had them over a barrel because they were her criminal co-conspirators. They did not need her to steal, but she wanted ongoing revenue for her charity. She obviously had the skill to avoid capture, and she stayed silent on the consortium's role. In the grand scheme of things, her thefts were a very small part of their business, but for Laura it was the major source of income for her charities.

"The Russian company had a problem that the other companies are not facing – running out of diamonds. Its net revenues have been declining by thirty to fifty percent each of the last three years. Sometime in the next two to four years, the mine will run out of jewelry-grade diamonds. There are another two to three years where industrial-grade diamonds will be mined, and then the company will cease to exist. By the way, Ms. Bernard says our Russian counterparts shared this information with us as they have had their own watch on Mr. Bok for a variety of concerns. He seems to be unable to rationally deal with the loss of the mining operation. Personally he has enough assets that he'll not run out of cash in his life-time, so the problem seems to be more ego than financial desperation. He has so many accounts containing his assets that even the Russians feel that they have not traced all of them. These multiple accounts make it hard to find any payments made to men like our kidnappers. So that' all we have on Mr. Bok. Questions?"

"Not at this time let's move on. Overnight we received an accounting from Swiss authorities as to their accounts and the contents of their safe-deposit boxes."

"Great. Next we'll discuss Chloe. Like her cousin, she operated under a variety of names. She had assets in excess of ten million euros, and a house in Istanbul and ski chalet in Val-d'Isère. She contributes to the charities that Laura developed, and seems to have inflows into her account at about the same times as Laura. This would lead us to assume that they were partners in crime. She was a co-owner along with Laura of the jewelry store in Antwerp. She shows no spouse or dependents on any document. Really there is nothing remarkable about her finances other than she was well set.

"Moving on to Laura, as we said earlier she operated under a variety of aliases, but she used just one name for the Swiss bank account that we have been able to find so far. Wealthier than her cousin, she has some forty million euros in assets in Basel, Switzerland. Each cousin listed the other as heir to the account and the dissolution of the accounts with assets placed into Laura's charities if they were both gone. The safe-deposit box also contained an estimated thirty million in diamonds. Laura was a regular visitor to her box, visiting at least once a month. So we may speculate that she rotated her diamond cache between the jewelry store and the vault. The bank said her behavior was unusual as most customers visited far less frequently.

"There are some documents inside an envelope addressed to the Antwerp police that seem to duplicate what was on the chip, although they may not be as up-to-date. She lays out in great detail her theft operation and the role the individual consortium members play in it. Included in that notebook were detailed discussions each time Laura fought for an increased percentage of the value of the diamonds. I'm no attorney, but this seems like solid evidence to prosecute someone."

"So really, no new information, just more solid proof of the consortium members' roles in these crimes," Willems commented.

"Actually we saved the best accounting document for last," said Jo with a huge grin on her face. "The final item in the box is a list of politicians, customs, police, insurance, and Interpol agents in the employ of the diamond consortium in Belgium and other countries, including the euro amount used as bribes for matters relating to the diamond business. We cross-checked some of those amounts with bank records, tax records, and corporate filings on Euronext, the European stock exchange. We have just scratched the surface, but we can see the fund transfers between several people listed in this document. It's quite an explosive finding. How Laura learned about it is anyone's guess, but I bet that's why Mr. Bok was so angry – not only was she taking him for a ride on the diamonds, but she likely used her information on their political 'contributions' to maintain her own safety.

"The political contribution list was found only in Laura's safe-deposit box and not Chloe's. From some of the notes in the box I've had the impression that the remainder of the consortium was opposed to killing Laura, but Mr. Bok was out of control. When you really look at the situation, he had nothing to lose. His company would soon stop production and then he would have no company reputation to worry about preserving. I guess he thought he wouldn't get caught as her death would be classified as an allergic reaction, so he didn't worry about the criminal charges related to this case."

"Mr. Bok should be arriving at this building at any moment," announced Dubois. "We have a lot of material to question him on. In addition to the extraordinary work you have done with Laura's documents, we will question him on a few other issues including Chloe's death and Jill's queries from earlier in the day. As I indicated earlier, you ladies are not allowed to participate in the interview of Mr. Bok. I am not even sure which language we will conduct the interview in – English, French, or Russian. I expect this interview will take several hours. I would prefer that you stay in this building until we have more clarity on the role of the consortium."

Jill looked at her three friends just to reconfirm that they were all on the same page. "Since we're on vacation here, we'll pass on the opportunity to stay within this building. There are a couple art museums that we'll be visiting while you're doing the interview. Officer Dubois, please text me when you're done and ready to discuss the findings of that interview."

Dubois nodded his agreement and the meeting broke up. The Belgian police and Interpol needed to quickly strategize on the handling of the interview of Alexei Bok. They discussed whether they needed to inform the Russian embassy at this particular time, and decided they could delay that diplomatic courtesy. The fewest bribes on Laura's list went to the Russians. Likely this was a reflection of the diamond company's diminishing impact on Russian politics, with its power being as hard to find as the diamonds in the dying mine.

Nick asked Officer Dubois to direct them to a back-alley exit from the building. If indeed someone wanted to kidnap the women, there was no reason to make it easy for them. They paused before exiting to decide which museum to visit first. In the end, they decided to visit the Chocolate Museum and the Musical Instruments Museum. If there was time, they would visit the Royal Museum of the Armed Forces. They liked that all three museums were unique to Brussels and were not classic art museums. Exiting the building, Nick and Nathan each flagged a cab for the ride to the Chocolate Museum.

There was a café across the street from the museum and the group decided it would be best to have a real meal before potentially indulging in chocolate at their museum stop.

"It looks like we'll be able to leave here tomorrow as scheduled," commented Marie. "Nick, are you going to come visit us in the United States? Have you ever traveled to the U.S.?"

"Yes, I've visited New York and I plan to visit the U.S. in the near future. I've had so much fun getting to know you Americans, and I've been thinking about expanding my company. I would like to explore offering my services in America, and have actually started researching to determine where I might want to open my first office. Can you suggest some cities where hotel security has not been taken to the next level? I am thinking that large city hotels are already well organized from a security perspective and small city hotels may not have a need at this time for better security. So, Marie, Jo, and Angela, I would be looking at cities like Milwaukee and Madison. Jill and Nathan, sorry, but you don't seem to have any medium-sized cities in California. I'm just starting my research of what it takes to open a business in America at this time, so I'll have to see what further information tells me.

"Maybe you could consult for the Green Bay Packers," Angela suggested. "I am sure that they have worries about player security when they're on the road in a hostile city."

"That's actually an interesting proposition. I have a friend who is an executive with Manchester United. I'll check in with him as to what precautions their soccer team takes when they're on the road playing an opponent. Maybe that will be a new source of business in Europe."

They finished their lunch and crossed the street to the Chocolate Museum. Their visit ended up being a short forty-five minutes with a warm chocolate sample being provided at the end. Next they headed for the Musical Instruments Museum. None of them were able to read music or play an instrument. An audio tour guided them through their headphones, around the four floors of the collection. There were some amazing instruments on display, some dating back over one thousand years. Emerging two hours later, everyone in the group was better educated on music and instruments. They'd had fun trying out a few of the instruments that the public was allowed to touch, and that experience confirmed the lack of musical ability in the group.

With no word from Dubois, they caught a bus to the Royal Museum of the Armed Forces, which had received rave reviews. Jill had two favorite museums in Washington, D.C. – the National Archives and the Museum of American History. To some degree she was reminded of those museums while learning European history from the Belgian perspective. A couple years earlier, she and Angela had visited Gallipoli while on tour in Turkey. Like on the Gallipoli visit, she felt the emotional impact of the two World Wars from a non-American view.

Upon the museum tour's completion they discussed where to go eat their final meal in Brussels. They wanted Belgian food as it was not a cuisine readily available in the states. Nick consulted with a friend who recommended a restaurant relatively close to their present location. They'd started walking down the street toward their destination when Jill received a text from Dubois indicating there would be a meeting in thirty minutes.

Jill announced, "There's a meeting in thirty minutes at Interpol. We could decline to attend and enjoy a wonderful Belgian dinner..."

"Jill, are you nuts?" exclaimed Marie. "For the amount of work we've put in on this case, gratis, we need to see it through. I would rather go to the meeting and find out what Bok said during the interview."

"I have to agree with Marie," Jo concurred. "I want to hear his explanation for killing Laura."

"Okay, I guess I am happily outvoted. Just checking in with you guys; you have to admit that this has been our strangest vacation ever. Yet, I think for the most part, we've seen everything that was on our must-see list. We just haven't had much downtime."

Nick and Nathan again hailed cabs to take them back to Interpol. It had been an uneventful day and Nathan hoped it would continue to be quiet. They reached the building, went through the usual security precautions, and were escorted upstairs to the conference room. This time it was just Ms. Bernard, Willems, and Dubois in the room. The group figured the others must have already heard the results of Bok's interrogation.

"We were just about to head for dinner when we got your text," commented Jill as they entered the room. "Did everyone else go home already after they heard your report?"

"Actually no, everyone is following up on some piece of information in this case," Dubois replied. "Between the information that we received during our interrogation of Bok and what was in the political contribution letter this morning, we have a lot of work to do to break open the diamond consortium and its bribes worldwide. Your own FBI is interested in this case as there were some American politicians named in Laura's list.

"Let me start with what we learned from Bok. I'll start with the question that has bothered you, Jill, from the beginning. The day that Laura consumed the chocolate with nuts in, she'd an altercation with Bok in her store earlier. He timed it perfectly as she typically had an hour in the afternoon where she was the only person in the jewelry store. He entered the store, pulled a gun on her, and before she could hit her silent alarm button, required her to open her safe. He wanted to take the raw diamonds that she had in the safe as they weren't traceable; in fact, he wanted to take everything of value from Laura. She'd taken a bottle of water with her into the room where the safe was located. When he said he wanted the diamonds, she quickly moved them from the tray to her mouth and swallowed them with the water. She knew that even if he shot her, it would not give him the diamonds back.

"He left the store enraged, as she'd thwarted him once again. He walked immediately to Mr. Jacobs' shop and demanded he sell her the nut extract-tainted chocolate the next time she stopped in his shop. He told the shopkeeper he would stop by every two days to re-inject freshly made chocolate with the extract. He lucked out because Laura stopped by the chocolate store later that same day. She was mad, because for the first time in her life she would have to figure out the process for extracting the diamonds from her own body's waste system. She was fuming and stopped at Mr. Jacobs' shop on her way to meet Chloe for dinner. She normally wouldn't eat chocolate on the way to dinner, but it was her go-to solution when she was having a bad day. She ate the chocolate as she strolled through the streets to the restaurant. I think you know the remainder of the story."

"Did either Bok or Jacobs comment on the missing EpiPen?" asked Jill.

Willems and Dubois looked at each other for a few seconds before Willems responded, "Neither gentleman commented on the EpiPen, nor we did we specifically ask what happened to it."

"Did Bok indicate whether he was involved in Chloe's killing?" asked Marie.

"We asked if he was responsible for her death, and it seemed to me he was genuinely surprised to be told she was dead. He saw her as an assistant to be dismissed as his attention was focused totally on Laura."

"Then was Bok not aware that Chloe was Laura's partner in crime?" probed Jo. "I find it hard to believe that consortium members would claim ignorance of Laura's method of thievery and who her accomplices were on the job."

"I guess we'll know the answer to that question when we bring the remainder of the consortium members in for questioning," said Dubois. "We have issued a blue notice to all Interpol offices worldwide to work with local law enforcement for these arrests. As you can imagine, our first effort is focused on finding these men, as we don't necessarily know where they are and they have the financial resources to be anywhere on earth."

"It seems that our work here is done," said Jill. "There are still unanswered questions, but it sounds like you'll find those answers when you question the consortium CEOs. You have Laura's killer in custody and you have the basis for a prosecution started. You don't have Chloe's killer, but then that is not the case we were brought in to consult on."

"We leave for home tomorrow. It has been a pleasure getting to know you gentlemen and the financial systems of Europe," Jo declared.

"It has also been a pleasure working with you," Dubois replied. "I think Interpol will likely be following up with you through our U.S. office to see if we can arrange training on background checks and financial records examination like Marie and Jo provided during this case. While I think we would have gleaned the same information eventually, you ladies were so much faster at arriving at conclusions and we would benefit from your knowledge."

"Likewise, from the Belgian State Police, we appreciate your expertise and likely we will be participating in whatever training is arranged by Interpol," said Willems.

The group shook hands and left the conference room working their way toward the front door with a restaurant destination in mind. Nick had figured out that the spot his friend had recommended was within walking distance, and they set out on foot for dinner.

They were about four blocks away from the Interpol building in a deserted industrial area when a delivery van slammed on it brakes beside the group. Six men jumped out, each holding a Taser and pepper spray canisters, as they quickly surrounded the group.

A thousand thoughts were running through the heads of Jill's group. Nathan was doing calculations as to whether he could get off any kicks before being hit by pepper spray or a Taser stream. Nick spent seconds retrieving his cellphone out of his pants pocket and preparing to dial 1-1-2, the emergency number in Belgium. Jill was thinking about how wrong they had all been that the case was over. Jo was trying to escape in her mind to a safe place, while Marie was readying her large purse as a swinging weapon. Angela was capturing everything she could on camera. Most of all, they felt like they were in slow motion, as though time was standing still.

There was heavy breathing by the captors and captives and for a few additional seconds the outcome hung in the balance. Then it disappeared in a puff of smoke as the captives decided individually not to fight the men from the van.

Relieving them of their cellphones, the men tied each member of the group's hands in front of them and they were ordered into the back-end of the vehicle. Inside, the lights were bright and there was a collection of bean bag chairs to sit on. Two of their captors got inside the back with them. The captors stood in harnesses, which still gave them aim with the pepper spray but lent them stability for the ride. No one was man-handled in any way, so Jill viewed the situation as that whoever wanted them at the moment, wanted them alive and well.

The men's English was accented with a Slavic tone, Jill guessed. She was trying to figure out who was after them – there'd been a few loose ends when they'd left Interpol, but this seemed like overkill.

"What do you want with us?" asked Jill. "Who hired you? Are you Russian? Where are we going?"

Not surprisingly, they received no answers.

Nick had the nerve to grin at the ladies and said in a low tone, "I told you I haven't had this much entertainment in a long time."

Angela thought *silly man*, but said, "Did you miss the Taser and pepper spray? We're not being invited to a picnic."

"Snarky comments aside, what do we do next? I've never been kidnapped before," said Marie. "You ladies at least had some prior trouble in Puerto Rico. Jo and I are newbies at this."

"Let's put our heads together and discuss who wants us for perhaps a conversation, and is it somehow related to this case?" suggested Nathan. "Jill, what are the loose ends in this case? Let's start there."

Jill smiled and leaned over to kiss Nathan's cheek since she couldn't hug him with her hands tied, and murmured "you're the best, my rock, thank you."

"In answer to your question, we don't know who killed Chloe; we don't know who hired the men that surrounded the Interpol building were. We don't know who dropped a smoke grenade in our hotel room. It doesn't seem likely that it was Mr. Jacobs or Mr. Bok."

"I agree with Jill," Jo said. "I think we've a few other loose ends but they are much smaller when compared to the ones that Jill mentioned."

The van's walls had no windows, so they had no idea where they were traveling. They were moving at a good speed, so they must be on the highway. They were all racking their brains wondering who wanted them. Less than two hours later, according to Jill's watch, they slowed and seemed to leave the highway. After another ten minutes, they slowed again and then continued for another short distance.

The van doors were opened and the group was escorted into a house. Nick and Nathan viewed the lands around the house looking for an escape. They knew all of the women could run if need be, but they had no phone, no weapons other than their martial-art skills, and four women to guard.

Inside the house, they were shown into a parlor, seated in very heavy armchairs, and offered refreshments. The ties were removed from both wrists and each wrist was re-secured to the arm of the chair they were seated in. If they were going to run, they would have to take the chair with them somehow. There was enough slack in the rope that they could hold a glass and drink, but they couldn't untie the other hand. Jill, worried about any drugs that could be added to the beverages, advised the others not to drink. Their captors, overhearing this, exited the room and returned with a sealed drink that they could hear pop when the seal was broken prior to pouring.

A few minutes later, the door opened and a gentleman walked in. None of the six recognized him. He smiled at them and said, "Good evening. Sorry to bring you out to this house with your hands tied, but I needed to have a conversation with you before you leave tomorrow for the United States. I mean you no harm."

"Who are you?" asked Jill. "You know you could have left a message at the hotel requesting a meeting with us. Why are our hands still tied if you mean us no harm?"

"I am Laura Peeters' husband. My name is Henrik Klein and you are at my country home in Germany, about ninety minutes from Brussels. Laura and I were married seven years ago in your Las Vegas."

Jill, surprised by his statement, exclaimed, "Throughout all of the computer searches that we did on the case, we never discovered that Laura was married!"

CHAPTER 15

"Well you wouldn't have discovered that since we were married in the United States and Laura listed herself as deceased in Belgium. The reason your hands are still tied is, I want to have a conversation with you and I need you to stay seated until I am finished with all of my questions. You will be returned unharmed tonight to your hotel in Brussels."

Jill just shrugged and said, "Go ahead and ask your questions then, since it will be the middle of the night before we are returned to Brussels. Before you start, can you allow me to use a bathroom?"

Henrik responded with a nod and replied, "I'll do more than that since I understand my men interrupted you on the way to dinner. If you would all like to use the water-closet, then we will adjourn to my dining room and I'll feed you while we talk, no?"

Jo, ravenously hungry by now, and feeling no eminent threat to her safety spoke for the group. "That's a good idea. I'll request that you leave the handcuffs off while we dine as I need both hands to eat."

Henrik, having no faith in the Americans' remaining docile, said "I'll move the tie to one of your legs, and your waists. That will still leave you bound to the chair, which will make it difficult to attack me or depart."

Resigned but not surprised by his answer, they made use of the bathroom one by one and were then escorted and tied to a chair in a dining room. It was apparent that Henrik had zero trust in their compliance.

A server brought in two bottles of wine that Henrik proceeded to uncork in front of them and pour into glasses. "See, I just opened these bottles, no drugs have been put in it." Obviously his men had told him of their conversation earlier.

"Laura was excellent at sleight-of-hand, and she had the time to teach you the same skill. You could have poured something into the bottle and I would not necessarily have caught that." Jill reached over and said, "I'll swap glasses with you, just to be on the safe side."

"None of this really matters. We're entirely at your mercy as our phones have been removed, and your men are armed," Nathan lacked the patience to play whatever games were going on in this room. "So maybe we should stop the bullshit, and just move on to what you want to know."

"You are a man of few words, but clearly you have a need to protect your women. Hopefully you understand my desire to find what little justice I can after the killing of the love of my life."

Servers entered the dining room, delivering bread and butter to the table, followed by bowls of soup. Henrik described what was to be on the menu for their conversation.

Despite being tied to the chair, Jill felt that Henrik in the present situation was of no threat to her and her friends, other than a potential risk of missing their flight in the morning. So she decided to plunge in with her usual aggressive questioning behavior.

"Is this beautiful house, complete with servants, where Laura spent the proceeds of her diamond heists?"

"I'll tell you a little about my relationship with Laura," Henrik replied. "We met over her one and only failed diamond heist. Yes, she tried to steal from this house while I was here. It was love at first sight.

"I manage a global computer and identity security company. A company engineer created an algorithm that could predict when thieves were casing an individual. I was beta testing the algorithm on myself since I wasn't sure of the commercial appeal of the technology. I think the science on identity theft points to it being random, rather than targeted. Our algorithm was developed for use in targeted thefts."

"It was during that beta testing period that Laura began investigating this house with a plan to steal the diamonds in the chandelier over this dining-room table. She studied blueprints of my house from the local planning authority. She also studied my movements. So I began studying her in return, assessing whether she acted alone or she had help, trying to guess when she planned to hit my house. The more I studied her, the more intrigued I became. I could tell that the identity of Julie DuPont was fake, but I didn't know her real name. In the end, all I could do was add some secret security measures to my house, and generally put out the word that I would be gone for a particular month.

"Two weeks into that month, she made her attempt to steal the chandelier. I had also given my staff vacation time for that month. I have a twin brother who is an actor on a German crime show. We had arranged for him to be photographed as me in the French Riviera, just to cement the appearance that no one was in this house. I had stocked the house with food for the month and was working in a room serving as my office that I knew was not on any blueprints that the city had on record. I went to elaborate trouble to meet this thief in person, planning on turning her over to the authorities when I was done.

"Instead I ended up marrying her. I had installed camera monitors in my office, which alerted me when she finally stepped onto my property. I quickly hid in that china storage area," said

Henrik, as he opened the door to the storage area to reveal the space.

"I served in the German Intelligence Agency prior to starting my own security company and felt quite felt quite comfortable confronting the thief and protecting my property. Imagine her surprise, and that of her cousin Chloe, when I stepped out of that door. Instead of trying to run, Laura went on the attack about the blood diamonds in my chandelier. The nerve of the woman – I was in a perfect position to turn her over to German authorities. Instead, we sat down and had a very intriguing conversation. She and her cousin eventually left and we started dating. What you see in the chandelier now is cubic zirconia. I sold off the original diamonds and donated that money to her charities; she wouldn't have dated me otherwise."

Angela asked the question that had been top of her mind since Henrik began his story. "Why did she continue to steal diamonds after she met you? It seems as though you have sufficient funds to support her charities for the miners."

"You do not understand Laura and her irrational belief that there should be no market for blood diamonds in the world. At the base of everything was a desire on her part to change the business model for diamonds. It may seem to you that she strictly stole diamonds to fund the charities for the miners, but what she was really trying to do was bankrupt the consortium owners and the people that bought the diamonds to begin with.

"I had endless conversations with her on redirecting her passion, but nothing I suggested convinced her to change her course of action. So I just learned to accept her as she was, do what I could to keep her from getting caught, and now in the end, since I'm convinced that the diamond consortium caused her and Chloe's deaths, I will seek justice for her killing."

Henrik's story was very engaging. It was so powerful that the man continued to love Laura despite her huge flaw relating to diamond thievery.

Marie was pulled into this love story and asked, "Did you have children?"

"No, it was a point of contention in our marriage. We both wanted children, but Laura, despite her long-term success as a thief, thought she was fated to get caught and spend the rest of her life in prison. She did not want to subject any children to their mother's fate."

"Your story is so sad, and I can't believe I'm in sympathy with Laura," Jo grumbled, expressing the conflicted emotions that the women felt towards Laura and now Henrik.

Nick, unlike the women, was not particularly moved by Henrik's story. He was a law-and-order kind of guy. He didn't care about Laura's passion for the miners. He saw her as a criminal and Henrik as her accomplice.

"Your story is interesting, but why did you kidnap us and bring us here? You said you wanted to ask us questions, yet all you have done is talk about yourself. We would like to be released from our bonds as soon as possible and be given a ride back to Brussels," Nick said.

Angela frowned at Nick for the abrupt shift from the romantic notion of Henrik and Laura to whatever questions Henrik had for them. It was like hearing a record get scratched.

Angela reached over and put her hand on Henrik's and said "Henrik, just ignore Nick for now; he has been slow to grasp how attractive strong women are, and how important it is that we follow our passion to make the world a better place."

Nick couldn't help himself; he made eye contact with Nathan and rolled his eyes. Nathan kicked him under the table. If Nick wanted any chance of a future with Angela, he needed to stay out of the conversation. He just didn't realize what a force the four women could be when they jointly decided to do something, and clearly they all had reached some sisterhood agreement to help Henrik.

While Henrik had been sharing his story, the ravenous

captives had consumed an aromatic and tasty soup. It was a ham broth with the smell of hickory and bacon rising up. These dishes had been replaced with the main course: moist and tender pork roast with vegetables and potatoes. The food was excellent, and Nathan, their resident wine expert, had been impressed with the wine selections that had accompanied each course.

Jill's mind had been running a hundred miles a minute trying to put the loose ends that formed this case together. "Henrik, how often did you have us followed? Were you a friend of Chloe's and do you know who killed her?"

"My operatives followed you from that first morning you took the train to Bruges. At first, I just wanted to thank you for trying to save Laura. Then when you assisted Dr. DeGroot with the case, I stayed close with your findings. Chloe was like a sister to me. We tried to get your attention to ask you some questions, but then someone else was tailing you. Sadly, I lost Chloe to the same person that killed Laura."

Jill needed to correct his perspective, "Henrik, I don't believe they were killed by the same person. Interpol has Alexei Bok in custody. He confessed to putting the nuts in Laura's chocolate and forcing the chocolate store owner, Mr. Jacobs, to give her the product. Bok was weirdly focused on Laura – he blamed her for his mine running out of diamonds. He assumed Chloe was her assistant at the store and nothing more. A question we forgot to have Interpol ask him was whether or not he was the person who sat her up in the hospital, and if he removed the EpiPen from her purse."

"I'm not sure I follow your questions. What do you mean someone sat her up in the hospital and that killed her? How does sitting up in bed kill you?"

"She died from empty vena cava syndrome. When someone has an allergic reaction and their blood pressure drops, the treatment is to give them epinephrine. The danger with those patients is if you sit them up after they have regained a heartbeat, all of the blood in their ventricles runs out and they die. Laura survived her initial allergic reaction, thanks to the quick action of the first responders and the CPR administered by Marie and I, and was doing well in the emergency room, talking to hospital staff. About half an hour after her arrival a major traffic accident distracted the staff and someone got in Laura's room and sat her upright. That someone had to know something about allergic reactions, to know he or she could so easily kill Laura."

"I was not aware of this part of the story. My investigator must not have looked into what happened at the hospital. Apparently Chloe didn't know that, either. We had both thought that Laura didn't make it alive to hospital." He took a moment to swallow and gather his emotions. Eventually anger overcame his grief and he focused on Jill again.

He motioned to one of his security people and directed, "You can remove the ties from them. Jill, I would like to hire you to complete this investigation," said Henrik naming a fee that would easily fund their next two vacations. "I need to know who killed my wife and Chloe, and Interpol doesn't seem to be getting close to an answer. Will you work with me and my men to solve these crimes?"

"I'm not one to turn down a job offer, but why do you want our help?" Jill asked. "You obviously have your own staff already, so why would you need us? Really, you said you did a stint in the German Intelligence Agency, doesn't that make you more resourceful than an amateur team from America?"

"You've told me more details about Laura than my own staff found," replied Henrik. "Also, you sat with Interpol and the Belgian police, which privileged you to more conversations than my men were involved in. So, I repeat, I would like to hire your team."

"Angela and I must return to the United States tomorrow; our jobs require that we be there," Marie replied. "We can assist long-distance in a few days, but I'll return to a large in-box that will require more hours at work my first few days back."

"Actually, I had a change of plans. When I checked my mail earlier today, I had a note from the family I was supposed to photograph. Since, the kids just went back to school, they are passing illnesses back and forth to each other. This family has a five-year-old and an eight-year-old. This shoot was to be their picture for their Christmas card this year. Unfortunately, the five year old has a case of chicken pox and so they have rescheduled for three weeks from now, hoping the pox marks will no longer be visible and he'll be released from quarantine. My next photo shoot is two days after that, so I can stay an extra two days in Belgium."

"That's about what I can afford to take off work," said Jo. "Two days is a hard deadline that I can't extend."

"I'm good for a week," said Jill. "I hope that if we have your intelligence resources, and we work full-time on this case, that we'll resolve it in the two days, before we lose Angela and Jo."

"I would like you to stay here at my estate, both for your own protection and because it is well wired and you'll have the resources you need. I'll provide you with a car to take you anywhere you need to go for in-person investigations. Gentlemen, I'll leave it up to the ladies as to what your role is here, since I understand that neither of you are employed by Jill."

Jill, looking out for Angela's interests, said, "Nick, you're welcome to join us in the investigation if you can afford the time away from your own business and if you want to join us. Nathan, I'm sure you'll find some wineries in the area to visit while we work from this base."

"Henrik, is your estate close to the Rhine Valley?" Nathan did not have a sense in his head of where in Germany they were presently located.

"Yes, we are in the Rhine Valley. My intelligence report about you indicates that you're the premier wine label designer in the world. I would imagine that you have clients in this vicinity."

"Yes I think I have about six clients in this region and it is always good to visit them. Once I've assured myself that you have adequate security on this estate to protect the women, I'll spend my day visiting my clients with this estate as a base. We'll need to check out of our hotel and have our luggage brought here."

"Why don't I escort Angela back to Belgium, where we can pack up everyone's luggage," proposed Nick. "Marie, what time does your plane depart tomorrow?"

"It leaves at noon."

"This estate is about a ninety minute drive from the airport, which is located on the northwest side of the city, and that's the direction from Brussels of my home," explained Henrik. "You can spend the night here with your friends, and I'll send you by car in the morning to the airport if that is acceptable."

"I would like to stay here and lend a hand to my friends," replied Marie, "if you'll take care of that ride tomorrow."

"Do you have a room we can begin work in tonight?" asked Jo. "I would like to start by re-booking my airline tickets, and Angela, I'll take care of your ticket change as well."

"Can I just say this weird vacation, just got weirder and the beer mystery has deepened? I'll have to be creative in describing this part of our vacation in our photo album," said a smiling Angela. "Thanks, Jo, for making the flight change. I'm ready to head back to Belgium with Nick, if your driver is available."

The group broke up at that point. Angela and Nick headed outside to be driven back to Brussels to pack up everyone's things. Henrik showed everyone else to a beautiful conference room where they could work. It contained more computers than users, a white board, and a projection screen. Adjacent to it was a small kitchen filled with snacks and drinks. From there Henrik toured them around the house, showing them the bedrooms that they could use.

ALEC PECHE

Henrik also demonstrated the security measures present in his lovely home while they waited for Nick and Angela to return with their belongings. After their luggage arrived, Nathan would have his own laptop, which had the graphic-design software he needed for work, as well as the information on his clients. Now that he was satisfied the women would be safe, he was looking forward to setting up appointments to meet his clients. He had been to three of the wineries before, and it would be great seeing the vineyards of his three newer clients.

Jill loved the setup of the conference room that was designated for them to work in, especially the white board. She hadn't realized how much she missed organizing her thoughts about a case on a white board, but then up to this point on this case she had been a casual crime- solver, an accessory to law enforcement's efforts. Now she was about to morph into full-time on–the-job consultant.

She began by arranging as many facts as she could on the board. She printed pictures of Laura and Chloe, the consortium CEOs including Mr. Bok, and Mr. Jacobs. Then she added pictures of the men who attacked them in Amsterdam and Brussels, and the Russian Interpol agent to the white board. Next she added a section of the board that had the unknown facts. What was Laura's relationship with the consortium members over time? Who had forced Laura into an upright position? Jill realized that she needed to prepare a list of questions about Laura's and Chloe's thoughts, behaviors, and actions. She would wait for Angela to return before they questioned Henrik, because she knew Angela would do the best job extracting information from him. Given the loyalties of the Russian agent in Antwerp, she supposed she would keep a separate side list of all the law enforcement people they had worked with so far on the case. Finally, she added a timeline of Laura's life and when it had begun to intersect with the women's vacation.

"Can you think of anything else to add?" asked Jill of Jo and Marie.

212

"After we fill in the timeline, we should add financial transactions between all of these parties," Jo replied. "I would also add the chip that Laura dropped into your jacket. Are we sure we got all of the facts off that chip, or were we diverted by the payment to various politicians? Speaking of which, I think we should add their faces up there, too."

"Good suggestion; I'll add their names as they seem to have had the most to lose if Laura had revealed their payments to the world."

Jill's cell phone, which Henrik had returned, began ringing. Looking at the phone face, she said to Jo and Marie, "It's Nick."

"Hi Nick, what's up?"

Then there was silence as Jill listened to Nick's voice.

"Oh no!" Jill covered the mouthpiece and said "our rooms were ransacked." Speaking back into the phone she said to Nick, "Is anything missing?" She listened a while longer, then ended the call.

"The hotel rooms were ransacked; they got both our suite and Nick's room. Since Angela and Nick aren't sure what belongs to whom, and the suite is a mess, they are just going to pack everything up and bring it here. We'll probably have to do some sorting of stuff so that we can make sure it is back in the appropriate suitcase. He wasn't even sure about the electronics as he didn't want to waste time looking for stuff."

"How about the room safes? Were those broken into?" asked an anxious Marie. "My passport was in our safe, and I'll need it to leave the country. Let me call him back on your phone, since you have his number."

She took Jill's cell from her. "Nick, it's Marie on Jill's phone. Are the safes opened? Is my passport there?"

After listening to Nick's response, she ended the call and handed the phone back to Jill. "He said the safes were opened and he did not see my passport. Once the luggage gets here we'll have to sort through the stuff. It's going to be close to two in the morning when they return. At this rate I should just stay awake until it's time to leave for the airport."

"Maybe you'll have to stay and help on the case until you can get a replacement passport," suggested Jill. "Perhaps that is fate telling you to stay in Germany for two days. Once you sort through your stuff, we can make a call to the embassy to find out what the processing time is. Maybe you'll still be able to make your flight. You could leave early and swing by the embassy on your way to the airport."

"It's not the end of the world if I return two days late; things can be rescheduled, and they might have to be if I don't have a passport. No one will believe me when I tell them the stories from this vacation – from CPR in the restaurant, to our performance in the red-light district, to Jo's introduction to a knife, and our kidnapping earlier this evening. As Angela said, it's been a weird vacation."

Henrik and Nathan returned to the room. Nathan was very satisfied with the security of the house, the property, and the computers. Henrik stopped and stared at what Jill had put up on the board. He was quiet and thoughtful as he reviewed every piece of information. Finally, he looked over at Jill. "This is helpful, laid out this way. I will learn from you and I am pleased you agreed to work for me."

"Thank you for the compliment. I find I can think better about a problem when I lay it out like this. My brain doesn't waste time reassembling the facts every time I think about the case."

Jill changed the subject. "We have a new problem. While we were gone from our hotel suite, it was ransacked. According to Nick, our stuff is scattered everywhere. Marie's passport may be missing. I told them to pack everything they could in suitcases and bags and bring it here and we'll sort it out to see what is missing. They should be on their way now."

"Wow, it seems like the case is far from over," said Jo. "My passport may also be missing; I'll have to check my purse, but I think I have everything else in my possession. Fortunately, as this is the end of trip, I wasn't leaving cash in the room safe. Other than some beloved jeans and a prized hair dryer, there is nothing that I'll miss."

"I hope my laptop has not been stolen as it be more difficult to get work done without it," said Nathan. "Hey, I wonder if Nick had been successful setting up a camera on our suite. After the smoke grenade incident, I thought he was going to rig that."

"Good idea - let me call and ask." Jill walked over to the table and grabbed her cell phone to dial Nick.

"Nick, it's Jill. Are you on your way back? Yes? Good. Say, do you remember you mentioned setting up a camera focused on our suite door after the smoke grenade? You did, awesome. Maybe we'll learn something from that tape. We'll see you soon."

Jill ended the call and faced the others, "They're about one hour away according to your driver," she said with a nod at Henrik. "Nick did rig a camera on our suite door and he collected the camera and its tape when he left the hotel."

"Did they report the theft to the police?" asked Jo.

"No, Nick did not think that was a good idea. I wonder why he would say that, given that he's a former police officer. Maybe the problem was it would have delayed them at the room and by not knowing which stuff belongs to whom, they may not know yet if anything has been stolen. Fortunately whoever went through the room did not damage the furniture; it was just our stuff that was flung everywhere."

"Well, it seems like we're just waiting for them to return. Nathan, if you and the ladies would like to relax, there's an indoor pool and whirlpool and I have spare suits in the pool area," offered Henrik.

"That sounds like an excellent idea, although I may fall asleep if I step into warm, swirling water," said Marie. "Nathan, you'll watch out for us, and get us out of pool if you see us falling sleep? We know you're the night owl among us."

"Yes, Marie, I'll watch out for you. We could discuss motives in this case and that might keep your brains running."

The three women frowned at him as Henrik led them to the pool area. A few minutes later, they were all relaxing in a beautiful whirlpool. They had bathrobes that they could throw on once Angela and Nick arrived, or their skin became prunes - whichever came first.

A little bit later, Angela and Nick were shown into the pool space.

"I can see you guys worked up quite a sweat while we were in Brussels," quipped Angela. "Sadly, it's a sweat from hot, swirling water rather than applying your considerable brainpower to solve this case."

"Actually, we have quite a layout in the conference room. Even Henrik was impressed with it," said Jill. "We needed to know if you had a new clue on the tape from the camera aimed at our suite door. We'll get out and adjourn to our room, so we can sort through and organize all the stuff. First order of business is to find our passports and then our electronics."

They all returned to one of their bedrooms and sorted their belongings into five piles. Since Nick's room had also been ransacked, although his possessions were in disarray, they were luckily all in his own hotel room. While they sorted out the stuff, Nick took the hallway camera to the conference room and worked on reviewing the film. Within fifteen minutes, they'd returned every garment, bag, and suitcase to its rightful owner. Marie and Angela's passports were not located. Jo and Jill carried their passports in their purses at all times, so they had them. Marie would call the embassy in a few moments to find out how soon they could obtain replacements.

They also discovered that Nathan's and Nick's laptops were missing, as was Jill's iPad. Marie had her iPad with her all day. They each carted their stuff to their respective bedrooms, and then headed back to the conference room. It was way past Jill's bedtime, and as soon as she had the answer as to who broke into their hotel room, she would be heading for bed. She was feeling woozy. Although she was participating in conversations, her brain was so tired, she wasn't exactly sure what was real and she doubted she'd remember any of it tomorrow."

They arrived at the conference room to find Nick blinking rapidly as the tape moved forward at a fast speed. Jill then recognized that it wasn't just her that was exhausted -they all were. "Nick, let's call it quits. I really wanted to see who went into our rooms, but you're trying so hard to stay awake while you are looking at that tape that you must be missing sections. We can start fresh in the morning." With that comment she headed toward her bedroom, dragging Nathan with her.

Jill wanted everyone to take a break. It had been a hard day, starting with the early meeting at Interpol, the three museums, the evening visit to the Interpol building, the abduction, and the drive from Brussels. Nick and Angela had done even more in making that round-trip drive and packing up everyone's belongings. They all had to be very tired.

Jo and Marie followed after a minute's hesitation.

Angela said to Nick, "She's right it's been a long day and you're struggling to watch the tape. Let's get back to this in the morning." She tugged his hand and he stood up and began following her out of the room.

Henrik saw the exhaustion in the Americans, but he wanted answers. He would have a couple staff stare at the boring tape to see if they found anything while everyone was sleeping. They would get a faster start in the morning if something was located. He was still seething with anger to find out that Laura had made it alive to the hospital, where a second person had ended her life when no one was watching. Posing as a distant relative, he'd retrieved her body from the Antwerp hospital and buried her on the grounds of the estate in a private ceremony with just Chloe in attendance.

His business friends and associates had rarely interacted with Laura. They were considered a commuting couple, each running their interests in a different country with rare time spent together. Laura had spent most of her time alone, but she passed at least four nights a week with Henrik when they were both in town. She had refused to stop stealing – it wasn't about the money; rather, it was supporting the miners that continued to be taken advantage of by the mine owners. She had resented the retail shops that had continued to buy diamonds for resale, knowing that the miners who had mined the stones lived in very poor conditions.

With a heavy sigh, Henrik left instructions to his men to review the tape to see if there were any unauthorized room entries recorded on it. Once the staff were briefed, he proceeded to his own lonely bed.

CHAPTER 16

As usual, Jill was awake first the next morning, followed by Marie. They both headed out seeking coffee, hoping to find the kitchen in this very large house. They found a woman working in the kitchen. She spoke only German, so between gestures and words like café, they managed to get a great cup of coffee and proceeded toward the conference room.

Jill said, "I forgot to ask you last night how do you and Angela go about getting replacement passports? Will you make your flight on time today?"

"There's a decent chance I could make the flight, but I would rather not stress about it so I called the office and left word that I had been robbed and it would take me an additional two days to return. It just seemed easier than sweating it out at the airport. I'll return with Angela and Jo. I believe there's a closer consulate for us to get a new passport in Dusseldorf. I'll have to ask Henrik which city is closer to this house."

They entered the conference room and Jill walked to where Nick had been reviewing the tape the previous night. She looked at the set-up but had no idea how to operate it. She would just have to wait for him. She didn't know if he was an early riser, but she was sure she would not see Angela, Jo, or Nathan for at least another two hours. Henrik had graciously given Nathan a loaner laptop to take to his meetings with clients.

Henrik entered the conference room and said, "Good morning ladies. I see you have coffee. Would you rather have breakfast served in this room or the dining room?"

"I'd like to start work as soon as possible, so this room is fine. Angela, Jo, and Nathan won't likely appear for at least another two hours. I don't know if Nick is an early riser. I hope so, as I would like to start viewing the tape this morning."

"Ah, yes, the tape. I had my man who works security here at night view the tape. Let me see if he found anything," said Henrik as he walked over to a house phone and dialed. After a short conversation in German, he returned to them.

"My security guy watched the tape and gave me two different times on the tape to look at," said Henrik as he walked over to the set-up that Nick had been using to look at the tape.

"Two areas? Were there two separate incidents of someone going into our rooms that looked suspicious, or was it the entry and exit of the same person?"

"I don't know. Let's watch the tape and see what my man has seen," Henrik leaned in as he began to move the video forward to the first time-stamp mentioned by his man.

The three of them crowded closer and watched. It was a maid dressed in the hotel's uniform with a housekeeping cart. She spent about twenty minutes in the suite, and at first Jill didn't register anything as wrong, but then she saw what Henrik's man saw – the maid had not touched anything on the cart the entire twenty minutes she was in the room. How do you clean a room with no linens, vacuum, or cleaning supplies? She exited, carrying a plastic garbage bag with something inside of it that she dumped into the trash hamper on her cart. She moved the cart to the service elevator and left, cleaning no other rooms on that floor."

"No wonder Nick didn't see this as a problem last night,"

remarked Marie. "It's a good act until you think about what she's supposed to be doing as a maid. It also points to how tired he was after that very long day."

"Let's go to the second part of the tape," Jill suggested. "Your security guy is good. I might have skipped over this section since she behaved so like a maid."

Henrik moved the tape forward by six hours to see two gentlemen, not in any hotel uniform, enter the room.

"Marie, isn't that Inspector Graaf from the Netherlands branch of Interpol?" asked Jill.

"Yes, it is. And I think the second man looks like our fake hotel security guard who stole Angela's camera during the smoke grenade farce."

"Interpol has an internal problem in this case," Jill explained to Henrik, "There was a Russian member of the Interpol office that was caught on film in one of Angela's pictures. These two must be the rogue agents in the Antwerp office. No wonder Inspector Graaf was so unfriendly when we met with him. What possible reason could he have to search our room? To be fair to him, we don't know if the woman or Inspector Graaf made the mess. The camera shows the woman carrying a bag out of the room, but the inspector could have put small stuff like our passports in his jacket pockets."

Jill frowned. "This really irks me. Who are the honest souls in law enforcement in this case? I would like to say something to Dubois, but I can't trust his agency. Perhaps Willems is safe to trust," she mused. "What do you think Marie?"

Henrik spoke up, "My experience is that there are good and bad cops in any agency. So you have to decide based on who their superiors are, and your gut feel as to whether they are crooked."

Nick had been leaning in and listening at the door, and now he proceeded into the room. "As a former Dutch police officer, I would have to agree with Henrik's comments. There's no real pattern to determine who's honest and who is not. I also agree with your assessment that of all the people we have met on this case, Willems seems like the most reliable."

"Let me call him then," responded Jill. "I feel good about Dubois, but I worry about his superiors, as Henrik so wisely stated. There seem to be holes in Interpol in regards to this case and there's no saying who is on the take." She picked up her phone and dialed Willems' number.

"Officer Willems, this is Jill Quint. Is this a convenient time to talk? Good. Are you by yourself at the moment?" She paused and then continued. "After the smoke bomb grenade, Nick put a camera on our suite door. When we got back to the suite last night, it had been ransacked. We captured on camera several persons that did not have a reason to enter our room. One of those persons was Inspector Graaf from Interpol's Antwerp office, so I haven't notified Officer Dubois of last night's activity. The other person is the fake security guard at the hotel."

Jill listened to Willems for a while and then replied, "We changed our plans and are staying with a friend in Germany at the moment. We've delayed our departure by two days."

There was another pause on Jill's side of the conversation. Then Jill said, "Please hold for a moment," and put her phone on mute.

She looked over at Henrik and asked, "Henrik, do you mind if I give the Belgian police this location? I think we can avoid revealing who you are in relation to Laura Peeters."

He nodded his okay, so Jill un-muted the phone and said to Willems, "We're outside of Dusseldorf, and this is the address. It's about a ninety-minute drive from Brussels."

Another pause occurred in Jill's conversation and then she ended the call. "Willems is going to drive here just as soon as he notifies his superior, which he has to do since he is leaving Belgium.

"Now we need to think of a plausible explanation for being at Henrik's house. I think the real answer would be a considerable distraction to solving this case. So Henrik, you're going to be a distant cousin to Jo. We had tried to meet you for dinner our first night in Antwerp, but you were called away from home for a work issue. Last night, we finally connected. After dinner we moved the conversation to our suite only to discover it was ransacked, and so you invited us back to your home."

"The hole in our story," Marie analyzed, "is why didn't we call the police when we discovered the condition of the hotel room?"

"Good question," replied Jill. "How about our impulse was to immediately not trust anyone when we saw Inspector Graaf on the tape? This morning after having a discussion, we concurred that we trust the Belgian police rather than Interpol."

Henrik and Nick had been listening to the women work out their story. "The other option is that Henrik and I are friends and we ran into him last night at the restaurant," suggested Nick. "Regardless, I don't think they will look too deep into Henrik as I don't believe they did so with my friend Max in Amsterdam. Then again, this is the Belgian police, not the Dutch police."

"Let's wait until the others appear this morning and get their input," said Jill. "Now, going back to the tape, how do we figure out who the maid is?"

Henrik replied, "Let's go back and study her a few times. Nick, you haven't seen this, and I think as tired as you were last night, you might have missed her performance."

They all sat around the monitor, reviewing the tape.

"Do you think it's really a woman?" asked Marie. "I mean, she looks like a woman to me and her hands seem female, but I'm just asking the question, given some of the disguises we've seen so far."

They watched the tape a few more times and agreed it was a woman in the maid's uniform.

"Throughout this vacation, we've had a variety of people that wanted to harm or kidnap us," stated Jill. "Some of the people were sent by Chloe, Henrik, Interpol Antwerp, the Russian consortium CEO, perhaps some other Russians, and one other person or group. This woman on this video must belong to the last group."

"She doesn't look familiar," observed Marie. "I don't remember seeing her in the last ten days, but I admit that on some of the crowded streets, I wouldn't have noticed her."

"I have facial recognition software on my computers," interjected Henrik. "It doesn't have the depth of faces like you would find in one of those secret U.S. spying agencies, but it may have her face. Some of the companies that I provide security for choose to use facial recognition software to control access."

"I wonder if I'm in your system," said Marie.

"Let's find out if you are. Sit in front of this camera and let's see if I can find Marie Simon."

About three minutes later a match came up for Marie.

"Okay, that's scary. Does your system match to driver's licenses and passports worldwide? I think those are the only pictures I have in a database anywhere in the world."

"The software uses many sources that are growing every day, including Facebook, Instagram, and other forms of social media. Let me try entering our fake maid's picture into the system and we'll see what pops up. I take it that depending on whom she is, you may tell Willems about her appearing on the video."

"Yes, I think that's the right strategy," affirmed Jill.

"I'm guessing the inspector will be here in about forty-five minutes," Henrik said. "We need to brief your friends on the latest development so they don't blow our story. Do you want to wake them and brief them on the plan?"

"Henrik, that's an excellent suggestion. Nathan's a bear in the morning and I think he'll avoid being around Willems or saying much as that's his nature," said Jill. "I'll go brief Angela and Jo."

Jill stood up to leave the room when Henrik's facial recognition beeped that a match was found. They all walked over and surrounded the monitor.

Jill read aloud, "Her name is Jessica Rathbone and she's from

South Africa. Will you guys do a search on her while I go chat with Jo and Angela? I bet Jessica has a connection to one of the South African mines."

Jill went upstairs to knock on Angela's and Jo's respective doors. Angela was nearly finished getting ready and walked with Jill to Jo's room. Jo had been awake and thinking about getting up. Jill relayed the morning's discoveries and Willems' impending arrival. They agreed on the story that Henrik would be Jo's distant cousin. Angela needed another five minutes and she would join them in the conference room. Jo always took longer to get ready, so she would not be in the room when the inspector arrived. She went further down the corridor to her own room to see if Nathan was awake. He was just barely awake, his brain not engaged. Jill left and went to the kitchen to fetch him a carafe of coffee. He would be alert and ready about the same time as Jo. She knew she could tell him the Henrik story and he would hold it in his memory until his brain was alert enough to process the plan.

Jill returned to the conference room to see what Henrik, Nick, and Marie had found on their internet search of Jessica Rathbone. Angela walked in on her heels.

"Good morning, everyone," said the typically cheerful Angela.

She received greetings back and Henrik offered Angela her favorite breakfast – tea and a chocolate croissant.

"Everyone has been briefed upstairs, but I don't expect to see Jo or Nathan for another hour. Tell us about Jessica."

"Jessica is a thirty-five-year-old resident of Pretoria, South Africa," began Marie. "Her name is likely fake as there is no history of her beyond about ten years ago. There's no record of where she was born, or went to school. She was a minor actress in her twenties, mostly commercials. She dated Liberian warlord Charles Taylor several years ago, but there's no recent mention of a relationship."

"Do you think Laura - and now the four of us have a warlord after us?" asked Angela. "From what I've read about conflict diamonds, the warlords are nasty customers engaged in rape, torture, and murder, and make the consortium members look like nice guys."

"Before Willems arrives, let's decide if we're going to tell him about the woman on the video," Jill said. "I would suggest that we do tell him as this case just got more complicated. Furthermore, a warlord may require international assistance and someone in Interpol would be helpful. It may be Dubois; I just don't know with that agency who is loyal to Interpol's mission."

Angela and Marie nodded their agreement with Jill. Henrik and Nick, after a moment's hesitation, agreed as well. It was perfect timing, as Willems had arrived at the gate of the estate and was being let in. Jill and Henrik went to the front door to meet the inspector and brought him into the conference room.

"Nice place here," Willems said. "You never mentioned that one of you was of German heritage."

There was something in his voice and body language that told them he wasn't fooled by this last-minute relationship. However, as it wasn't relevant to the reason he had come to this estate, he would let it go for the moment.

"Inspector Willems, this has been a complex case from the start, and it just got worse in our estimation," said Jill. "As I mentioned on the phone, we have Officer Graaf from Interpol Antwerp entering our room yesterday while we were gone. You're the only person that has been notified of this search of our private property. Interpol seems to have several bad players. This has us doubting Officer Dubois and his motives.

"What I didn't tell you this morning, was there was a second person that entered our room hours before Officer Graaf. Henrik operates a security software company and identified the woman as Jessica Rathbone. She apparently stole our electronics and passports. Let me play the tape for you now and then we can talk."

Jo and Nathan entered the room at that point and they joined the inspector to view the tape for the first time. Henrik ran the tape twice, speeding through the twenty minutes that Jessica was in their rooms.

Fifteen minutes later, after intensely watching the video, Inspector Willems sat back in his chair and said to Jill, "I would guess that you don't know who to trust in this case. For some reason, you mostly trust me. I say mostly because you didn't trust me enough when you called to tell me about the first person, but in finding out who she might be connected to, you now know you have to trust someone. Do I have the situation correct?"

"Yes, Inspector Willems, that about sums up all of our feelings regarding this case. I feel you haven't shared everything available in this case. However, if any African terrorist organization knows my name, then we need your help. Yesterday you were in agreement with Officer Dubois that the case was closed, but I think today hopefully you can see that it's far from closed. We haven't looked into the background or financials of Officer Graaf or Officer Dubois or yourself for that matter, but those are our next steps. This case has been so cloudy from the start with multiple people having multiple agendas for wanting to speak with us or harm us and it's getting very difficult to tell them apart."

"I understand your perspective, but know this: I have been Officer Dubois' colleague for at least fifteen years. I have never seen him have anything but the highest integrity. I don't believe he knew about Graaf, nor would he condone that behavior as he believes in upholding the law, and there was no cause to search your rooms.

"You're correct that we have been holding something back. In Belgium we are quiet about our dirty laundry, so to speak. We thought there was a problem within Interpol, but we didn't know who was behind it or how many agents were involved. I can assure you that Officer Dubois is not one of those agents; he is actually the one in charge of the internal investigation. It will help him to have Officer Graaf on tape. I need to bring him in on the case. I would like to request he travel here, and then we'll move on your second person of interest – Jessica Rathbone. You mentioned she was connected to an African terrorist organization?"

"You're sure he's a good guy?" asked Marie. "We've had so many people chase us on this trip that we're starting to feel like Madonna facing the paparazzi, or at least how we think she would feel. It's not that I don't trust you, but I guess I don't trust your judgment in regards to Dubois. I'll do a quick five-minute search and see if he comes out clean."

"Did you do a search on me?" asked Willems.

"No, we went with our gut feeling on you," replied Jill. "Please don't prove our gut was wrong in regards to not being an honest representative of the law.

They waited in silence while Marie worked her internet search magic collecting what she could on Dubois. In the end he seemed to be exactly what he was, so they agreed to bring him into the case. Willems left the room to place the call to his trusted colleague; despite what the Americans desired, he would have included Dubois in this latest finding. He returned about ten minutes later, obviously having taken the time to explain the bigger story to Dubois.

CHAPTER 17

"*H*e'll be here in about ninety minutes. If indeed an African warlord has entered this picture, Interpol will be most interested. They have been trying to bring a rather evil warlord to justice for nearly twenty years. If he's connected to this case, it might be Interpol's chance to finally convict him."

"Let's go back to our unknowns for the Laura Peeters and Chloe Martin case," Jill prompted. "We don't know who hired the seven men that blocked the entrances to Interpol two days ago. The seven did not identify the Russian diamond company CEO as the person who hired them. We don't know who killed Chloe and what their motives were. Lastly we don't understand Jessica's role in our lives at this time. Is it accidental, or is it related to Charles Taylor, the warlord?"

Marie added, "And now we have one more question – what do we have in our possession that anyone wanted? Obviously, someone thought there was something on those computers that would be of interest to someone. The loss of the two passports is probably just to create a nuisance for us."

"Let's talk about the computers," Nick suggested. "We lost the two laptops provided by my company, Jill's iPad, Nathan's laptop, and my personal laptop. It's a shame that I didn't put a camera outside of my door to know if both groups visited my room.

"I think we can assume that Jessica got all of the computers from your rooms, but it's unknown if she got mine. On all of the computers, someone with a little computer expertise could look at the browser history to see what we were looking at. I'm thinking they would find the consortium CEOs and companies, conflict diamonds and mining, Laura Peeters and her aliases, Chloe Martin and her aliases, and the men arrested in Amsterdam. What they wouldn't find was the documentation of what was on Laura's chip as Dubois wisely kept that documentation in the Interpol building. They also wouldn't find the information on Jacobs or any of the financial searches done since those were conducted on Interpol computers. Do I have this correct?"

"Nathan's computer strictly would have his work on it, though a computer expert could hack into his email and see my comments on the case," Jill imparted. "Since none of those comments occurred after we learned of Laura's chip, it won't be too helpful to someone trying to figure out what we know."

"Good thing Officer Dubois had us shred the paper copy that the lab produced for us," said Angela. "I didn't think much about his request that we shred the documents at the time he asked."

"I believe our next steps lie with Officer Dubois answering questions about what Interpol knows and doesn't know in regards to what started as a death by nut allergy case and may now be the tip of an opportunity to bring down a large organization," Jill declared.

Looking over at Henrik she asked, "Is there a path we can take to walk around this estate? I feel a need to stretch my legs, and I bet that Angela, Jo, and Marie will want to join me."

"Yes, there is a loop that is slightly longer than three kilometers if you follow the path from the library door. I'll take you there now and point you on your way."

"Text me if we aren't back by the time Dubois arrives, but I would think we would be back before then as it will take us probably fifty minutes to walk with Angela snapping pictures along the way."

"Jill, you can thank Nick for loaning me his camera so I can keep documenting our vacation," said Angela.

The women left the room to grab jackets, sunglasses, and their lone remaining camera. Upon their return, Henrik guided them over to the start of the path with a few words about what they would see along the way.

The group enjoyed a brisk walk around the estate. The trees were again brilliant in their fall colors. The path curved near the tip of a small lake, fed by a creek. Further on, a gazebo with indoor seating was added to enjoy the bubbling water flow of that same creek on its way to the lake.

A distance from the gazebo, they saw the back of a stone monument and went over to explore. It depicted a woman wearing a jeweler's eyepiece holding a very large carat diamond in her hand. It had Laura's name and birth and death dates on it. There was also an inscription in French that they couldn't read. They might ask Henrik about it later. Jill wondered how he had arranged to have the body brought home, since she was officially listed as not having a family. She hadn't checked in with Dr. DeGroot to ask if someone had retrieved Laura's body. The gazebo must have been their favorite spot, and likely Henrik wanted Laura close by.

They were coming back to the house when Jill asked Angela, "Are you going to label these pictures as beautiful fall trees on the estate of the man who kidnapped us from Brussels'?"

"You're too funny. I thought I would label them as stunning fall leaves on an estate near Dusseldorf and hope my scrapbook viewers wouldn't wonder how or why we ended up in Germany."

They shortly returned to the conference room and found that

Dubois had just arrived, and Jo and Nathan were already seated in the room.

As it was approaching lunch, Henrik had left to make arrangements with his cook for lunch for nine guests.

"Hello, Officer Dubois," said Jill upon entering the room.

He stood, nodded at the women, and said "Hello. It seems like you continue to have problems with your own safety. I arrived a few minutes before you, and Nick and Inspector Willems were about to show me the video-tape of Interpol entering your hotel room yesterday. I want to assure you that Graaf's entry was not authorized by anyone in Interpol or the Belgian police force.

"'I've also been informed that you did not trust my honesty and integrity. I am sorry that I gave you any impression that your safety and the truth in the Laura Peeters murder investigation were not my top priorities."

"Officer Dubois, you didn't do anything personally to make me think that you weren't trustworthy," said Jill. "Rather, it's the agency you represent. As you can imagine, it feels like Interpol has a few rogue agents, making it hard to know who to trust. Inspector Willems has basically sworn in his own blood that you've always viewed upholding the law as your top priority. His endorsement got our agreement to bring you here today. Thank you for making the drive. Let's move on and view the tape."

Henrik had connected the video player to a projector, and they sat around the conference table watching the recording play out on the large screen. It was again played and reviewed several times before Dubois was satisfied that he had seen everything on the tape.

"I had hoped you Americans would have left Belgium before any more attempts on your lives or your property were made, but I can see that I was wrong to underestimate this group of criminals. I assume that what I am about to say will remain confidential; if it doesn't, then we may never get to prosecute Laura Peeters' killer."

He looked around the room at the participants individually, looking for a nod indicating confidentiality. Satisfied that they understood the gravity of the situation, he paused, not comfortable with the new member of this group – Henrik. There was something off about the guy, not criminally off, but there was some raging emotion just below the surface. Dubois would just have to trust the women as they had thus far shown excellent judgment of character.

"Interpol has had a small secret group focused on the diamond consortium for about six years," began Dubois. "We were aware of the problems in the mines and the violation of the Kimberley Process. Interpol, in conjunction with the governments of South Africa, Botswana and the Congo, formed a group to improve their lot about twelve years previously. The deal with the Democratic Republic of the Congo fell apart as they descended into a civil war. The country is so rich in natural resources that its government appears to swing from one corrupt leadership regime to another. In regards to the diamond industry, Congo holds thirty percent of the world's diamond resources. Word of our secret efforts to improve the life of the miners and hold countries accountable to the Kimberley Process got out through our Congo representatives.

"The various warring factions in the Congo made life miserable for anyone touching the diamond industry. They killed off a few mine CEOs, and they required bribes not to harm the workers, or simply to let the workers pass unhurt on the road to the mine each day. Recently they have gotten bolder in their demands and their spies. Sadly, Laura Peeters has had so many individuals wanting her death in this past year that it all converged on her. The consortium members were tired of her taking their profits; the Congo leaders and there have been many, have wanted her dead for a long time for keeping the world's focus on their inhumane treatment of the miners; and then there were all the politicians on her list who were at risk of being embarrassed.

"Interpol tried to reach out to Laura. We knew there was a woman running a charity with a connection to Antwerp and the diamond industry, but we didn't know her name or even what she looked like. Thankfully, she told you her name at the restaurant, or she would have been identified as Julie DuPont. I'd had a trace on her name for probably the last decade as I was convinced that she wasn't dead. Between the diamonds in her stomach at death and the name, many pieces began to fall in place for our secret group investigating this mess.

"Unfortunately, at the same time, we learned of the leak in the Antwerp office. I was saddened but not surprised by the leaks within Interpol. Any of the players in this diamond scheme had the funds to influence the average person's morals."

"Unlike Jacobs, who was forced to choose between losing his beloved wife or supplying Laura with chocolate containing nuts, Inspector Graaf had no higher motives. I had another team member delve into his finances and there are cash payments in his accounts over the last two years. He will lose his job and spend some time in prison, as will his Russian counterpart. However, at the moment we are keeping quiet about our knowledge as we need to smoke out other rogue agents. I want it all this time – the rogue agents, the consortium CEOs, the warlords of Africa, and the politicians that took bribes. I think with a little planning on our part, we can take them all down."

"How do you plan to do that?" asked Jill.

"I planted false information in several Interpol offices over the past week. Basically it was Laura's spreadsheet altered with different names and quantities of euros flowing. That must have been why they went after your rooms – to verify the authenticity of the documents. The document details what everyone's bribes were in amount and for what activity. I mixed the truth and the lies."

"You're wise to shred the initial paper copy you gave us of her disk," mentioned Marie. "I thought your request at the time was a little strange, but then I didn't dwell on it."

"I think that Laura evolved over time as to how she wanted to improve the life of the miners. I'm guessing she started out thinking she could simply steal the diamonds, sell them and give the money back to the miners. However, I'm sure she quickly discovered that money did not fix any long-term problems such as slavery and children being forced to work."

"Yes she did discover that she hadn't fixed a single social problem for the miners," said Henrik. "I know this because I was her husband."

Jill, Angela, and Marie had discussed Henrik's role as Laura's husband and how it might solve this entire case if Willems and Dubois were informed of his status. They'd been in agreement that it would aid the case's resolution, but it was Henrik's decision to inform the two law enforcement officers. They'd quickly decided that morning that he couldn't be prosecuted for kidnapping if they refused to say they were kidnapped. She didn't know the rules of German or Belgian law, but as long as Henrik wasn't living on Laura's diamond profits, he was likely not going to face prosecution.

"None of our research uncovered a marriage," said Dubois after a long silent pause. "Do you have proof of that?"

"I have a copy of our marriage certificate for a ceremony performed in Las Vegas in the United States in my safe." With a sad smile, Henrik said, "We met when she tried to rob me of my diamond chandelier, so you can cease your worry that everything in this house was bought with her diamond theft money. We kept separate accounts. My global security business funded my assets, and her funds from the sales of diamonds funded her efforts for a better life for African miners. And before you ask, I knew Chloe as well."

"Well that certainly brings complications and new information into this case. Mr. Klein, I doubted that you really were a relative of Jo. Jill, how did you meet Mr. Klein and how long have you known each other."

"We met at a restaurant last night after we left Interpol. He suggested we move here to finish the investigation and remove ourselves from harm's way. We brought you and Willems in the case when we saw who was on the tape."

"Somehow I don't think that's the full story and you're withholding something from me," said Dubois. "However, we are at a critical junction in the case at the moment and I can't afford to dwell on that point especially if Mr. Klein has new information."

"Please call me Henrik. Let me tell you a little about Laura. Her one significant flaw was her passion to make the world fair for diamond miners. I could not convince her to retire from the increasingly high-stakes game she was playing. It was the only bone of contention between us in our marriage. To accept a life with her, I had to accept her occupation. I used my security forces to make her world safer, but ultimately I couldn't keep her safe. She was adamant that I would be a widower someday and so she worked very hard to keep the diamond thefts off my radar. She didn't want me or my company dragged into her criminal history once she was gone, her words, not mine. If you did a search of this house, and you won't, you would find her clothes, her fingerprints, and her grave, but really nothing more. One of the reasons I loved her was the passion she had for helping others.

"Sadly, she infused Chloe with the same zeal to save the miners. Chloe and I laid Laura to rest last week, and I hope to obtain Chloe's body after the medical examiner is finished. Will you help me with that?"

"I should have checked where Laura's body was released to; I might have found you sooner Henrik," Willems said.

"You could have checked but my path was well covered and even if you had followed Laura's departure from Dr. DeGroot's examination table, you wouldn't have found me," Henrik replied.

"Yes, I'll see that Chloe is released to you."

"Thank you."

There was a brief moment of silence as everyone in the room thought of the futility of Laura's approach to helping make the world a better place for the miners. She'd made many improvements, but she had not saved them all.

CHAPTER 18

"*H*enrik, let's go back a bit in the proceedings of this case," directed Willems. "Were you aware that Laura kept an odd computer chip in her possession likely at all times to pass on in the event that she was in some kind of desperate trouble?"

"Yes when we would argue, she would talk about that chip. She obsessively updated it. In a weak moment I showed her how to do searches that would elicit the kind of information she kept in her spreadsheet – namely bribes that were traded among the mine owners, politicians, and what I would call 'militia units' within these mining communities."

"Where did she do the research for that spreadsheet?" asked Willems. "Was it on the computers here in this house, or in her apartment in Antwerp or in her retail store?"

"She did her work at the retail store in Antwerp. She had all kinds of extra security on the internet line because of the credit card transactions. She thought that security would prevent her from being tracked; I had repeatedly told her she was living in a fool's paradise. There was simply too much money and power at

238

stake. She thought if she played the parties against each other, she would stay safe."

"You mean the consortium did not know what she looked like or that she operated the retail store?" asked Jill. "I am impressed with her bravery that she would take these powerful people and companies on in a game of wits – she would only stay alive if they all lived in fear of what she would reveal upon her death."

"Laura was very successful at being unidentifiable, and that made her feel safe," explained Henrik. "It kept her free from prison and safe from anyone who wanted to kill her. She never negotiated face-to-face. When she walked around Antwerp, she changed her appearance. If you speak to her staff at the jewelry store, you will find that she had a series of wigs that she changed frequently. She made out to the staff that it was a fashion quirk of hers. She also stole from her own shop and filed an insurance claim for the theft to keep up the appearance of being nothing more than a jewelry store owner."

"She had some fifteen years, and perhaps your help, Henrik, in staying ten steps in front of everyone," commented Dubois.

"I learned early in our marriage not to help Laura with her schemes. I made the mistake of showing her in great detail what was wrong with her approach to her own security. Instead of being suitably frightened, she spent the next week figuring out a way to close the breach I had shown her. After that lesson, I never again discussed her schemes. Instead I used my own security team and computer algorithms to keep her safe. We had a few near-misses that I was able to detect in advance and pass along to her. She would then reach out to the consortium members that would typically serve as the communication point between the militia folks and the politicians. If one party took her down, they would all go down, so they often policed each other as far as not killing her."

"So what happened this time? It seemed to all disintegrate, with Laura and Chloe losing their lives and all of the parties coming out of hiding and targeting our American tourists," Willems mused.

"I think what happened was the Russian. He had tried to convince his fellow consortium members to kill her in the past, but they would always stop him. As his production and profits waned, he was increasingly ignored by the other five members and they lost control of him."

"How do you know about all of these events?" asked Dubois.

"Mostly I know the events because of my conversations with Chloe after Laura's death. We discussed in great detail what to do to avenge Laura."

"Avenge, Laura? Willems and I are not here to avenge Laura. We are here to gain enough details to seal the coffin of all of the players in this diamond game. If we could have captured Laura and Chloe alive and sent them to prison, then we would have. While I can appreciate that no one was particularly clean in profiting from the efforts of miners working in poor to awful conditions, she is first and foremost a criminal who could have chosen a different path to get her message across to the world. Furthermore, Henrik, if I could find evidence identifying you as an accessory, I would try to send you to prison as well. Just so we are clear on where my loyalties lie, they are with the law and it's a line you cannot cross."

"Just so we are clear on who you are dealing with, I never aided Laura in a single crime. All I'm guilty of is knowing her real name," Henrik replied.

"Gentlemen, now that you have cleared the air, can we move on to figuring out who killed Laura and Chloe?" asked Jill, knowing they needed to stop wasting time.

"I suggest we break up into two groups with one group focusing on Jessica Rathbone and the other group researching our fake hotel security guard-cum-companion of Graaf," suggested Marie. "At some point today, Angela and I need to visit Dusseldorf to renew our passports. Inspector Willems, will you provide us with your official signature that our room was robbed? I know that we don't know for sure that was when our passports were stolen, but the tape doesn't show anyone else entering the room. We know they were there at the time of the smoke grenade, we just don't know when they disappeared from the room. While we could say we were pickpocketed on the street, I would think the process would go faster with your assistance, even though this is Germany."

"Yes, I can assist you with that. If you have the consulate's number, I can call and give them my badge number to prove you have made a report to law enforcement. That is usually all they need. They'll verify with my office that I am for real, and usually they quickly reissue you your documentation. I have always wanted you ladies to go home and I'll do whatever I can to get you on a plane to return to the U.S."

At least Willems offered a cheeky grin when he added the final bit, which mitigated the two women's rising hackles.

"Back to Marie's suggestion, while you all work on solving this mystery, I'm going to visit some vineyard clients in this area," said Nathan standing up and preparing to exit the room. "Henrik, thanks for the loan of the laptop. Would you mind if I downloaded my graphic design software on to it?"

"If you'll tell me what you need, I'll have my assistant, who's in the library, set it up for you. Give her about twenty minutes and then she'll have it ready for you, as well as a car."

"Thanks, Henrik, I'll drop off the laptop to her and get the car key. Thank you for keeping the ladies safe. Have a great day," said Nathan departing the room with a wave.

As no one had a better suggestion than Marie, they split into two groups, gathering intelligence on both people. Jessica had a particularly disturbing background.

Marie worked her usual magic, cutting through layers of false identities to the real Jessica, or in this case, the real Mary. Jessica was born Mary Smith in South Africa. Her parents were killed during a terrorist bombing in Pretoria when she eight years old and from there she was raised by an aunt. After high school she entered a trade college and received a nursing degree. For the next six years she worked at a series of long-term care facilities.

Marie began her report. "Five years into her six-year career, the nursing homes started sharing data and discovered that their mortality rates climbed by four-hundred to five hundred percent when she was working. After an extensive review of the medical records, they thought she might be connected to twenty to thirty deaths at each facility."

"At each facility?" several people exclaimed at the same time.

"Yes, at each facility. So over time, she took the lives of perhaps one hundred to one hundred fifty residents. What an astounding murder rate! She was no angel of mercy, either, since she used an overdose of potassium by itself with no sedatives. It said in one of the articles that the death would be fast, in four to six minutes, but the pain excruciating."

"Since she's running free, it means that officials have not caught her," Dubois commented. "How did you know that Mary and Jessica are one in the same person?"

"Nick was so tired last night he forgot to tell us of his moment of brilliance," said Angela. "When he saw that both rooms had been ransacked, he had his staff from his Brussels branch come and dust the room for fingerprints. While we were sleeping overnight, one of the sets of prints in both rooms matched her prints, which were on record from when she got her nursing license."

Nick added, "She could have stayed in one of the rooms as a tourist recently and not be our visitor yesterday, but then why were the prints inside both rooms? The chances of her being the fake maid are very high. Also, her prints were on the safe in both rooms."

Both Willems and Dubois nodded their agreement with Nick's theories. There was a sense of urgency and energy in Henrik's conference room, at the thought of not only solving Laura's and Chloe's murders and likely bringing politicians and diamond mine CEOs to justice, but now they might also get a mass murderer in their sweep.

"As a nurse, she would have likely had the knowledge about the empty vena cava syndrome that killed Laura," said Jill. "I think the pathologist dusted her body for prints and ran them through Interpol, but if this Jessica was smart she would have worn gloves in the hospital, and no one would have considered those out of place. We should check with Dr. DeGroot to see what print results his office got back."

"In regards to Chloe's death, she was found leaning against a trash container close to the Church of Notre Dame," said Marie. "What evidence did your crime scene people collect on her death that might indicate whether or not Jessica was there?"

"Just a moment and I'll check on both cases, since they were investigated by the Belgian police" said Willems. "Go ahead and continue the discussion while I pull up the report on her. I'm interested to see if Marie can detect where and what Jessica did after she thankfully left the nursing profession."

Marie put two pictures up on the screen; one of Mary Smith and the other of Jessica Rathbone. On the surface they were two different people. The images were likely ten years apart at least. Everyone studied the pictures, noting the differences. She looked to be a natural blonde with very pale skin and no freckles. Looking at the two pictures, the hairline was the same, as was the creamy skin. In one, the nose was thinner, the cheeks a little fuller. In both pictures she had dimples. Overall, she looked like a friendly sort of person.

"Dimples are hard to get rid of surgically as the cheek is attached to deep muscles underneath which engage when someone smiles," said Jill. "That might have been a vanity point for her as well. I think she is the same woman based on the skin color, hairline and dimples, but it would be interesting to see what computer software says about the two faces, if there is such a type of software."

"As you can see from this case, an amazing number of criminals have plastic surgery," said Dubois. "Our French headquarters developed software that was an extension of facial recognition programming about two years ago. With input from plastic surgeons, we use probabilities that a difference in a face is real or surgically enhanced to develop an overall probability that two faces are the same. While the eye socket can be changed, it is difficult to change the size or shape of the eyeball without drastically affecting vision. Teeth are also another area of match – while you can have them straightened or capped, unless you're willing to pull out all your front teeth, you don't change the proportions of each tooth. We'll send these two pictures to Lyon, and we should have an answer back within an hour."

Marie looked at the group to see if they were ready to return to the data she had on Jessica, and she got the nod to continue. She'd completed most of the computer search on Jessica, with her team members adding follow-up questions to complete Jessica's profile.

"It appears that after the South African government issued a warrant for Mary Smith's arrest, she went underground for a few years. I would guess that was when she had her surgery and recovery. I don't know if you can make all of these changes in a single surgery or if it takes multiple surgeries."

Jill shook her head that she didn't know either, so Marie resumed speaking.

"Mary reappeared as Jessica, did some small acting jobs, and was occasionally photographed as Charles Taylor's girlfriend. As he was wanted for crimes towards the people of the Democratic Republic of the Congo, she was also wanted for questioning. Up to this point in time, no one had reason to think that she might be more than his girlfriend as it's hard to envision a woman participating in his atrocities, let alone be an accomplice to a man raping and killing as his disciples did. But if she killed over a hundred people in nursing homes, then I certainly think she could have participated in brutalizing villagers and miners. She must know that she's wanted in connection to her relationship with Taylor, or perhaps that relationship ended because there have been no more photos or stories about the two of them for awhile."

"I believe he was captured and is being held for trial," said Dubois. "I'll check on that. It would account for the lack of pictures of the two of them. Maybe she's running his empire in his absence."

With a little clicking on his keyboard, Dubois had his answer in seconds.

"Charles Taylor was arrested about a year ago and has been imprisoned the entire time. It looks like she is wanted by the Congolese government and Interpol as an accessory to Taylor, and notes on this file indicate she is presently thought to be running his organization at his direction. There is suspicion that he is passing messages through his attorney to her."

"I am relieved that she is not the person that held me at knife-point in the shoe store. It sounds like she would have slit my neck for the sport of it. If you give me a few minutes, I'll see what I can find on her finances and those of Mr. Taylor," Jo offered.

"One final comment from my research on Jessica: she stole anything of value her nursing- home victims possessed before she killed them. Perhaps that's what gave her the funds for the plastic surgery and to stay in hiding for a while."

"She might be nastier than a woman from our previous case in California. Her name was Lark Sumac and she was the CEO of a black ops global company that provided a wide range of security personnel services. She commanded several of her black ops heli-copters to shoot up a sheriff's station and a highway rest stop while I was in the vicinity. And she certainly didn't kill as many people as Jessica," Jill remarked.

"I think we have an advantage on her since she doesn't know

that she was captured on video or that we have put the two persons together," Willems said. "I looked into the prints that were lifted from Chloe's body, and there is a match to Mary Smith, aka Jessica Rathbone. Since those prints were lifted from her head and neck area, I think it is safe to assume that they weren't friends – for instance, if that were the case, the prints could have been left as a result of shaking hands with each other. Also, since some of the prints were smudged, they may have been left as part of a struggle.

"I would issue a warrant for her arrest, but I want to coordinate this with Interpol efforts. I think we have enough evidence with the prints to issue a warrant for the questioning of Mary Smith, but leave out the connection to Jessica Rathbone. Dubois, would you agree? We could take the original picture and modify it under the guise of 'aging it to a more appropriate photo' and provide the photo from the hotel. Would any of the bad seeds that remain within Interpol see through that pretext?"

"Let me check with someone else on the task force. As bad a mass murderer as she is, I hate to lose the opportunity to apprehend her. However, if we can have her and all the other criminals, that would be my preference. I think the only question is, what picture do we release? We certainly want to release the first picture as it correlates to the prints. Do we want to at least leave her second picture with any airport customs agents? Give me a moment to check –in with my fellow task force members."

"While, he makes that call, why don't we all take a quick break for lunch," Henrik suggested. "There's a buffet set up in the dining room. Let's grab something to eat and bring it back here so we can continue working."

They all stood and stretched their backs and legs. Dubois and Willems were given directions to the restrooms. Soon they were filling their plates with the feast that Henrik's staff had laid out.

CHAPTER 19

*E*veryone was soon back in the conference room. Jill nibbled on her food as she rearranged some of the pictures and relationships of the characters in the case on the white board. The activity gave her time to think about next steps. Whatever Interpol did with Jessica would have an impact as either they would capture her and hopefully get her confession to Laura's and Chloe's deaths, or she would run free, which would allow more time to identify all of Interpol's rogue agents.

After Dubois returned with his plate, they would either listen to the report on the fake security guard, or hear what Interpol's plan for Jessica was.

Dubois entered briskly a few minutes later and announced, "We decided we are moving out and trying to detain Jessica Rathbone, aka Mary Smith. My superior in Lyon is speaking with Willems' superior to gather the resources of the Belgian police and Interpol to find and detain her. She is simply too much of a risk to the rest of humanity. We have enough evidence on the major players in this case, except the rogue Interpol agents. We may still be able to figure that out with some financial sleuthing. I hate to mass-search all of the employees worldwide, but we will design an algorithm to find any employee with an unexplained addition of ten thousand euros or more to their bank account. Hopefully no one would sell out the agency for less than that amount."

"That is good news indeed," said Jill. "I think it is important to get her into custody. At the very least, the nursing home patients deserve justice."

Willems held out his smartphone and said, "A wanted notice has been issued for the search and capture of Jessica Rathbone/Mary Smith and includes her picture from the hotel room."

There seemed to be an air of satisfaction that the work they'd done in that room today led to the identity of a serial murderer, as well as perhaps the identity of Laura's and Chloe's killer.

Jill, always wanting to keep the case moving forward, said "It feels good to have identified Mary/Jessica. Let's move on and discuss our fake hotel security guard. He has an interesting background, though not nearly as gruesome as Mary/Jessica's. He's an employee of the consortium, has been on their payroll for fifteen to twenty years, and carries the title of corporate/regulatory director. His name is Michael Williams and he is from Belgium. I'm guessing that it was his job to track changing regulations throughout the world and use the power of the industry to avert any changes that would hurt the diamond industry. I think he was likely behind arranging the contributions to the politicians on Laura's list."

"Did you locate any criminal history in his background?" Willems asked.

"No criminal history, not even a speeding ticket," Jill replied.

"We could issue a notice that he is wanted for questioning," said Willems. "Between the smoke grenade and capturing him on film, we have enough to hold him. I am sure he will have the fanciest of lawyers to argue his way out of trouble and he will try to claim some sort of diplomatic immunity, but the video is pretty hard to argue with."

"I wonder what, if anything, Williams knew about Smith," reflected Angela. "Are they working together? With Laura gone and her spreadsheet available to the world, is the balance of power now gone? Did the threat of all she could reveal keep everyone in check? Was Jessica, on behalf of Taylor, trying to get the spreadsheet from us so they could use it to blackmail the consortium members and the politicians? They had the deepest pockets and the most to hide. Taylor's organization already had a low reputation in the rest of the world."

"Officer Dubois, can you get us a copy of the information on the computer chip?" asked Marie. "I would like to look at the names and transactions on it in light of the new information we have about Taylor, Jessica, and Interpol's agents. I know you were planning on a global round up of the people on the list, but it would help to see them up on Jill's whiteboard."

"Actually, I distributed a flash drive to each of the secret task force members with the requirement that they carry it on their person at all times. I simply could not afford any additional leaks. So I'll load it on to the screen now."

Jill stood at the whiteboard while Marie and Dubois called out names and where they belonged on her diagram. In the end it was like viewing an incestuous family tree, given the crossovers in relationships among all the players on Laura's chip. The diagram really helped them understand the balance of power and how it had shifted over time. Obviously, Taylor's power had peaked just before his arrest.

Jill said aloud, "he started by controlling the miners in just his native country the Congo, but once he found the trick of requiring the diamond company to pay him to allow their workers safe passage to the mines, he recruited other mercenaries and duplicated his behavior at the other five mines owned by the consortium including the one in Russia. Every time the mine owners threatened to end payment, he would counter with the threat of exposing the still-harsh conditions of the miners, information that would hurt their sales."

Marie picked up Jill's line of thought. "The consortium members had no leverage with Taylor, as he could also hire more workers and he wasn't trying to protect his reputation. Laura could continue stealing conflict diamonds and force payback percentages because she had the leverage of the public release of the bribes and the reimbursement for her stones from the thefts. Laura hated Taylor because as bad as the mine owners were, he was ten times worse."

"Let's circle back to Mr. Bok," said Angela. "If Jessica was Laura's killer, then she had to know when Laura got the tainted chocolate, and that makes me think she was in the restaurant that night. I don't think I took any pictures of the crowd, but let me go check," she started to make her way to the door.

Dubois halted her, saying he could have his lab send him the first fifty pictures from when she had downloaded her memory card a few days ago. She returned to her seat, and Dubois had the email about five minutes later.

Angela was correct; she had not taken any pictures of the crowd overall, but she did get one of the Brabo Fountain in the Grote Market shortly before they entered the restaurant. Jessica could be seen in the background leaning against a building, holding a map.

"It's just too coincidental that Jessica was this close to where Laura was planning to dine that night," Henrik said. "I want to make sure that when this woman goes to trial, she can't be found innocent. Do we have any word on where she is at this moment? Any update from your officers?"

Both Dubois and Willems viewed the status of the hunt for Jessica on their smartphones. Willems looked up and said, "We have many cameras in major public places in Belgium. We're running her latest picture against what cameras are seeing across the city to no avail. So we are going back and trying to trace her exit from your hotel yesterday. Of course, by now she could be back in the Congo."

"How about Williams?" asked Marie. "Any clue as to where he might be?"

"Jo, you have been quiet for a while," Jill murmured. "Have you found anything in the financials that will help find or hang any player in this case?"

"Actually, I did find some information on both of them. Money is going back and forth between the two of them, which is surprising. Based on what you and Marie were talking about earlier, I expected them to be on opposite sides of the table, so to speak. Instead, Williams sent Jessica money from a consortium account, and Jessica sent Williams money privately from her account to his.

"You also spoke earlier about Bok. His mine had better luck keeping Taylor out. You mentioned that Taylor expanded his operations to all consortium mines. That was true, but he was unable to maintain his presence in Russia. First, the mine is located in Siberia, so he had difficulty recruiting his thugs to that part of the world. There were a couple of problems with Russia. Second, Russian Special Forces didn't take kindly to Taylor and his thugs. Then there was the problem with the cold. Guns perform strangely in the cold. Their lubricants freeze and condensation interferes with some of the components of the gun when it travels from indoors to outdoors, so their guns would often lock or misfire. Taylor and his crew abandoned the Russian mine after two winters and retreated to hassle the other five mine owners.

"About two years after Taylor abandoned Russia; there was a single payment from Taylor to Bok. Taylor had concluded that if Laura ever went public with her spread-sheet, then all of his sources of cash would dry up. He needed the consortium members to pay his fees, and if they all went to jail, that would cease. He paid Bok five million euros, one month before he approached Mr. Jacobs. Again, is it a coincidence that the plan to kill Laura was hatched a month later? Two weeks after the payment, Taylor was arrested for crimes against humanity and has been imprisoned since his arrest. I think we have some questions to ask of Bok, and I wish we could ask Chloe some questions."

"Chloe!" exclaimed Henrik. "What does she have to do with the story at this juncture?"

"Mr. Bok transferred one million euros to Chloe shortly after he made contact with Jacobs," replied Jo.

"I can't believe that Chloe would ever consider harming Laura. I saw love and affection between Laura and Chloe, and it's why I wanted her final resting place close to Laura."

"Was she happy with the back-up role that she seemed to have?" asked Marie. "Did she have the same from-the-gut-passion' to help the miners that Laura had? Did Chloe ever want to donate the proceeds of their diamond thefts to another cause?"

"I'll admit I've been bothered by the fact that Laura's EpiPen was not in her purse when she first noticed her allergic symptoms," said Jill. "Henrik, do you ever remember a time when Laura did not have her EpiPen within reach? Perhaps during your marriage, you actually saw her react to nuts that were accidentally near or in whatever food she was consuming."

"Yes, she had a few reactions and you're correct that she always had her medication close by as she would have a reaction perhaps once a year."

Jill pondered aloud, "So who took the medication out of Laura's purse? Who was around her in the previous twelve hours? It seems likely that the medication would have been removed while she was at work that day. That question has bothered me from the start of this case."

"Chloe is not around to question, but Bok is in police custody," said Angela looking at Willems and Dubois. "It would be nice to have someone ask him these questions. Is that possible?"

Willems walked to another part of the conference room so as not to disturb the others. He retrieved his phone and called his office. They needed to understand a few more facets of what Bok had been up to the past year. So far Bok had been forthcoming in interrogation. He knew he was going to prison and had nothing to lose from telling the truth. Willems hit the 'end' button as he returned to the conference table.

"My men are going to ask Bok these questions. It will take a little time to arrange as we must give his attorney advance notice of our desire to question him."

"Perhaps we can also question him about Jessica and Taylor," Dubois suggested. "Ladies, I am sure you would like to give me a list of questions for him."

"Officer Dubois, while I can hear the hint of sarcasm in your voice, we'll give you a list of questions we would like to see asked of Bok," replied Jill. "Angela, as our expert interviewer, do you want to take a moment to compile a list?"

"Perhaps we all should take a moment to create the list of questions for Inspector Willems," suggested Angela. "I would like to take a break and get a ride to the consulate to get our passports. Inspector, I believe you agreed to make a call on our behalf verifying the legitimacy of our passport theft?"

"Yes I'll do that right now."

Jo was still chasing something in someone's finances. Jill, Marie, Nick, and Angela put their heads together to come up with a short list of questions for Bok to give to Willems.

Dubois and Willems added to the list when they were done and transmitted the list to the Brussels jail where Bok was being held. Henrik arranged a ride for Angela and Marie to the American consulate in Dusseldorf to replace their passports. Henrik guessed they would be gone for an hour. Jill was ready for another walk and asked Jo if she wanted a break. As Jo was tired of staring at a computer screen, she was easy to convince. She'd been trying to follow the money of Charles Taylor's organization, which wasn't easy, given the currency and international boundaries of where money flowed for him.

Dubois and Willems took the opportunity to catch up on their email, as did Nick and Henrik. Both managed their own companies, although Henrik's company had a much larger scope in the computer security area while Nick's was more focused on his staff at the various hotels and the processes they followed to ensure the safety of the hotel guests. They both had common ground in security, but they had little overlap in their focus and nicely complemented each other's strengths.

Angela and Marie had left and Nick, Jo, and Jill were about to step outside when Henrik got a call from his security people. He quickly had his three guests step back inside the home.

CHAPTER 20

"*I*'ve just received an alert from my men about an intruder," Henrik said urgently. "As you know, I operate a software company, among other things, and so I have a server farm located on this property. Because of the need to secure that server farm, I have extraordinary security. I explain this as the farm was only added about five years ago, several years after Laura broke into this home. I won't waste time telling you about all of the technology and staff that guard the farm and, indirectly, this house.

"When the car carrying Angela and Marie left the gate, an intruder stealthily entered before the gate closed. My men are transmitting the video feed of this person to my computer in this room." Henrik clicked on a few computer keys and suddenly they could see a person in all black steadily progressing across the estate.

"Can you zoom in on the face?" asked Willems. "Is there just one man?"

"The face is covered up and there just seems to be one intruder," replied Henrik as they stood watching the screen. "The question is whether the intruder is here for the server farm or for this house."

They watched for a few more moments. "There, we likely have our answer," said Henrik, pointing to the screen. "The person should have made a turn on the property if they wanted to find the server farm."

"Henrik, are your men armed?" asked Willems.

"No. But I like to experiment with various security measures, so we'll see if any of them work." Henrik was rubbing his hands together and had the appearance of a man relishing a forthcoming battle of wits.

Jill couldn't resist asking, "What is your estimate of when this man will reach the house at his current pace?"

"If this man makes it through all of my challenges, it will take about seven minutes. He's approaching the first challenge in about a minute."

After a slight pause, Henrik said, "Damn, he beat me on the first challenge." He had the energy of someone watching a soccer match. "He must have spotted the trip wire and hopped over it. Let's see if he misses the next four wires."

"Wow, you have five trip wires," said Jill admiringly. "I feel lucky to have survived our walk this morning."

"I have five course obstacles and many more trip wires to engage those obstacles. I had the wires turned off for you. I figured I would be a bad host if I allowed you to be strung up in a tree."

"Is that what is going to happen to him if he misses seeing a wire?" asked Dubois. Both he and Willems had taken guns out of their holsters and were loading their chambers while watching the screen.

"That is one of several surprises. He should trigger the second obstacle now."

Viewing the screen, which had no audio feed, they watched as the man seemed to have heard a sound and squatted, aiming a gun in a shooters' stance. Dummies dressed in camouflage dropped from the trees around the man. He took a step forward to fire and stepped on a hidden net, which sprang over him, leaving him covered with its webbed netting. The net was designed to get caught on as many protrusions as possible and it caught the man's waist holster, his fingers, and it even was sticking to the knit stocking covering his face. Jill couldn't help but clap and gave Jo a high five. She would have offered the same gesture to the men, but she wasn't sure it was in the culture of Europe to high-five each other.

The man took a knife out of his pants pocket, got free of the net, and starting moving forward again.

"Wow, I would have given up and tried to leave this property," commented Jo. "It wouldn't take more than that experience to tell me I wasn't wanted here."

"You, my friend, wouldn't make a very good criminal," Henrik replied never taking his eyes off the screen.

He began clenching his fists and shifting back and forth in an excited fashion. "Here comes the next opportunity."

This time they watched as the man seemingly sunk into something.

"I have several quicksand bogs that I keep covered when there's no security risk, so that animals don't get trapped in it. When we caught him on camera, the covers on the bogs were removed automatically. Let's see if he knows his physics lessons on how to get out."

"Should we just send Inspector Willems and Officer Dubois over to arrest him?" suggested Jill.

"No, as I don't want to disengage my security and they would be at risk for some of the traps I've laid. I know where all the traps are laid out there, yet I would have a hard time negotiating the path. If the man doesn't figure out in twenty minutes how to get out of the bog, then it's game over and they can go arrest him, but some of my other surprises should leave the man more disabled than he is at the moment."

They watched the man struggle some more. When it was clear that the man was tiring or getting cold since the quicksand was likely in the fifty-degree range, the struggle slowed. Finally the physics kicked in and the man either remembered or recognized that slow movements were the way out. After another five minutes, he had crawled out of the bog.

He sat winded on the ground, examining it for a safe place to sit and undo his boots to get the muck out of them. He was lucky they laced up his calves; otherwise, the bog would have kept his shoes.

Again Jill thought, 'Give it up and go home', but the man stood up and continued on his path toward the house.

"Henrik, what else do you have planned for our unwelcome guest?" asked Nick, who was clearly in the same entertainment zone as Henrik.

"Have patience, my friend, and wait and see."

Then they saw the next obstacle that Henrik had rigged. He had seemingly heavy vine overgrowth in this part of the forest that surrounded the house. The vines were an extremely convincing fake of the real foliage. These vines were special, though: they were rigged with electricity, so each time the man tried to move a vine out of the way he got a few jolts. After taking a few shocks, he pulled something out of his waist holster and used it to slide the vines away. It reduced the man's shocks but he couldn't completely avoid the vines and continued to get shocked on camera.

"You know, Henrik, I have a few enemies that I would love to let loose in your obstacle course," commented Nick with a huge grin. "Do you rent it out?"

"A lot of what you've seen in my obstacle course is computer-generated, a creative side effort of my programming staff. I probably shouldn't be showing this to Dubois and Willems as perhaps it's not entirely legal to shock people."

"Actually, I partially agree with Nick's comment," said Willems. "This might serve as a good course to train our special forces on. Will you rent it out to law enforcement? As to shocking people, I'll just plead ignorance of German laws."

"That might be a win-win for both of us. My company can learn how to make it more difficult, and your men can learn how to conquer it."

After this little side conversation, they again focused on the screen. The man cleared the forest and they could see him at nearly two hundred yards away, heading for the house.

"Gentlemen, what are we going to do now that he has cleared the course and is getting closer to the house?" asked Jill, amused by the men's behavior yet cognizant of the seriousness of an assailant coming for them.

"Who said he cleared the course? I believe I have one more obstacle up my sleeve, if he takes the bait I've planted."

Sure enough, about a minute later, the finale of Henrik's obstacle course was reached. The man had been zigzagging from tree to tree, getting closer to the house, when he hit Henrik's last trap. One moment he was moving with stealth from tree to tree, and the next he was hanging upside down from one of the tree branches.

"Henrik, we definitely need to rent this course from you," said Willems.

"Do you think the man is armed?" asked Jo. "How will you get close enough to cut him down and arrest him without being hit by some weapon?"

"My team discussed that exact problem. If the person caught upside down had access to a gun, knife, or even pepper spray they could do damage to someone approaching. Shooting upside down is surprisingly difficult, but I wouldn't want to place anyone's life at risk."

"How did your team solve this problem?"

"Nickelodeon," replied Henrik.

"You have Nickelodeon in Germany?" asked Jo, surprised.

"What is Nickelodeon?" asked Dubois and Willems, their voices in unison.

Jill and Jo thought they knew what was coming: green slime. Seconds later, they saw they were correct.

Henrik explained, "The pulley that arranges our stranger so also has a bucket of green slime that oozes down the person. It makes it impossible to get a grip on any weapon. My goals in this course were to stop an intruder, not harm them or the environment in doing so, and allow me to be entertained through the whole process."

Nick clapped Henrik on the back and said, "You did a great job achieving all of those goals. Let's go meet him."

Jill said to Jo, "Angela and Marie missed a great show. Maybe Henrik taped it and we can watch it again when they return."

The four men went outside to get the intruder out of the tree. Henrik had placed a call to the German police and their ETA was about ten minutes. There would be many explanations required when they arrived, as they would want to know why the Belgian police and Interpol, who were out of their jurisdiction, were present at the German estate.

Jill wanted to know how someone had followed them here, and asked that question of Jo.

"Good question, Jill. We would not have been here unless we' were kidnapped. Someone had to know precisely where we were located to attack this estate. I'm starting to get this covert business and I would suggest that one or more of us has a transmitter planted in our purses or in our possessions."

"My thoughts exactly; let's ask Henrik if he has any technology that senses trackers rather than doing a manual search of our stuff," suggested Jill. "It looks like the intruder is on the ground and handcuffed. Let's go and see if, by chance, we recognize him, and ask Henrik our question."

They ventured outside to look at the person that was face-down on the ground. Henrik and Nick were standing over someone with long hair, while both Willems and Dubois were on their cellphones. When Jill and Jo got closer, they saw why.

Now that the ski mask was removed, they could see it was Jessica Rathbone, aka Mary Smith. This would be the arrest of the decade, perhaps of the careers, of the two law-enforcement officers. In the distance they could hear the siren of an approaching German police car. Things were about to get messier, and Jill wished that Angela was here to question Jessica.

They decided it was best to leave Jessica where she was until the German police arrived. Given the green slime all over her, she would make a mess out of whoever had to take her away to prison. In the meantime, the woman was beginning to shiver from the time spent in the bog and the cold green slime.

Jill motioned Henrik aside and asked him if he had a tracker sensor. He quickly arranged for one of his security people to assist Jill and Jo in looking for a tracking device. Jessica might confess that she had followed a tracker, but there were so many more major questions to ask her. Jill would rather just get the question answered with technology instead. Shortly thereafter, with the assistance of Henrik's man, they discovered sensors in two suit-cases, Jo's purse, and in Nick's luggage.

Marie and Angela arrived back at the estate with new pass-ports, amazed at what they'd missed. Nick had replayed the video for them, and with the knowledge that the intruder was in custody, they could fully enjoy Henrik's obstacle course. They even watched it a second time just to enjoy the green slime at the end.

Angela took the lead on compiling a list of questions they wanted Jessica to be asked by her interrogators. There would be a fight as to which country would prosecute her, but the odds were on South Africa, where she had killed so many nursing-home residents. Before she was extradited, she divulged everything. She might in the future be labeled criminally insane since she was so proud of her work. In that pride, she bragged about each death, describing how good she had felt when she sat Laura up, and gazed into Chloe's eyes as she choked her to death.

Jessica was so thrilled to have an audience to boast about her killing skills to that it was difficult to divert her to other topics, like money, the relationship with the other consortium members, Charles Taylor, and Williams. Much to Henrik's relief, Jessica revealed that she put one million euros into Chloe's bank account, hoping to drive an ax between Laura and Chloe. When Chloe had told Laura what Jessica was trying to do, Laura sent word back through the consortium to Jessica to get out of their lives. Henrik was happy that he not misjudged Chloe's genuine affection for Laura.

There would be months of questioning ahead for Jessica as she had been involved in so many crimes in several countries. Even tiny Sierra Leone wanted to interview her on the atrocities she committed against its villagers near their diamond mines.

After the briefest of jurisdiction squabbles, it was agreed that Jessica would be returned to Brussels to be charged in the deaths of Laura Peeters and Chloe Martin. The Belgian police had a paddy wagon that could be hosed down to get rid of any of the still-dripping slime.

Mr. Bok had been questioned that same afternoon and gave investigators new material for questioning Jessica. They'd learned that just after Laura swallowed the diamonds, Bok took the EpiPen out of Laura's purse and crushed it under his boot. She must have cleaned it up before she went left for the day, because no one mentioned finding broken glass in the store. Laura probably thought she would replenish her EpiPen supply once she met Chloe for dinner, since Chloe carried a spare for Laura in her purse.

They group was sitting on a terrace at Henrik's house after law enforcement had left with Jessica. His security staff had reset the obstacle course so it was ready for the next intruder.

"Henrik, it looks like we've wrapped up your case in a much shorter time than expected," commented Jill. "Perhaps we should re-do that contract since I didn't put as much work into the case as we expected."

"I would rather attribute your success to you and your brilliant team, and for knowing who to bring in from law enforcement. I am happy that the world is safe from Jessica. I've also made some new friends. I hope you will return here on your next visit to Europe."

"Henrik, we're so sorry about the loss of both Laura and Chloe. You seemed to have had a wonderful relationship with both women that I would guess has left a large hole in your life. Although it's a tiny filler of an empty heart, I think you should invite law enforcement here to train, as it will intellectually engage you and give you respite from your grief."

"Jill, you may be right. It felt so good to have my security system tested today. It's the first time I have smiled in weeks."

Jill received an email later that evening from Willems. He wrote:

Jessica continues to talk about her exploits. Our police psychiatrist has never seen the degree of narcissism he sees in her. If we didn't already have Laura's list, Jessica would be a great source of tracking all illicit payments over the years. She has even verified 90 percent of the agents we thought had been bought off in this case.

Mr. Williams was captured as he tried to leave the airport in Stockholm, Sweden. He apparently took a series of ferries to get out of Belgium in preparation to fly home to South Africa. He had fake identification, but Interpol had put a facial recognition alert out to all EU members to stop him from trying to leave.

Upon questioning he knew of Jessica's role in the death of the two women and her position in Taylor's organization, but simply didn't care.

Williams' only goal was to protect the consortium, and his role was simply removing any documents of their involvement with Charles Taylor. Now, he sat in jail in Sweden, waiting to be extradited to the location of the trials for the consortium CEOs.'

Jill, Jo, Marie and Angela had packed their suitcases and would be arriving back only a day later than their original itinerary.

Nathan had been invited to stay with Henrik until he finished visiting his clients. Nathan liked Henrik and agreed to his suggestion.

The five friends and their new acquaintance, Nick, had their last quiet night together, enjoying drinks in Henrik's spa and chatting about unimportant things. It was the perfect end to their most unusual vacation.

EPILOGUE

$\mathcal{J}$ ill said goodbye to her friends at the Brussels airport. With the commission they'd earned from Henrik, their vacation account was well padded for their next holiday. They hadn't decided where they were going next year in the spring; there was just so much of the world to see.

While they'd lost a lot of sleep due to several late-night adventures, and there were more than a few tense moments, the four women all agreed that they'd really enjoyed Belgium and the Netherlands, and had seen everything on their list of attractions.

Nick had added value to their vacation by taking them to restaurants they would not otherwise have been to and showing them the beautiful park in Brussels. The added days in Germany had given them a glimpse of spending time in Europe more as a resident than a tourist. Jill thought they would see more of Nick in the future, as it appeared he wanted to pursue a long distance relationship with Angela. He'd also discussed his plans to set up a business in the United States, perhaps with Henrik as a partner, or subcontracting himself to Jill as cases came her way.

Jill thought they would be back to Europe for work soon as they'd made a positive impression on both the Belgian police and

Interpol. Certainly from Jill's perspective as a former medical examiner, she would like to see Belgium improve their autopsy process to reduce the opportunities for the perfect murder.

She would be picking up Trixie, her beloved Dalmatian, from a friend's house later that day after she landed in San Francisco. Tomorrow she would take Trixie for a run and see if she could reduce the impact of all the beer she had drank in the last two weeks. She hoped she had a little time to get over her jet lag before she took on her next suspicious death, but in her line of work she almost always had to start a case within hours of a death or she'd lose valuable information.

Jill was looking forward to reviewing Angela's scrapbook of their vacation; she thought it would likely take her friend to new literary heights explaining some of the photos. Thankfully, there were no photos of their brief appearance in the red-light district in Amsterdam. That would have been the one photo none of them ever wanted to see on the internet.

Life was good. They had a great vacation, brought resolution to Henrik, and helped to take down one of the worst female serial killers of all time. The four friends had renewed their friendship, and perhaps one of them had found a new love.

The End

ABOUT THE AUTHOR

I reside in Northern California with my rescue dog and cat. I love to travel, play sports, read, and drink wine and beer. I enjoy the diversity of the world and I'm always watching people and events for story ideas.

If you would like to sign up for my monthly blog and announcement of new books, please follow this link: https://www.AlecPecheBooks.com

While you're waiting for the next story, if you would be so kind as to leave a review for this book, that would be great. I appreciate all the feedback and support. Reviews buoy my spirits and stoke the fires of creativity.

Readers that sign up for website receive a free prequel novelette for the Jill Quint Series.

Amazon Author Profile

Author Profile on Goodreads

Author Profile on BookBub